The dog melte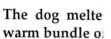 warm bundle o would let the pup sleep with her in the pink room tonight. Then she realized that for the first time since her grandfather died, she would no longer be alone in the house where she grew up. Before she could stop it, a lone tear of gratitude fell from her lashes.

"Thank you," she breathed.

Joe nodded and his gaze glowed with understanding. Not pity, or even sympathy. The expression his coffee eyes bore was one of shared grief. "My pleasure."

Goldie sniffed and shifted from one foot to the other. She really needed to hold it together. But she had to ask him one last question before the two of them went inside and she lost him in the whirlwind of all the other guests. "Why?"

Joe looked up from the dog with a questioning glance. "Why what?"

"Why are you doing all of this for me? You hardly know me." Her voice cracked with emotion.

Joe's fingers wrapped around the shiny silver tag on the dog's pink collar. He turned over the tag, ran his thumb over the engraving and showed it to Goldie. "Because something told me this might be exactly what you need right now."

Bliss.

The dog's name was Bliss.

Cup of Joe

by

Teri Wilson

To Cheryl, Rhy + Cricket, love + blessings, Teri Wilson XO

Contact Information:
titleadmin@whiterosepublishing.com

All scripture quotations, unless otherwise indicated, are taken from the HOLY BIBLE, NEW INTERNATIONAL VERSION®. NIV®. Copyright © 1973, 1978, 1984 by International Bible Society. Used by permission of Zondervan. All rights reserved.

Cover Art by *Tamra Westberry*

White Rose Publishing,
a division of Pelican Ventures, LLC
www.whiterosepublishing.com
PO Box 1738 *Aztec, NM * 87410

Publishing History
First White Rose Edition, 2009
Softcover ISBN 1-60154-708-0

Published in the United States of America

Dedication

In loving memory of my Grandpa,
Robert K. Wilson
Dec. 22, 1915 - Oct. 25, 2006

And for Jesus Christ, You are ever Faithful and True.
Rev. 19:11.

Praise for Teri Wilson

Cup of Joe: 2nd Place Merritt Contest Winner
~Sponsored by the San Antonio Romance Authors

Hoofbeats & Heartstrings series from
The Wild Rose Press

Do You Hear What I Hear?

Using horses, aromatherapy and a love story, Teri weaves a tale that is more than a novel, more than a love story, it is THE love story in human history revealed. Read this book, you won't regret it!
~Dr. Kim Bloomer, veterinary naturopath, author, and host of Animal Talk Naturally

I was so enchanted with this charming tale that I read it straight through in one sitting. This story is my first taste of the work of Teri Wilson but it will not be my last...Do You Hear What I Hear? is a must read Christmas story. I highly recommend this enchanting, magical tale! ... I can't wait for the next installment!
~Stephanie B., Fallen Angels Reviews

Love, Lilies & the Unbroken Straw

In one word: sweet! This chaste romance was a breath of fresh air... I'd recommend this story for those looking for something closer to a true romance. And, in fact, I already have.
~Janelle, You Gotta Read Reviews

"The Lord is close to the brokenhearted and saves those who are crushed in spirit."

Chapter One

Three days had passed since Goldie Jensen's grandfather died.

She could tell because that's how many full coffee cups stood on her front porch, neatly lined up like brave little soldiers. A caffeinated army.

Goldie, on the other hand, wasn't feeling so brave. Or caffeinated, for that matter. Feet shoved into pink fuzzy slippers, she parked herself on the sofa and stared at the television with bleary eyes. Her doting Grandpa might be gone, but she still had *Judge Rudy* and *Name that Price* for company. Hardly the usual television fare for a young woman in her late twenties, but give her a break. Old habits die hard, and she'd lived with an elderly man all her adult life.

Until three days ago.

She tucked her pink, fluffy feet under her legs, clad in her favorite Sponge Bob pajama bottoms, and yelled at the television. "Under. Under!"

Sheesh, the ionic blow dryer was obviously less

expensive than the exorbitant price the host, Cary Anderson, was motioning toward with his little stack of note cards. Still, Agnes from Oklahoma wrung her hands and looked longingly at the audience for help.

"Under!" *What's the deal? I'm pretty sure they have blow dryers in Oklahoma, Agnes.*

Agnes shouted "over," and Goldie moaned in disgust just as the doorbell rang. She grabbed the remote and muted Cary with the touch of a button.

"Goldie, I know you're home," a distinctly male voice boomed from the other side of the front door. "I heard the television. Please come to the door."

He was back.

Again.

Coffee Guy.

Goldie gnawed on her thumbnail and remained glued to the sofa, her gaze darting back and forth between the door and the television. To her astonishment, it appeared as though Agnes had actually made it to the showroom shootout. The frazzled contestant was already wielding her pricing gun, preparing to aim it at the extravagant prizes in the final round. Goldie un-muted just to check.

"I'm not going anywhere. I'm going to sit right here until you open the door." Coffee Guy's voice was softer, but still carried a distinctive note of determination. "I can wait for quite a while. There's plenty of coffee out here to keep me going."

When the screen switched from the kitschy game show set to a commercial for Depends, Goldie dragged herself from the couch to the peephole. Through the tiny circle, she saw the distorted figure of Coffee Guy resting casually against a pillar with yet another cup of coffee in his hand. His long legs crossed at the ankles, he was the perfect picture of patience. She really needed to stop calling him Coffee Guy. He had a real name, after all, but she couldn't bring herself to remember what it was. Like everything else these days, the effort it took was overwhelming. Why did even the simplest of tasks make her feel so tired?

A swig of caffeine may not be such a bad idea.

Before she changed her mind, and before Cary had a chance to start the showroom shootout round without her, she swung open the door. Astonished, Coffee Guy nearly tumbled backwards off the front porch.

"Goldie! You opened the door." He tugged at the neck of his navy sweater, clearly unprepared for a face-to-face meeting.

"That's what you wanted, isn't it?" Goldie's voice was flat, void of all emotion. She scarcely recognized it herself.

"Um," he stammered. "Well, yes. Yes, it is."

"So, what's so important?" Strains of "come name that price" drifted from the living room and Goldie resisted the sudden urge to slam the door in his face.

The lure of the television, coupled with the way Coffee Guy looked at her, was almost too much for her to bear. His melting irises were…well, coffee colored, and they bore an expression of empathy so intense it left no doubt he knew the magnitude of her grief down to the core. But how was that possible? She barely knew the man. He was her Grandpa's friend, not hers. And, since her grandfather's passing, she'd kept her feelings tightly under wraps and shared them with no one. Not even God. And certainly not with near strangers who left unwelcome gifts on her porch.

He tugged at the collar of his sweater again, ran a

hand through his rumpled chestnut hair and sighed. "I'm worried about you. I want to make sure you're OK."

A lump lodged in Goldie's throat, making it all the more difficult for her to squeak out her response with any sort of authenticity. "I'm fine."

The corner of his mouth lifted ever so slightly. "You don't look fine. Cute maybe, but not your usual put-together self."

Goldie felt his gaze as it landed on her pink slippers and slouchy p.j. bottoms. *Blast you Sponge Bob! Blast you and blast your square pants.*

She lifted her fingertips to her cheek as she felt a pink flush crawl up her neck and tiptoe toward her temples. How would he know what she normally looked like, anyway? Granted, he'd been coming here every morning for months, delivering coffee to her grandfather once he was too ill for his regular morning walk to the coffee shop. But Goldie had usually moved about in the background, content to let the two men chat, enjoy their java and play checkers. Sure, Coffee Guy was undoubtedly closer to her own age than her Grandpa's. Goldie wasn't blind. She'd become keenly aware of his broad shoulders, kind smile and strong jaw months ago. How could she not? But she couldn't remember ever exchanging more than a couple words with him in the past. She honestly didn't think he'd ever noticed her.

Before the coffee starting showing up three days ago.

Coffee she knew was intended for her.

"I'm OK. Really. I was just getting ready to, um, clean the house." It was a plausible scenario. Right?

"Mmm. That's right. You're probably expecting

4

company. The funeral is tomorrow, isn't it?"

Goldie didn't trust herself to talk about the memorial service without breaking down, so she nodded in silence.

Coffee Guy shrugged and glanced up and down the empty street. "The coffee shop is pretty slow this morning. I could stay if you'd like some help."

Goldie felt her eyes widen at the suggestion.

"I mean," he continued. "I'm pretty good with a mop and a dishrag. I've got lots of experience cleaning up at the shop."

"Oh, no!" Goldie couldn't imagine a more awkward scenario, even if she had been telling the truth about needing to clean house. What did he expect from her? Small talk while they scrubbed the toilet together? *No thanks.* "I couldn't ask you to do that. Everything is under control."

"It's no bother. I could use the company. I kind of miss the old guy myself, you know?" There it was again. That intangible quality—something in his eyes, in the subtle downward slope of his mouth—carried the silent message that he knew her pain. That perhaps she had more in common with this casual acquaintance than she would have ever guessed.

Despite her great effort to hold it together, Goldie's bottom lip quivered with rebellion, and her vision misted over with unshed tears. It would have been so easy to lose it altogether and dissolve in a weepy puddle right there on the porch. In the back of her mind, she wondered what Coffee Guy would do if she just gave in and let it all out. Let her sorrow fall like rain, turning all the paper coffee cups at her feet to mush. Would he say what she knew all her friends were thinking? That the man had been 90 years old and lived a long and happy life? That he'd hung around a lot longer than anyone ever expected? Why the shock? Why the overwhelming urge to just climb under the covers when her alarm sounded in the morning?

She knew all these things. Believed them in her mind. The problem rested squarely in her heart.

Goldie blinked at Coffee Guy and decided if she did, in fact, give up the fight against her emotions and let him see the turmoil inside, he wouldn't find her so cute anymore. The ugly truth would make the Sponge Bob pajamas and fuzzy slippers seem like red carpet-worthy glamour. She swallowed it all down and let the numbness take over again.

"I've got it taken care of. Mission accomplished." She nodded for extra emphasis. "I'm sure you need to get back to work anyway."

Hint, hint.

He held her gaze for a long moment, as if trying to send her a secret message with his warm cocoa eyes. Whatever it was, she didn't want to hear it, so she broke the silent connection and looked away—over her shoulder toward Cary and showroom package number two. It was a good one. Goldie thought she saw his-and-her jet skis, but she couldn't be sure.

"OK then. I guess I'll see you tomorrow."

She hoped with every fiber of her being he was referring to the funeral and not another morning coffee delivery.

Speaking of coffee, there it was, a mere two inches from her chest. Coffee Guy had thrust it toward her, a grin dancing on his lips. "Well, here you go. Your morning coffee. Nice, fresh and hot."

Goldie looked down at the cup and the steam

rising from the little hole in its lid. "Listen, you really don't need to keep doing this. Grandpa is gone. He was the coffee lover in the family."

"I know." He nodded, that glimmer of sympathy flickering once again in his eyes. "But I want to do something nice for you. This is yours. Please take it."

Was there no getting through to this guy? Did he not see his previous offerings scattered on the front porch, full to the brim and untouched? "The thing is...I don't like coffee."

A look of utter disbelief washed over Coffee Guy's features. He looked as shocked as if she'd just told him the earth was flat. Under normal circumstances, his gaping mouth would have made Goldie laugh. She would have teased him that if he didn't close it soon, flies might buzz right in.

But these weren't normal circumstances. Nothing would be normal ever again. So, instead, she huffed out an irritated sigh.

It was enough to jolt him out of his stunned trance. He blinked at the coffee cup and his gaze shot back to Goldie. "You're joking, right?"

Do I look like I'm joking? "No."

"But everyone likes coffee." It sounded a little like a slogan rolling off his tongue.

"Not everyone. Not me." Finally, she'd found the words to rid herself of this situation once and for all. Maybe now he'd scoot on back to his coffee shop in time for her to catch the beginning of *Judge Rudy*. She'd already missed the end of the showroom shootout round.

"Goldie?"

Goldie shook the cobwebs loose in her head. Why did this keep happening? "I'm sorry. What were we talking about?"

Coffee Guy took a step closer and lowered his voice. "You just told me you didn't like coffee." He grinned. "Say it isn't so."

Oh that's right. Goldie stood straighter and tried to look serious. As serious as she could look with an animated sponge prancing across her backside, anyway. She cleared her throat and added a final phrase to urge him on his way a little faster. "Never liked it. Never will."

He lifted a brow. *"Never?* That's an awfully strong word."

Uh oh.

"We'll see about that." He set the coffee on the top step beside the pink fuzz of Goldie's foot. "Tomorrow, then."

With that, he turned to go and shot her a full-tilt, thousand watt smile that made her insides churn. Goldie clutched her stomach.

What was that?

She must remember to eat. Had she had anything for breakfast? Simple hunger had caused the fluttering in her belly. It had to be.

Coffee Guy reached the end of the street and waved. When he turned the corner, she bent down to pick up the mess of paper cups at her feet. Her fingers wrapped around the one closest to her. The warmth of the fresh brew seeped through the walls of the cup and spread outward from the center of her palm. Goldie brought the cup closer to her face and took a whiff from the opening. She closed her eyes and took in the comforting scent she associated so closely with her grandfather.

When she opened her eyes, simple block letters

flooded her vision.

Joe's Coffee Shop.

Turtle Beach, North Carolina.

That's right. His name was Joe. Joe Montgomery. How could she have forgotten?

❧

The chimes on the door to the coffee shop tinkled as Joe crossed the threshold, rousing Java from his slumber on the plaid dog bed in the corner.

"Hey boy, did you miss me?" Joe gave the Siberian Husky a good scratch on the scruff of his neck and smiled.

Java answered him with his signature *woo-woo* yodel. Joe interpreted that as a *yes*. He took a crunchy dog biscuit from his pocket and waited for the big dog to politely sit and offer his paw for a shake. Joe gave the biscuit to Java with an open palm. Treat clenched firmly in his jaws, the Husky returned to his bed, turned three slow circles and plopped down with his tail wrapped around his body in a tight hug.

"Joe, you're back!" gushed the slender young woman behind the counter.

Joe nodded to the regular morning customers sipping their coffee from the shiny red stools at the bar. Then he turned his attention to his employee. "Good morning," he replied, making every effort not to wince at the tiny diamond stud sparkling in Cinnamon's nose. Joe doubted the glittering stone was real, but that's OK because her name wasn't either.

C'mon, was anyone really named Cinnamon? He'd met a few dogs with such a moniker, especially since he'd started hosting monthly pet adoptions for the Turtle Beach Animal Shelter in the coffee shop parking lot, but never an actual person. Not even one with flaming red hair like Cinnamon's.

If the scrawl on her employment application could be trusted, her real name was Jane. A perfectly respectable name as far as he was concerned. But the moment he'd hired her, despite the nose piercing winking at him from its place next to her nostril, she'd insisted he call her Cinnamon. According to his new employee, it was a much more suitable name for a barista.

Barista—yet another label Joe found himself reluctant to use. What was wrong with *counter help*? He supposed it didn't make a difference, so long as baristas and counter helpers earned the same hourly wage.

"The shelter called to make sure everything is still set for tomorrow's pet adoption." Cinnamon frowned in concentration and scrubbed an invisible spot on the counter. Nose rings and aliases aside, she was hands-down the best employee he'd ever hired. She could change her name to Paprika and Joe would still give her a job.

"Sounds great. I'll give them a call." Joe's gaze swept the counter and he raked a hand through his hair. "Have you seen today's paper?"

"Yep. Right here." Cinnamon pulled the thin, small-town paper from a shelf beneath the counter. She handed it to him. "Are you looking for your friend's obituary?"

Joe frowned and flipped open the local news section, spreading the flimsy pages open on the Formica. "Mmm hmm."

He turned the pages until he saw faces peering

back at him from the neat columns of the obituary page. Faces he mostly recognized as either acquaintances or customers. Turtle Beach was a small town, after all. But none of the faces tugged at his heart quite like the one beneath the army cap with the captain's bars. The photo had to be at least fifty years old, but Joe could still see the eyes of his friend on the fresh face of the young soldier in the World War II photo. They were the same cat eyes that sometimes watched him from behind thick, feminine, lashes. Eyes that kept him spellbound. Eyes that now held the vacant glimmer of pain and loss.

Goldie's eyes.

"Interesting," Cinnamon commented as she peered over his shoulder. "I wonder why his family chose such an old photograph."

Joe cleared his throat, pressing down the lump that had lodged there. "It's his military photo. He belonged to one of the first Army units to go in and liberate the concentration camps during World War II."

"Oh. Wow." Over his shoulder, Cinnamon's voice carried a note of reverence, which made the lump grow even larger.

"I know. He was a really special man. We're all going to miss him, especially his granddaughter." In his vulnerable emotional state, he didn't quite trust himself to say Goldie's name aloud.

"Teresa?"

Joe knit his brows, unsure who Cinnamon was talking about until he saw her bright red fingernail pointing to the tiny words of the obituary.

Robert K. Jensen

December 22, 1918 — October 23, 2008

Robert K. Jensen, "Bob" to his friends and family, died peacefully at his home in Turtle Beach, NC, at the age of 90 after a long illness. Bob was a retired Army captain who served his country for 22 years. He is survived by his loving granddaughter, Teresa Jensen, and predeceased by his wife of 30 years, Annabelle Jensen, and his son, Robert K. Jensen, Jr. Memorial services for Bob are scheduled for noon, October 27, at Turtle Beach Community Church.

"He will swallow up death forever,

And the Lord God will wipe away tears from all faces…"

Isaiah 25:8

Hmm. So it appeared Cinnamon wasn't the only one with an alias. "She goes by Goldie."

"Goldie?" The corner of Cinnamon's mouth lifted, causing the diamond nose stud to twinkle and glisten. "That's sweet."

"Yes, she is," Joe muttered, almost to himself.

Cinnamon cut her gaze sideways toward him, suspicion washing over her features. He focused on the black and white print of the newspaper, particularly the Bible verse at the bottom of the paragraph. He imagined tears rolling down Goldie's porcelain cheek. His gut clenched and he prayed, *Lord, work through me if it is your will. I want to wipe the tears from her face and bring the sparkle back to her eyes.*

"She's his only survivor. He told me he raised her after her parents were killed in a car accident when she was just a little girl. She took care of him these last months while he was sick."

Cinnamon stopped watching him with that

suspicious gleam and knit her brows. "So, she's all alone now. That's so sad."

Joe grabbed a pair of scissors from next to the cash register and cut a neat square around Bob's obituary. He tacked it up on the wall next to the flier announcing the following day's pet adoption.

They both tilted their heads and looked at the photo on the wall of Bob Jensen as a young, vibrant soldier. After a quiet moment, Cinnamon broke the respectful silence. "Well, I'd better get back to work."

Joe nodded his understanding until he remembered the important matter he needed to discuss with her. "Wait a sec, OK?"

"Sure. What is it?"

"Well, I've been thinking." Joe leaned his back against the counter and crossed his feet at the ankles. "Maybe we should add a few new things to the coffee menu."

Cinnamon's mouth dropped open and the dishrag in her hand fluttered to the floor.

Joe ignored her shocked expression and continued, as if he did this sort of thing every day. "Nothing too crazy. Maybe some latte. Or some cappuccino." His gaze flitted to the unused milk steamer and fancy espresso maker sitting in the corner. Items that had been purely decorative up until this point. "And I think we should start tomorrow."

"Are you serious?" Cinnamon's voice quivered with excitement. She looked like a kid on Christmas morning. "But I've been bugging you about this since I started working here. I've begged and begged you to let me come up with some more modern menu choices. You always say 'no.' I'd finally given up."

Joe couldn't help but smile at Cinnamon's

delighted reaction. He was suddenly very glad she fancied herself a barista because he didn't have the first clue how to make a latte. Or what *skinny, foam, whip, no whip,* or any other of those words he never thought he'd ever utter in his own, old-fashioned coffee shop meant. "Well now I'm saying yes."

Cinnamon crossed her arms and cocked an eyebrow at him. "What's going on? You always say we don't need to serve anything but plain, old coffee. You even have a mantra." She gave a mock salute. "Everybody likes coffee."

"Not everybody." Joe sneaked a final glance at the photo of Goldie's grandfather tacked up on the wall. "Nope. Not everybody."

Chapter Two

Joe eyed the paper cup topped with a generous mountain of something that resembled whipped cream. He held it to his nose and took a whiff. It smelled, and looked, much more like a dessert than a coffee beverage. "What is this again?"

Cinnamon rolled her eyes. "A latte macchiato." An exasperated sigh followed the eye rolling. "With foam."

He took another whiff, then a tentative sip. "This is phenomenal."

She grinned from ear to ear. "I told you I knew what I was doing. Honestly, it's shameful you've never had one of these before."

"I mean, it's really, really good." Then he just had to ask, "Are you absolutely sure there's coffee in here?"

Cinnamon jammed her hands on her hips. "Yes. As a matter of fact, it has espresso in it."

"Hmm, no kidding?" He took another sip. He would have never guessed something as strong as espresso. Sure enough, there was a hint of coffee mixed in with the creamy caramel goodness. But it was subtle. Subtle enough that someone who didn't drink coffee just might like it, too. Someone like Goldie.

"This is perfect. Let me get a lid for this one…" His voice drifted off, and he cleared his throat.

Cinnamon shot him an amused grin. "What was that?"

He felt his face redden and he squared his shoulders. Why should he try to hide his feelings? Cinnamon may have a nosy streak at times, but she was his employee. "I said, can you please make another one? I'm going to take it to Goldie. She's got a tough day ahead of her." He looked straight at Cinnamon, willing himself not to wince, and waited for what he knew would probably be a teasing remark.

Instead, her expression softened. "That's really sweet, boss."

Joe shifted his weight from one foot to the other. Having prepared himself for teasing, he almost felt even more uncomfortable with her sincerity. "Um. Well, she might not like it. She's not a, uh, coffee drinker."

"Yet." Cinnamon pointed at her new creation. "If she doesn't like that latte macchiato, I'll be shocked. But don't worry. If she doesn't, we'll find something she likes. I've got more delicious recipes up my sleeve." She winked at him knowingly, and he ran his hand through his hair as he always did when he was nervous.

How in the world had he ended up in this situation? Taking love advice from a young girl with a nose ring?

"OK. Well, thanks." He added for good measure, "And, good job."

"No problem, boss." She flicked a lever on the shiny espresso machine and a loud hiss filled the air.

Less than half an hour later, Joe stood on the now-familiar territory that was Goldie's front porch. In one hand, he gripped a fresh, warm latte macchiato and in the other, the end of Java's leather leash. He looked down at Java. The dog's pink tongue lolled out of the side of his mouth. "Behave, OK?"

Java just blinked. Joe wondered, once again, if he should have brought the big Husky along. It seemed more than a little presumptuous. But Cinnamon had absolutely insisted on it. *Take Java*, she'd said as she shoved the leash into his palm. *Chicks dig dogs*.

Joe glanced up at the blue morning sky.

Forgive me, Lord.

At once, he regretted ever letting Cinnamon figure out how smitten he was with Goldie. Now, his genuine attempts to cheer her up, to take away at least some of the grief dragging her down, felt wrong. Like he was taking advantage of her sadness, which he never, ever would do.

He was half-tempted to turn around and walk back to the coffee shop, but he couldn't. He'd made a promise to her grandfather. A promise he intended to keep.

So, instead of slinking back to the coffee shop, he rang the doorbell with the hand that held the whipped coffee confection. Java sat completely still and let out a dramatic yawn. Joe wished he felt half as calm as his dog.

"Who is it?" Goldie's monotone voice was barely discernable coming from the other side of the door. But at least she hadn't pretended not to hear the bell. It was progress, right?

Joe spoke loudly enough so she could hear him through the door, but not as forcefully as he had yesterday. He didn't want to seem pushy before she even laid eyes on him. "It's me. Joe."

The door opened a crack. Through the tiny sliver, he saw her groggy eyes widen as she took in the large dog standing next to him. Joe held his breath in anticipation. And as Java's tail wagged and beat against the wooden steps of the porch, Goldie's features flickered to life. Then, to his utter astonishment, she actually smiled. "Who's your friend?"

Joe had never seen such a glorious vision as that subtle smile. His heart leapt to his throat at the sight of her standing there, dressed in black for her grandfather's funeral, smiling as she pat his dog on the head. Yes, it appeared Goldie did, in fact, dig dogs. Cinnamon was right. And if Java brought her even a moment of happiness on this solemn day, he was glad he listened to Cinnamon's advice. He sent up a silent prayer of thanks. "This is Java."

The smile lingered on her lips, faint as a whisper. "He's so sweet. Is he yours?"

"Yep. I adopted him a couple of years ago." He watched as Goldie scratched Java behind the ears. She looked like a ballerina, elegant and lovely, in her sweeping black skirt and ballet flats with tiny bows on top. A vision of grace and beauty. But she was dressed this way because today she was going to bury her grandfather. He wished he could take her place, and she could climb back in her Sponge Bob pajamas and fuzzy slippers and spend all day curled up on the sofa.

"So, I brought you something." As he spoke, her gaze flitted to the paper cup in his hand. Her bow-shaped lips lifted into a subtle upturn as she saw the cursive letter *G* drizzled on top of the whipped cream in caramel sauce. Another smile!

"Is that coffee? Don't you remember what I told you yesterday?" The smile lingered, giving her words a teasing quality.

"You don't like coffee. How could I forget?" He clutched his chest in a mock heartbroken gesture. "Just taste it. One little sip. That's all I ask. Please."

She took the cup from his hand. "Well, I'm not sure how it will taste, but it's awfully pretty."

He had to admit Cinnamon knew more than her fair share about coffee. The caramel *G* had actually been his own idea. He'd practiced a few times on a napkin before tackling the mountain of whipped cream atop Goldie's latte macchiato. Penmanship had never been his strong suit, but he'd kept at it until the *G* was perfect. "So, you're going to try it, right?"

"OK. But no promises." She wrinkled her nose as she brought the cup to her lips, red and smooth as a shiny satin ribbon.

Joe held his breath as she took a tiny sip. He relaxed slightly when she took another, longer, taste. "You like it, don't you?"

"It's not bad." She peered at him over the coffee cup and took another sip, decorating the tip of her nose with a small dollop of whipped cream.

Before he could stop himself, Joe reached over and dabbed at her nose with the tip of his finger. "Admit it. You love it, don't you?"

"Love?" She raised her eyebrows. "Like hate, love is an awfully strong word."

The blood in Joe's veins stood still. He knew she was only joking—turning his own words around from the day before. But hearing the word *love* fall off her lips gave him the strangest sensation inside.

Because he loved her. Yes, he did. And that is why

he'd promised her grandfather he would look after her. To make sure she was OK. And one day, God willing, he would actually tell her how he felt about her. Someday…when she was ready to hear it.

"It's good. Quite yummy, actually." Goldie ran her tongue over the edge of the cup, capturing the last bit of whipped cream. The simple gesture stole the breath from Joe's lungs.

It took him a moment to remember what they were talking about. *Oh yeah. The latte macchiato.* "I knew it. You do like coffee, after all."

She just took another sip and ran her hand over Java's pointy ears.

Unsure how to interpret her silence, Joe decided to quit while he was ahead. "Well, I guess I'd better let you get ready for…"

She completed his sentence when his voice trailed off. "The funeral."

Joe nodded and pretended not to notice that her eyes had suddenly become very bright blue and shiny with unshed tears.

"Are you coming?"

"Yes," he replied. "I'll be there."

"I'm having a reception afterward. Here at the house, if you'd like to come." She looked at the ground and sighed, but her fingers remained buried in Java's fur.

"I'd like that very much."

"OK then." Goldie retreated back to the crack in the doorframe, the glow in her face growing dim.

Joe would have drawn the entire alphabet in caramel letters if it would have made the moment last longer. "Bye, Goldie." As he turned to leave, Java whimpered, drawing her attention once more.

"Thanks Joe. Thanks for everything," she murmured as she closed the door with a click.

Joe paused on the top step. "It's my pleasure," he whispered to Java, to God, and whoever else might be listening.

❧

Goldie's eyes traveled the length of the dining room table as she tried to remember the last time she'd ever seen so much food all in one place. If only she were hungry. There were deli trays, home baked cookies, fresh fruit and a most impressive assortment of casserole dishes. Seriously.

She blinked at the neat rows of corning ware overflowing with King Ranch chicken, green bean casserole, tuna casserole, macaroni and cheese casserole and hamburger casserole. *I'd bet money that Piggly Wiggly is clean out of every variety of Campbell's creamed soup.*

Southerners knew the secret to dealing with grief—comfort food. And it seemed every resident of Turtle Beach who owned a spatula had turned out for the reception at Goldie's house after the funeral. She eyed the macaroni and cheese and tried to will her stomach to growl. Nothing. Not even a whimper.

"Ohhh. Arrrrg."

Goldie's head snapped from left to right as she looked for the source of the sudden groan. It wasn't her tummy. She wondered for a moment if the table had moaned from the sheer weight of all the casserole dishes. Then she realized where the sounds of agony came from. She just smiled. "Have you had enough to eat, Peggy?"

"I've never eaten so much at one sitting in all my life." Peggy, Goldie's neighbor, blushed. Her snowy white hair served as a stark contrast to the crimson glow of her cheeks.

"I know. I have no idea what I'm going to do with all this food." Goldie shook her head and motioned toward the table. The fact that it still stood on all four legs astounded her.

"It's for you to eat, child." Peggy patted her on the shoulder with a gentle hand. "That's what it's here for."

Goldie sighed. She knew she needed to eat something, but just the effort it took to lift a fork to her mouth seemed impossible. In fact, the last thing she'd eaten had been the generous mountain of whipped cream atop the delicious coffee drink Joe had brought her this morning. She touched the tip of her nose, remembering when he'd dabbed at it with his own fingertip, and her cheeks flushed ten times redder than Peggy's.

"Here, have a taste." Peggy waved a piece of what looked like banana bread under Goldie's nose.

Goldie wanted to appease the older woman, so she took a bite and swallowed. It felt like a lump of sand going down her throat.

"Maybe I'll bring some of this food over to Care Group this week," she managed to choke out.

At the mention of Care Group, a strange look washed over Peggy's features. Then, as quickly as it came, it disappeared. "Well, dear. We old folks certainly don't expect you to keep coming to Care Group. You were there to help your Grandpa...to make sure he got there OK."

"I know. But I've really enjoyed worshipping with

all of you." It was the truth. Goldie felt right at home at the weekly Bible study group Peggy held in her living room and referred to affectionately as *Care Group*. Besides, wherever would she find a church service as convenient as Care Group? All she had to do was walk right next door. Even in her current pathetic state, Goldie thought she could manage to pry herself off the sofa and trudge the 30 feet to Peggy's front door. "So maybe I'll just pack up some of the leftovers and bring them with me on Thursday."

Peggy opened her mouth to respond, but before any words could emerge, Goldie's friend Eve bounced into the conversation. Eve had a tendency to do that.

Bounce, that is.

Usually Goldie found her bubbly personality sweet and endearing, but today it only made her tired. Weariness settled over her as Eve squeezed Peggy's shoulders and gave her smacking air kisses beside both cheeks.

"*Bonjour*! Have you ever seen such a spread of food in all your life? People really turned out for the big guy, huh?" She flashed Goldie a wink. Her grandfather and Eve had always shared a fun relationship, with plenty of teasing back and forth. She'd started calling him "big guy" back when she and Goldie were in middle school.

"Yes, this is becoming quite the shindig." Eve's emerald eyes sparkled beneath her long, sweeping lashes as she fiddled with the classic string of pearls around her neck. Her gaze swept the room with methodical precision.

"You can stop looking around, Eve. Most of the people here are at least 30 years older than you are. I don't think you're going to bump into any eligible bachelors." Peggy smirked and bit into something covered with melted cheese.

"Please! Like I would try to look for the love of my life at the big guy's funeral." She rolled her eyes and feigned innocence.

"Well, technically, the funeral is over," Peggy said in voice tinged with a teasing lilt. "So, it wouldn't be entirely inappropriate to meet the love of your life now. You just never know. I hear George over there is looking for someone."

She pointed to George Brown who was bending over the punch bowl at the small, round table in the breakfast nook. George was a member of Care Group. Like Eve, he loved dancing, pizza and long walks on the beach. Unlike Eve, he was seventy-five years old.

"Don't tempt me," Eve chided. "I'm getting desperate."

This was the moment in the conversation when Goldie would normally remind her that she was sure to find someone. After all, Eve was sweet-natured and beautiful. And, as the French teacher at Turtle Beach High School, she possessed a certain stylish sophistication that most guys found irresistible. Far from desperate, Eve had certainly had more than her fair share of dates. She wasn't looking for dates any more, though. She wanted to settle down with just the right man. But Goldie suddenly could barely keep her eyes open, much less remind her friend that Mr. Right was out there somewhere for her, waiting for God's perfect timing.

"I think I'm going to go lie down for a minute," she blurted out. Peggy and Eve, whose conversation had progressed from man-hunting to how navy was the new black, turned their heads in unison and looked at her with concern.

"Are you OK, *mon ami*?" Eve furrowed her brows.

"Yes, I just want to rest for a bit. I...I haven't gotten much sleep lately." *Unless you count lying on the sofa in my pajamas and staring at the television as sleep.*

"We'll be right here if you need us, dear." Peggy gave Goldie's hand a comforting squeeze as she walked away toward her bedroom.

It was all she could do to make it to the bed without her legs collapsing beneath her. She didn't even pause to close the door to her room. She simply kicked off her ballet flats and curled up in a ball on top of her bedspread. Instinctively, she reached for the afghan folded in a neat rectangle at the foot of the bed—the one her grandmother had crocheted even before Goldie was born—and spread it over the folds of her black dress. The worn yarn was soft and comforting, like an old teddy bear. As Goldie fingered the intricate loops and stitches, her gaze swept the old rocking chair in the corner and the antique dresser lined up against the rose-colored wall. Her room had looked exactly the same for almost as long as she could remember. All at once, she realized that now her grandfather was gone. Everyone would probably expect her to move into his bedroom. On the surface, it made sense. His bedroom, the master, was far more spacious than her tiny pink room. But the very thought of leaving the space where she'd lived since she was nine years old was too much to bear. Not to mention the unimaginable task of cleaning out her grandfather's things.

Tears blurred her vision and threatened to spill over onto her cheeks. She sniffed and willed herself not to cry. *Not now. Not here.*

Friends, neighbors and acquaintances milled about the surrounding rooms. Nothing but thin walls separated her from nearly everyone she knew. Now was not the time for a breakdown.

"Goldie? Are you awake?" Eve's whisper and the soft rap of knuckles on the open bedroom door helped keep the tears at bay.

Goldie sat up, the crocheted blanket still wrapped snugly around her. "Yes. Come on in."

Eve sat on the very edge of the bed, a strange smile tugging at the corners of her lips.

Goldie shifted on the mattress to make more room for her friend. The thought crossed her mind that Eve had spent many a night in this room herself throughout the years. They'd been close friends since elementary school, often having sleepovers at one another's homes. More often than not, they ended up here. At her grandfather's home. Her Grandpa was always there to offer them a platter full of hot buttered raisin toast and his legendary root beer floats. "What is it? You look like the cat that swallowed the canary. Oh my gosh...you're not really going on a date with George Brown, are you?"

"No. I'm not. Not yet, anyway." She looked down and examined an invisible chip in her perfect French manicure. "But you certainly seem to have something up your sleeve."

"What are you talking about?"

"I'm talking about the gentleman caller waiting for you on the front porch." She peeked at Goldie from behind her thick lashes and paused for dramatic effect. "He says his name is Joe Montgomery. As in Joe's Coffee Shop."

Joe.

Goldie gulped. Her thoughts immediately turned to this morning and the dollop of whipped cream. Her nose tingled as if her skin itself remembered the sensation of his touch. She scrubbed at her nose with the side of her pointer finger. "Joe's here?"

"He sure is. And he comes bearing gifts." Eve smiled that mysterious little smile once more.

Coffee. It had to be. The man seemed to possess an unending flow of the stuff. "Why is he outside? Didn't you invite him in?"

"Yes, but he wants to talk to you in private. What is going on? You haven't mentioned this guy to me at all." Eve crossed her arms and raised her eyebrows, as if waiting for an answer.

Well, she'll just have to wait a little longer.

Goldie couldn't leave Joe out there on the porch. Certainly not after she'd invited him to the reception. "I'll explain it later, although there's really nothing to tell. I'm not hiding anything from you. He's a friend of Grandpa's. I barely know him."

"That's not what it looks like to me. He brought you a *chien*, for goodness' sake." Now Eve was grinning from ear to ear, which irritated Goldie to no end. She knew Goldie hated it when she lapsed into French.

Goldie threw the afghan at her in a wad and huffed off the bed. "I'm sure a *chien* is nothing more than a casserole. He's simply being polite, like everyone else."

Eve didn't respond.

Verbally, that is.

The twinkle in her eyes spoke volumes.

For reasons beyond Goldie's comprehension, she felt the need to defend herself. Honestly, what was Eve thinking? Her Grandfather had died only four days ago. "And just so you know, I have less than zero interest in romance right now. No interest at all. None. Whatsoever."

But even as she spoke the words, the events of the morning played out in her mind like a slide show—the swirl of caramel sauce in the delicate shape of the letter G, the swipe of Java's pink tongue against her cheek, Joe's warm cocoa eyes. And, for the grand finale, the tip of Joe's finger grazing her nose. Her hands shook as she reached for her shoes. As slide shows went, it was a pretty good one.

But really. The man was only being nice. Everyone was. She was the object of the entire neighborhood's pity. She had her body's weight worth of casseroles in the next room to prove it. In her heart, she knew it wasn't pity in the strictest sense of the word. More like good, Christian charity. Believers caring for her in her time of need. Of course, she wasn't sure if Joe even believed in God. But she suspected his intentions were along the lines of those of her friends and the rest of Turtle Beach.

"There's absolutely nothing going on between me and Coffee Guy." Goldie ignored Eve's raised eyebrows. "I mean, Joe. Nothing at all."

As if to emphasize her point, to put a big black exclamation mark at the end of it, she slid her feet into her ratty, pink fuzzy slippers instead of her ballet flats.

There. She wiggled her toes inside the fluffy shoes. *Like anyone could accuse me of trying to look alluring now.*

Eve grimaced at the slippers and Goldie knew she'd effectively made her point. Goldie strode out of the bedroom, Eve hot on her pink fuzzy heels. When she reached the front door, she found Peggy peering through the peep hole.

"Excuse me?" Goldie tapped her on the shoulder and she jumped a clear foot backward.

"Oh. My goodness." Peggy cheeks glowed crimson. Her curly bob looked even whiter than usual next to her flushed face. "I was just…um…"

"Never mind, I'm well aware of what you were doing." Goldie motioned towards the door. "Do you mind?"

Eve looped her arm through Peggy's and they wandered off toward the dining room. Goldie wasn't fooled. She knew the minute she stepped out on the porch they would pounce on the peephole like two ducks on a June bug.

She blew out a sigh and caught a glimpse of herself in the hall mirror. Curly blonde hair mashed flat on one side, her black dress crumpled from her all-too-brief nap, she looked like a mess. Joe would have to be insane to have any romantic interest in her. She was a walking disaster area. The idea was laughable at best.

She twisted the doorknob and stepped outside.

"Hi Goldie." He stood in his usual spot on the front steps, his hair rumpled in an endearing sort of way, with a small orange and white dog nestled in his arms. A different dog than the furry Husky with one blue eye and one brown one. The dog he called Java. Goldie thought how strange it was that this man, who she scarcely knew, now had a regular spot on her porch…in her life.

"Hi." She cleared her throat and instinctively touched the tip of her nose. When she realized what she was doing, she clasped both her hands behind her back.

"Are you doing OK? I mean, with the funeral and all?" Concern colored his features as his voice trailed off. His gaze swept downward and lingered on her faded pink shoes. The corner of his mouth lifted in a half-grin.

Is he smiling? At my feet?

"Oh, you know." She waved her hand toward the house and its closed door. "It's a little overwhelming. But I'm glad you came. You were always such a good friend to Grandpa. He would have wanted you to be here."

Joe nodded and the half-grin vanished for a moment. He looked almost disappointed until Goldie reached over and scratched the little dog on the chin. It licked Goldie's fingertips and wiggled to escape Joe's grasp.

"Can I hold it?" Goldie asked, reaching her arms toward the dog. It had a short muzzle and long, silky ears. Goldie thought she recognized it as some sort of spaniel.

"Sure." He lifted the pup and helped settle it in the crook of Goldie's elbow.

She nestled the pup against her chest and dipped her chin to nuzzle its silky head. The feather-soft fur felt oddly comforting against Goldie's skin. "Is it a boy or a girl?"

Joe beamed at her. "She's a little girl."

"I thought she might be a girl. She's so tiny and cute. Very feminine." The dog's wispy tail wagged against the inside of her arm. It tickled and a giggle escaped from Goldie's lips. For a moment, she nearly forgot about the mourners gathered in her living room. "How many dogs do you have, Joe?"

"Just one." He ran a hand through his thick, dark

hair. His expression turned almost sheepish and words like *adorable* and *dreamy* floated through Goldie's thoughts. She blinked several long blinks.

Convinced she was getting her impression of the sweet dog confused with her thoughts of Joe, she asked the obvious question. "Then who does this one belong to?"

He flashed that full-on, thousand-watt smile and took a step closer. Goldie was surprised to find he smelled vaguely of toothpaste. She would have guessed coffee. Not that she'd given it any thought up until this point. Because she hadn't. Right?

"She belongs to you," he breathed out in a minty whisper.

Goldie tried to respond, but found herself frozen in time, unable to move or speak. A surprising thrill ran up and down her spine, and then she realized it all had to be a big misunderstanding. Joe must have seen this dog wandering around the neighborhood and thought it was hers for some reason. Although, surely her Grandpa would have mentioned to him if they'd had a dog. And Joe had been in their home plenty of times in those last months. There had never been a dog in sight. "Oh no. I don't have a dog."

She held the little spaniel out toward him. The dog's legs spun in the air as if she were trying to keep afloat.

Joe didn't reach for the pup. He just shrugged, winked and shoved his hands in the pockets of his khaki dress pants. "You do now."

The shiver ran up Goldie's spine again, causing her to feel more tingly, more alive, than she had in weeks. Acting on instinct, she hugged the spaniel close to her chest again. "What? You bought me a dog?"

Joe shook his head. "No, I didn't buy her. She's from the shelter. I host a monthly pet adoption at the coffee shop."

Goldie nodded, as if anything he said made sense. What was happening? How did the shelter and its monthly pet adoption have anything to do with her? People just didn't go around giving dogs as gifts. Casseroles, yes. Dogs, no. Definitely not.

"Look, I know it may not seem appropriate, and if you don't want her I understand. I can take her back." Joe ran his fingertips over the crown of the little pup's head. She batted long doggy lashes and nudged against his hand for more petting.

She does seem like a sweetheart.

Goldie squeezed the little orange and white dog and held her close enough so that she could feel the thump of a doggie heart beating against her own. It was the closest she'd been to another beating heart in a very long time. "Well, I'd hate to turn her away if she needs a home."

Joe clasped his hands in front of his chest and closed his eyes for the briefest of moments. It looked almost as though he were praying. "OK. That's great. Really, really great."

The dog melted into the crook of Goldie's arm, a warm bundle of soft fur. Goldie thought perhaps she would let the pup sleep with her in the pink room tonight. Then she realized that for the first time since her grandfather died, she would no longer be alone in the house where she grew up. Before she could stop it, a lone tear of gratitude fell from her lashes.

"Thank you," she breathed.

Joe nodded and his gaze glowed with understanding. Not pity, or even sympathy. The expression his coffee eyes bore was one of shared grief. "My pleasure."

Goldie sniffed and shifted from one foot to the other. She really needed to hold it together. But she had to ask him one last question before the two of them went inside and she lost him in the whirlwind of all the other guests. "Why?"

Joe looked up from the dog with a questioning glance. "Why what?"

"Why are you doing all of this for me? You hardly know me." Her voice cracked with emotion.

Joe's fingers wrapped around the shiny silver tag on the dog's pink collar. He turned over the tag, ran his thumb over the engraving and showed it to Goldie. "Because something told me this might be exactly what you need right now."

Bliss.

The dog's name was Bliss.

Chapter Three

"You did *what*?" Cinnamon's hand froze mid-air until the coffee she was pouring into a cherry red mug spilled over the edges and onto the countertop.

Joe blotted at the mess with a paper towel. "I gave her a dog."

"A *dog*? You gave her a *dog*?"

"Yes." Joe made air quotes with his fingers. "Chicks dig dogs. Sound familiar?"

Cinnamon groaned and blew a puff of air toward her forehead, momentarily causing her red bangs to go airborne.

Joe furrowed his brow. "What?"

"Dogs are living beings. They're not meant to be gifts. I would think you, of all people, would know that." She waved a dishrag toward Java's dog bed in the corner of the coffee shop. The Husky's mismatched eyes followed the flailing motions of the dishrag. "How ever did you get the shelter staff to agree to it?"

Joe closed his eyes and rubbed his temples. For such a young girl, Cinnamon certainly had no problem speaking her mind. Even when her boss was on the receiving end of her lecture. "You have a point. But, don't worry. If for some reason it doesn't work out, I'll take the dog. And once I explained the situation to the shelter manager, she understood."

"And what exactly is the situation?" Cinnamon's voice rose, full of romantic innuendo.

Joe shot her a look of warning. "It's not what you think."

"Then what is it?" Her expression became contrite while she twisted her dishrag and begged. "C'mon, please. You've told me this much already."

Joe's gaze shot from one empty barstool to the next. They were alone, so he figured he might as well share his moment of epiphany with the bubbly barista. What could it hurt? "Well, as you know I went by Goldie's house this morning to bring her the latte macchiato…which she loved, by the way."

"Told ya!" Cinnamon flashed a smile, and the movement of her face caused her nose stud to glisten and sparkle.

Joe attempted to ignore it, although to him it was like trying to ignore a strobe light. "She really liked Java, too. When she petted him it was the first time I'd seen her smile since her grandfather's passing." His heart warmed as he remembered her brief instant of joy.

"Told ya so. Again."

Joe ignored her cocky smirk. "Anyway, on the walk back to the coffee shop I began to pray."

"Pray?" Cinnamon frowned.

"Yes."

"What for?"

"For Goldie. I asked God to make her smile again, like she had with Java. I know she won't stop grieving all at once, but I asked for another smile. Just one. Just one small moment of happiness."

Cinnamon became very quiet and seemed to be turning his words over in her mind. "Then what happened?"

"I got back to the coffee shop and the animal shelter was here setting up for the pet adoption. I saw the little Cavalier King Charles Spaniel all by herself in the exercise pen." A chill ran up and down Joe's spine as he remembered the events of the morning. "At first I thought how strange it was to see a homeless Cavalier. So, I went over to pick her up. Then I saw the tag, and her name, and I knew."

"Knew what?" Cinnamon bunched the dishrag in her hands, clearly engrossed in his story.

"I knew it was God answering my prayer. It was the perfect moment of clarity." He clutched his hand to his chest, remembering the scripture that had come immediately to mind. The words had been so clear, so perfect that it was as if an angel had whispered them in his ear right there in the parking lot. How could he possibly explain something so intimate?

"The dog's name was Bliss. Bliss, of all things." This part of the story always made him laugh and it did once more.

Cinnamon crossed her arms. "You're losing me, boss."

Joe turned to face her. "Ephesians 3:20."

"From the Bible?"

"Yes." He closed his eyes and spoke the words aloud. He'd heard them at church many times throughout the years, but never had they meant as much to him as they had this morning while he held the wiggly pup in his arms. "It says God is able to do immeasurably more than all we ask or imagine, according to His power that is at work within us."

He paused and let the scripture and its meaning soak in. "Don't you see? I asked Him for one smile, one sliver of contentment. But God wants to do more than all I could ever ask or imagine. He wants to give her joy, all-encompassing happiness. He wants to give her bliss."

Cinnamon gasped. "Wow."

Joe cleared his throat, now clogged with emotion. "So, I knew the dog belonged to her."

"That is the most amazing thing I've ever heard." Even Cinnamon sounded choked up. "You really believe in all that, don't you?"

Joe slid his gaze toward her and realized for the first time that she may not be a believer. After all, he didn't know that much about her personal life. She was his employee—a recent one, at that. "I do."

She twisted her dishrag in her hands, stared at it and chewed on her lip. Joe wondered what she was thinking and whether or not anyone had spoken to her about Jesus before.

"You know, Cinnamon, you're always welcome to come to my church sometime. It's very laid back. We meet right on the beach." And just to make sure she didn't get the wrong idea, he added, "I could introduce you to some of the other kids there your age."

She rolled up the white towel and hit him with it in the arm. "You sound like my dad. I'm not a child, you know. I'll turn twenty in a few months."

"Well, just know you're welcome. Anytime." There. He'd extended the offer. Maybe someday she would show up. He was unsure what else he could do and not cross some sort of imaginary boundary line. He was possibly crossing one already. But, he considered Cinnamon a friend in addition to his employee. Besides, were there really any boundary lines when doing the Lord's work was concerned?

She nodded, a wistful look crossing her features, before returning to her usual perky self. "Joe, tell me more about Goldie."

Perky and nosy, to be precise.

He grabbed another crimson coffee mug and filled it from the fresh pot of decaf. "Don't you think it's time we get back to work?"

She rolled her eyes and waved her arms around the empty coffee shop. "Hello? We don't have any customers right now. Good grief, Joe. You're such a *guy*. I'm not asking you to share your deepest darkest feelings, although your reluctance to talk about her right now speaks volumes."

Joe sipped his coffee and tried to ignore her raised eyebrows.

"One thing. Just tell me one thing about her." Clearly she wasn't going to relent.

"All right, one thing." Joe tried to inject some authority into his voice. Although at this point, he'd probably lost whatever power he'd once had over the conversation. "Then I'm disappearing into my office while you experiment with some more new coffee drinks. OK?"

Cinnamon held up her right hand. "OK. Scout's honor."

"Hmm. I didn't realize the scouts were allowing nose rings these days." He just couldn't resist.

She jammed a hand on her hip. "I'm waiting. One thing. You promised."

"OK, OK. I was just teasing." Joe paused, a warm sensation coming over him, like a tender embrace. There were a million things about Goldie he could share—countless little details he'd treasured over the years. The types of things other people may not even notice. But he'd taken each and every one and saved it in his memory for moments like this one. He realized he wasn't telling Cinnamon about Goldie because she'd pestered him. He wanted to talk about Goldie. "She likes to wear scarves."

"Scarves?" Cinnamon's hand flew to her neck. "Like knitted winter scarves?"

"No. Silk scarves, like you see women wearing all the time in old movies. Sometimes she wraps one around her ponytail and other times knotted around her purse. I've seen them woven through the belt loops of her jeans before, too." The last one he'd seen her wear was deep purple and it had caused her blue eyes to look almost lavender. When he closed his eyes, he could still see her lilac gaze peeking at him from behind blonde curls.

Cinnamon cocked her head, once again sending the nose ring into a dazzling fit. "That's so retro. And pretty cool."

"Yea, I think it's pretty cool, too." He frowned, the warm feeling in his heart now tinged with sadness. "I haven't seen her wear one since her grandfather died."

"I'll bet she'll start wearing them again. You know, when she's feeling more like her normal self again."

"You're probably right." Joe pushed off from the counter where he'd been resting his elbows, and whistled toward the dog bed. "C'mon Java, let's go do some paperwork."

Cinnamon's gaze followed the big Husky as he trotted toward him. "Joe?"

"Hmm?"

"I'm sorry about the way I acted when you first

told me about Bliss. Giving Goldie the dog was the right thing to do. It was a brave, bold move." She winked. "And the right one."

Joe took a dog biscuit from one of his pockets and offered it to Java. He smiled. "I think so, too."

∂∽⮌

"Well, it's not a casserole. That's for sure." Peggy watched Bliss tumble head over heels, as she charged across the living room and tackled Goldie's slipper.

Goldie squealed and, much to the Cavalier's delight, kicked off the shoe. The pup shook it in her jaws with fury, and then collapsed on top of the pink fuzz.

The post-funeral crowd had thinned to only the three women sitting in the den—Goldie, Peggy and Eve. Well, technically it was four if you counted the spaniel.

"I cannot believe he brought you a dog." Eve stared at Bliss as if she were an alien from outer space. "I mean, what was he thinking?"

"I, for one, think it's adorable. I think *he* is adorable." Peggy clutched her heart for emphasis. "Honestly, Goldie. That young man is a keeper."

Goldie bit the inside of her cheek to keep from grinning in tentative agreement. "I'm not *keeping* him. I don't even *have* him."

Eve lifted a brow at the romping Cavalier King Charles Spaniel. "I beg to differ."

"What?" Goldie's gaze flitted back and forth between the two women. She waved a hand in Bliss's direction. "This doesn't mean anything. He's a friend. Nothing more."

It didn't escape her notice that a week ago, she wouldn't have even referred to him as a friend. He was an acquaintance at best.

Or so she thought.

"That," Peggy pointed a finger at the dog, now nestled between Goldie's feet with her head resting serenely on Goldie's toe, "is not your typical 'friendly' gesture. I didn't see anyone else bring you a dog today. Did you, Eve?"

"Oh sure," she said with an eye roll. "There are about 15 of them or so piled on the dining room table next to the casseroles. Shall I put them in the freezer next to the other leftovers?"

Peggy and Eve collapsed into a fit of giggles.

"Don't you pay any attention to them, Bliss." Goldie scooped the dog into her arms and nestled her cheek into the downy, soft fur. "No one's going to put you in the freezer."

"Oh. My. Gosh." Eve's eyes widened as she watched Goldie snuggle with her new dog. "You're keeping it, aren't you?"

"Of course." Goldie held Bliss in the protective crook of her arm. "Why wouldn't I?"

"Maybe because your pal, your buddy, your 'friend' Joe, dumped it in your lap without even asking if you wanted a dog." She flailed her arms around and Bliss flinched. "It was a sweet gesture, but you shouldn't feel obligated to keep the dog just because he gave it to you."

"Her," Goldie corrected. "She's not an *it*. She's a *her*."

"Whatever. You get the picture. All I'm saying is you are not required to keep that dog." Eve pointed at the Cavalier, a look of disgust creeping into her features.

"I know." Goldie laid a hand on Bliss's back as the pup curled into a ball and her eyelids fluttered shut. "But she needs a home. And I need…"

Goldie paused. What exactly, did she need? Above all, she needed the comfort of knowing she wasn't all alone in her grandfather's house. She needed to finally talk to God about all she was feeling. She needed to know she still mattered. She needed a reason to get up in the morning. Bliss took care of all these needs. Except the God part. "…I need her."

She needed her. Plain and simple. The part that wasn't quite so simple is how Joe had known exactly what she needed. Of all people, he had been the one to look into her heart and see what would bring her back to life. Not her friends. Not anyone else in Turtle Beach. Not even Care Group. Just Joe.

The thought gave Goldie pause.

And a fluttering sensation deep inside.

"Why are you so skeptical?" She directed her question at Eve. "I thought you were rooting for some kind of love connection between Joe and me."

Joe and me. The very words tasted strange on her tongue, but not at all unpleasant. Perhaps it was something she could grow accustomed to, like the rich flavor of coffee.

"Hey, the guy is clearly enamored with you. That's all I was trying to say." Her wide-eyed look of faux innocence told Goldie that Eve longed to say plenty more.

"What?" Goldie's impatient voice caused Bliss to waken with a start in her lap. She patted the little dog's head in apology. "Go ahead. Tell me."

Eve sighed. "I love you. You know that. So, please

don't take this the wrong way."

Goldie swallowed and wondered what was coming next.

"For years now your whole life has revolved around the big guy. I know you loved him dearly and wouldn't trade all those years with him for the world." Eve nodded with sympathy.

Goldie buried her fingers in the warm scruff of Bliss's neck and resisted the urge to scream. *Love him, not "loved" him. I still love him and always will.*

"But, now he's gone and it is time for you to move on. You can do whatever you want. Go back to school, travel the world, get an exciting job. This is your opportunity to embark on whatever adventure God has planned for you."

"People with jobs have dogs," Goldie answered flatly. "So do people in school. And people who travel."

"I know. Keep the dog if that's what you really want." She shrugged. "I'm just not so sure if you should keep Joe."

"What?" Peggy, who had been uncharacteristically silent up until this point, almost jumped out her chair.

Eve held up her hands to shield herself. If Goldie hadn't been so drained by the topic of this conversation, she would have laughed at Eve's efforts at self-preservation. How many times had they joked before about how they were both secretly afraid of Peggy? Too many to count. She might be elderly, but she was no "little old lady." Not by a long shot. One time Goldie had even seen her threaten a pair of total strangers with her knitting needles when she overheard them make a racial slur about a nearby child. Goldie had recounted the scene in great detail for Eve on more than one occasion. Every time, Eve had shuddered with mock terror. Judging by the look of fear in her eyes now, Goldie thought perhaps some of that terror had been real.

"Nothing. Never mind," Eve squeaked out. Her gaze darted around frantically. No doubt looking for the pointy knitting needles.

"Oh, by all means continue. Tell us exactly what is wrong with that sweet man." Peggy crossed her arms and stared daggers at Eve.

"Well, first of all, I agree that he seems very nice." Eve flashed a shaky smile and perched on the very edge of the recliner, looking ready to bolt at the first glimpse of knitting needle. "But don't you find him the slightest bit, well, old-fashioned? I mean, have you been inside his coffee shop? It's like a museum. Hello? Has the guy ever seen a Starbucks?"

"Oh, please. This is Turtle Beach, not New York City," Peggy countered with a satisfied smirk. "Besides, there's nothing wrong with old-fashioned values. Things like kindness, loyalty and good manners,"

"Since when is it considered good manners to bring a dog to a funeral?"

That did it. Peggy and Eve bickered and talked over one another until Goldie couldn't tell who was saying what. There had never been so much yelling in the house since her Grandpa had accused George Brown of cheating at Checkers at their Fourth of July party when Goldie was in eleventh grade.

In the middle of it all, Goldie sat completely silent and stroked Bliss's long, copper ears. Part of her longed to add her two cents to the conversation. She wanted to tell them about the fancy caramel coffee drink Joe had brought her that very morning. If asked, she could describe the drizzled caramel *G* in excruciating detail. She would have explained how that exquisite beverage was the result of his daily quest to get her to drink coffee. Without ever realizing it, she'd come to rely on his presence every morning on the front steps. It gave her new lonely life one constant source of companionship, even though at times it was through a closed door.

She thought about trying to explain how something in his warm chocolate eyes told her he understood her grief down to its core. And that those same sensitive eyes always sparkled with humor when he looked at her Sponge Bob pajamas or fuzzy pink slippers.

Most of all, she wanted to say that it was Joe's presence—and his rather unexpected gift—that had gotten her through one of the worst days of her life.

But in the end, Goldie said none of those things. She didn't know what was happening between her and Joe, but whatever it was felt deeply personal. Almost sacred.

So she said nothing at all.

Chapter Four

Goldie wasn't sure how it happened. One minute, she was out for a morning stroll with Bliss bobbing at the end of her new, pink patent leather leash and the next...

Well, the next minute she found herself hovering at the entrance of Joe's Coffee Shop. What was she doing here? Her intention had been to head over to the Turtle Beach Library to check out some books on dog training and puppies, maybe even learn a bit more about Cavalier King Charles Spaniels.

Her eyes widened at the sight of the bright yellow awning with Joe's name marching across it in big letters. How had she gotten here? It was as if her feet had walked here completely of their own accord.

She glanced down at Bliss. "Please tell me this was your idea. You dragged me here, right?"

The spaniel looked up at her with melting, doe eyes.

Yeah.

Like this little thing could drag anyone anywhere.

Goldie took a deep breath and tried to acknowledge that she must have walked here of her own free will. While her mind had been a complete whirlwind of phrases like "it's time to get on with your life," her feet had chosen to follow her heart instead of her overcrowded head. And she'd ended up here. On Joe's front steps.

Quite a little turnaround.

Goldie glanced at her watch and noted that if she walked quickly she could get home in time to catch the beginning of her game show. But, when she looked back up, she noticed a young woman with a shock of red hair staring at her through the window. She stood behind the counter, dishrag in hand, and seemed to be waiting for Goldie to step over the threshold.

Sorry, Cary.

Goldie gulped and opened the door.

She was greeted with a chorus of woo-woos from Java, who shuffled over from his dog bed to greet Bliss with a wag of his tail.

"Morning, Java." Goldie scratched the Husky behind his pointy ears, all the while keenly aware of a pair of eyes watching her with great interest from behind the counter. "Good morning," she said to the red-haired girl.

"Oh, hi." The girl dragged her gaze from the white silk scarf tied around Goldie's ponytail and offered a warm smile. "You must be Goldie."

"Yes," Goldie answered, feeling more self-conscious by the minute. "Um, how did you know my name?"

"Joe's mentioned you a time or two. I'm Cinnamon, by the way."

Was it Goldie's imagination, or did Cinnamon seem exceptionally happy to see her? She looked nearly as excited as the audience members of the Oprah show when she gave out all the free goodies.

What did she call it? Her *favorite things* episode.

Good grief. I watch way too much daytime television. Everyone's right. I really do need to get on with my life.

Goldie, suddenly filled with the heady knowledge of what it must feel like to be the all-powerful Oprah, fiddled with the end of Bliss's leash. Before she could stop the flow of words spewing from her mouth, she asked, "He mentioned me?"

"Oh yes." Cinnamon nodded with a grin. Then she waved her hand in the direction of the large chalkboard hanging over the counter. "Plus you're on our menu."

"What?" She must be having some sort of hallucination. Either that or she'd been so distracted by the sight of Cinnamon's unfortunate nose ring, she'd heard wrong.

"Your drink. The one Joe named after you." She wiggled her fingers toward the chalkboard again, this time with a flourish. "See? Right here."

And there it was. In black and white for the entire world to see.

Goldie's Latte Macchiato. $3.00.

She was sandwiched right between *Black Coffee* and *Espresso*. And my, she wasn't cheap either.

"Oh. Goodness." Goldie read and re-read the words to make sure they were real.

She blinked. Hard.

They were still there. "I've never been a menu item before."

Cinnamon smiled even wider. "Would you like one?"

Goldie tore her gaze from the chalkboard menu and tried to form a coherent answer, which would have been much easier if she'd been paying attention to the question. "Excuse me?"

"Would you like one?" Cinnamon asked. "A *Goldie's Latte Macchiato*? Your drink."

A giggle escaped Goldie's lips. It was so strange hearing her own name in the title of a beverage. Strange, but nice. She decided she quite liked it. "Yes, please. I'll have one *Goldie's Latte Macchiato*."

"Coming right up." Cinnamon winked at her, then added in a tantalizing whisper, "And I'll let Joe know you're here."

"Um, OK." Goldie tried not to blush, but a warm flush crawled up her neck and made its way to her cheeks.

And, to top it off, her nose started tingling at the sound of his name.

Her gaze flitted once again to the blackboard and her name drawn there in white chalk. She tilted her head to admire it, as if it were an exquisite piece of art. It certainly stood out from the other offerings on the menu. There wasn't a single other name up there. Not even Joe's. Just hers.

What did it mean?

Was Eve right? Could Joe possibly be attracted to her?

"So, what do you think?" A voice snapped her out of her thoughts. The voice of Joe himself. She stopped gaping at the chalkboard and directed all her attention toward him.

He pointed at the menu and grinned. When he smiled, his eyes crinkled in the corners in a most appealing way. How had she failed to notice this before? "It's...quite a surprise actually."

He raised his eyebrows. "A good one I hope?"

"Of course. It's very sweet. Thank you." She

reached toward Cinnamon's outstretched hand, which held her steaming coffee drink topped with a generous portion of whipped cream. Of course.

"Wait just a minute." Joe intercepted and took the cup in his own hand, causing Goldie's fingertips to graze his with a feather light touch.

She pulled her hand away and wondered if he felt the same sizzle when their fingers met.

"You can't drink this yet. It's not finished." Joe picked up a slender bottle with a fine-tipped nozzle and drizzled a delicate stream of caramel over the top of her drink. His hand was remarkably steady and, before Goldie even realized what was happening, he'd created a perfectly shaped *G* atop the whipped cream.

So the initial had been his idea.

Wow.

"Here you go. All yours." He held the cup toward her. She reached for it, careful not to touch his hand this time.

"So do all *Goldie's Latte Macchiatos* come with the fancy *G* on top?"

Joe's smile turned sheepish. "No. That's a special touch."

Goodness gracious. "I can't begin to thank you enough for all you've done for me."

"No thanks necessary." There it was again. That familiar gleam in his eye. The one that made her feel as if he had really known her all along.

"I disagree. Plenty of thanks are required. Especially for this precious little creature." She nodded her head toward Bliss, now splayed belly-up on the ground.

Joe came around to the front of the counter and scratched her tummy while Java watched with a cocked head. "So you two are getting along?"

"Fabulously. She never lets me out of her sight. It's very comforting." Without warning, Goldie suddenly felt the sting of tears in the corners of her eyes.

Would this ever stop? Today she finally felt better. More like herself than she had in days. Then it was back. A fresh wave of grief.

If Joe noticed, he disguised it well. He stood from where he was crouched on the floor beside Bliss and glanced around the shop. "We're pretty slow right now. How would you like to take the dogs for a quick walk on the beach?"

Goldie felt the *yes* rise in her heart before she even had a chance to give the question any thought. It was at that moment she realized part of her hoped Eve was right about Joe. Not the part about him being all wrong for her—good grief, no! The part about him having feelings for her. "Sure. That sounds nice."

"OK. Let me grab Java's leash and we'll go."

Two new customers filed in while he disappeared for a minute. As Joe returned, worn leather leash in hand, one of them placed an order for a *Goldie's Latte Macchiato* in a booming voice. Goldie's head turned at the sound of her name, but no one seemed to notice.

Except Joe. He winked at her as Cinnamon went to work once again at the espresso machine.

This is so strange. Strange, but nice. She wondered if she sat here all day in Joe's Coffee shop listening to people order her drink, if she'd ever grow accustomed to it.

Somehow, she doubted it.

"You know what?" Joe said as he held the door open for Goldie and Bliss. "Your intense dislike for coffee may be the best thing that ever happened for my business."

Goldie took a sip of her drink and grinned. "So I guess that makes us even." Hardly. But it was the only clever response she could come up with on short notice.

Joe guided her along the winding sidewalk beside the coffee shop that led to the sandy beach dunes. Goldie could hear the ocean, even smell it, before she actually saw the sun's rays dancing on the crystal clear water. As far as she looked in either direction, Goldie couldn't see another person on the isolated strip of beach.

They walked over the dunes where the sand was soft, like fine powder, and closer to the water. The cool ocean breeze ruffled the dogs' coats and blew Bliss's ears straight backward. She looked as though she could fly. Once they reached the packed sand of the shoreline, Joe and Goldie fell in step beside one another. Bliss and Java crept out in front, trotting and wagging their tails. Every so often one of them pounced on a seagull shadow drifting across the sand.

For a long moment, neither Goldie nor Joe said a word. But it wasn't an awkward silence. It felt comfortable, peaceful. Goldie wondered if right then— walking on the beach with Joe and his dog—her own eyes held that familiar glimmer of affection she'd seen so often in his.

"Can I ask you something?" Joe asked, breaking the silence.

"Sure."

"I couldn't help but notice the obituary in the paper listed your name as Teresa." He paused. Goldie suspected he wanted to make sure she felt comfortable discussing the obituary. She nodded to signal she was fine.

Joe continued, smiling so his eyes crinkled in the corners again. "So how did you get the nickname Goldie?"

"Grandpa." A tender feeling came over Goldie at the memory. "From the time I was a little girl, he always called me Goldilocks. Eventually, it got shortened to Goldie. Now that I'm an adult, I guess it seems strange to be named after a fairy tale character."

"No. Not strange. I think it's charming. It suits you perfectly." His gaze traveled the length of her blonde ponytail and over the wispy curls that had bounced free in the salty wind. "Does it bother you to talk about him? So soon?"

"No. Strangely enough, it feels nice." It was the truth, she realized with a wistful sigh. "He was such a huge part of my life, I can't imagine not talking about him."

Joe stopped walking and turned to face her. His dark eyebrows and the tips of his thick eyelashes were laced with a fine layer of salt from the ocean breeze. At Goldie's feet, Bliss danced on her hind legs and batted her front paws for Goldie to pick her up. But Goldie couldn't seem to look away from Joe.

"You know I'm here if you ever want to talk. About him. Or about anything. *Capeesh*?"

Her heart almost leapt out of her chest. *Capeesh* had been one of her grandfather's trademark phrases. He'd picked up the Italian slang word while he was stationed in Europe with the Army. She couldn't remember hearing anyone else ever use the word. Somehow, it seemed fitting for Joe to take up the tradition.

Goldie nodded her agreement and answered back,

just as she did with Grandpa. "Capeesh."

"Let me take this for you," he said as he reached for her empty coffee cup. "It looks like Bliss might be running out of steam."

Goldie scooped the spaniel into her arms. "She just needs a little cuddle."

Java poked Joe's leg with one of his big paws and woofed. When Goldie and Joe responded with laughter, he barked even louder.

Joe wagged his finger at the Husky. "Don't even think about it. You're too big to be carried."

They fell in step with one another again, and not until Goldie's senses became enveloped with the rich aroma of coffee, did she realize they were once again right around the corner from the shop. "We'll let you get back to work. Thanks for the walk. And the coffee."

Joe paused. He raked a hand through his windblown hair, still tinged with salty crystals. Java's gaze flitted back and forth between Joe and the coffee shop, as if he were trying to figure out why they weren't already inside. "Um, Goldie?"

"Yes?" Something in his tone and the way he shifted his weight from one foot to the other caused a swarm of butterflies to take flight in the pit of her stomach.

He cleared his throat and continued, "Are you busy this Saturday?"

Oh. My. Gosh. Joe the Coffee Guy is asking me out.

Goldie froze for a moment, unsure how to answer. The flutter in her belly told her she certainly wanted to go out with Joe. But, was it too soon? Was she even thinking clearly?

Then she looked at Joe and remembered who he was. He was still the same Joe. The Joe who played checkers with her grandfather. Grandpa had adored Joe. He would have probably been thrilled to see her go out on a date with him. Especially now. What was her problem? Of course, she would say yes. Maybe she would even say *capeesh*. Yes, that would probably make him laugh. That would be her answer. Capeesh. "No, not really. No plans."

"Oh, OK. Well, I was thinking you might want to bring Bliss to a dog training class. Java and I go every Saturday afternoon. Would you like to come along?"

It took every ounce of strength Goldie possessed to keep the smile on her face intact. She was mortified to her very core. He wasn't asking her out on a date. He was inviting her to a dog training class. A dog training class! And here she was, planning a witty, flirty dialogue about their non-date. Emphasis on the *non*. How on earth had she misread the signals?

Horrified, she nodded and tried to force out an answer. "Uh, sure. That sounds great."

She listened and commented in what she hoped were all the right places as Joe explained all about the training class. All the while, she clutched Bliss closer to her chest like a life preserver.

"OK, I'll see you Saturday." Joe winked and walked backwards, his gaze never leaving hers until he'd disappeared inside the shop.

Goldie spun on her heel, still holding Bliss in her arms, and headed for home. Growing wearier with each step, she forgot all about the library. She just wanted to get home, crawl back under the safety of her covers and forget she'd ever stopped at Joe's Coffee Shop. She knew it would be difficult, however, with the sweet taste of caramel still lingering on her lips.

❧❦

"So, did you ask her out?" Cinnamon swirled her straw around in what Joe thought was a vanilla latte. He still couldn't keep all the new drinks straight. When he'd asked her to develop a few new menu options, it had been akin to unleashing a dragon.

He rubbed his temples and glanced up at the chalkboard. Overnight the number of offerings listed there had tripled. Yep, he was actually going to be forced to study his own menu to get it all straight.

"Hello? Joe?" Cinnamon's distinct note of impatience brought his attention back to her interrogation. "Are you paying attention? What happened on your walk? Did you ask her out?"

If Cinnamon ever grew bored of her career as a barista, she had a brilliant future as a detective. Or private investigator. Pretty much anything that involved large amounts of questioning. And snooping.

She swirled her straw again and took a giant sip of her latte. The slurping noise echoed off the empty walls of the coffee shop. Joe wagged his finger at her. "Don't slurp."

"Can't help it. This is so good. Do you want me to make you one?" Cinnamon's words came out in rapid machine gun fire and she hopped from one foot to the other. "Hey, you're changing the subject. You still haven't answered my question."

Joe grabbed the large, empty cup from her hand. "That's it. I'm cutting you off. Clearly, you've had enough caffeine."

Cinnamon shrugged, but Joe noticed her gaze followed the empty cup as he pitched it in the trashcan. "Hey, it got super-busy in here while you were out. I had to keep up somehow. But don't feel bad about leaving me here by myself during the rush. It was all for the sake of true love." Cinnamon plopped her elbows on the countertop and rested her chin in her hands. She fluttered her eyelashes and sighed. "So, did you ask her out or what?"

Joe shot an envious glance at Java, snoozing away on his dog bed. Anything to avoid looking Cinnamon in the eye. Or nose ring, for that matter. "No."

"No?" she shrieked. "What do you mean *no*?"

"You don't understand. It's not the right time." He'd wanted to ask her out. No doubt about it. Then again, he'd wanted to ask her out for the better part of a year.

"Are you crazy? Of course it's the right time." She drummed her shiny orange nails on the counter. Their pounding hammered her words into his head.

"And how would you know that? You've known Goldie for all of five minutes."

"I'm a woman. I can tell." She said it with an air of confidence that belied her young age.

"Is that so?" Joe doubted she possessed any special insight into Goldie's emotions, but hope tugged at his heart ever so slightly. "How can you tell?"

"Easy. She was wearing a scarf. Didn't you see it?"

Of course, he'd seen it. It wrapped around her ponytail in three precise loops. The silky ends played with her mass of curls, slipping in and out of the blonde ringlets with every subtle movement of her lovely head. He couldn't hide the smile that played on his lips as he remembered it. "Yes. I saw the scarf."

"So, she's ready." Cinnamon announced, as if the matter could be settled that easily, by the mere presence of a silky wisp of fabric in Goldie's hair.

"The scarf could mean something. I'll admit that," Joe conceded. "But it doesn't necessarily have anything to do with me. She's probably feeling better about things; that's all."

Even as he spoke his words of doubt, he secretly prayed. *Dear Lord, please. Please let it have everything to do with me.*

Cinnamon heaved an enormous sigh. "Boss, you can't be serious. Are you blind? She wore her trademark scarf for the first time in over a week to *your* coffee shop, to see *you*, with the dog that *you* gave her."

When she put it that way, he almost dared to believe it. Could it be that after all this time, with a few simple acts of kindness, Goldie had finally noticed him? "You do have a point."

"So what are you waiting for?"

It was a legitimate question. What was he waiting for? "It's complicated."

Cinnamon rolled her eyes. "How so?"

"Bob, Goldie's grandfather, was a friend of mine. I made him a promise. A promise I intend to keep."

Cinnamon's face fell, a look of horror coming over her. "Oh no. You didn't promise him you would never date his granddaughter, did you?"

Joe chuckled. "Good grief, no. That's not it at all." Hardly. In fact, now that he thought about it, he supposed it probably would make Bob rather happy if he and Goldie ended up together.

Cinnamon let out a puff of breath. "Then what was your promise?"

"I promised him I would always look after Goldie for him once he was gone." Overcome with reverence for his pledge to Goldie's grandfather, Joe lowered his voice. "That's easy to do so long as I'm her friend."

"And even easier if she's..."

Joe leveled his gaze at Cinnamon and spoke his secret hope, his dream, aloud for the first time. "...my wife."

Cinnamon gasped. "You really love her, don't you?"

"I do." Choked with emotion, Joe cleared his throat. "But don't you see? If she's not ready, if I push too soon, things could get very awkward. She might not even want to be my friend. Then how could I watch over her, as I promised?"

Cinnamon pondered this for a moment and answered him in a way he never expected. "Boss, where does your God fit into all this?"

The question hit him like a slap in the face. He gave himself a moment to recover before responding. "I'm rather surprised to hear you talk about God, Cinnamon. Pleased, but surprised."

She shrugged her shoulders and peered at him with wide eyes. Joe could scarcely believe it, but she looked almost bashful. "I've been thinking about everything you said the other day and how you believe that He answers prayers. If you truly think He provided Bliss for you to give to Goldie, why don't you believe He'll show you the way to keep your promise? Why don't you trust Him with your feelings for Goldie?"

Joe ran his hand through his hair, still damp from the salty ocean breeze, and paused. He couldn't answer the question. She was right. This girl, who readily admitted she wasn't sure she even believed in God, had somehow spotted his lack of faith where his romantic feelings were concerned.

Forgive me, Lord. Forgive me for not trusting in you

and for being a bad example for your child, Cinnamon. She's searching for you, Lord. Help me help her.

"You really have been thinking about God a lot, haven't you?"

She gnawed on the corner of an orange fingernail. "A little."

He wished he knew a way to be a better witness for Christ. Unsure what exactly to do, he said, "That invitation to church is still good, by the way."

Cinnamon grinned, and turned to him, the diamond stud next to her nostril shining like a beacon. "I'll make you a deal, boss."

"A deal?"

"Yep." She shoved her hand toward him and nodded, as though she wanted a handshake. "If I go to your church, you will agree to ask Goldie out on a date."

"Are you serious?" Joe was skeptical. It seemed wrong, almost like a bribe. But, then again, maybe God didn't care. Maybe this way he and Cinnamon both would be following His plan.

"Yes sir. Completely, one hundred percent serious." She clicked her heels together and saluted him.

"OK." He stuck his hand toward hers, but then drew it back. "But you have to come to church first. Then, afterwards, I'll do it. I'll jump in with both feet and ask Goldie out."

"Great. It's a deal." She took his hand in hers and pumped it up and down in a vigorous shake.

"Deal."

As Joe stood there in the coffee shop, shaking hands underneath the chalkboard with Goldie's name winking down at him, he thought once again about the scarf. What did it mean? He imagined touching it, feeling the delicate silk between his fingers. He dreamed of unwinding it from Goldie's thick tresses and letting her curls fly free in the salty wind.

And he wondered how many Sundays he would have to wait for Cinnamon to come to church.

Chapter Five

"Goldie Jensen, you are the next contestant on Name that Price!" The familiar baritone voice of the announcer boomed in Goldie's ear and she momentarily panicked. How could she possibly run down all the steps to the stage in her clumsy, pink fuzzy slippers? She hiked up the hem of her Sponge Bob pajamas and somehow found herself behind a microphone. Cary Andrews, the studio audience and all the viewers at home watched and waited for her to say something.

"Hi Cary," she muttered, casting furtive glances at the other contestants. Why was she the only one wearing pajamas?

"Good morning, Goldie," he gushed. "Are you ready for the next item?"

"Yes." Goldie nodded, with no small amount of hesitation. "Yes, I am."

Cary beamed at her, flashing polished white teeth that seemed even brighter than they were on television. "Then let's Name that Price."

Cary swept an arm toward the bright orange set, where a slender model with impossibly thick, frosted hair stood before a closed curtain. Every eye in the studio was fixed on that curtain, waiting for it to rise. What hid behind it? A pair of his-and-her motorcycles? A bicycle built for two? Perhaps a trip to some exotic location? Or, one could only hope, a new car?

The model swirled her wrist and, as if by magic, the curtain slowly began to rise. Goldie wondered if she learned that move in some sort of game show hostess school. If so, she must have gotten an A-plus.

Around her, the audience let out a collective gasp as the curtain rose to reveal sparkly gold letters above an enormous photo of Goldie, walking arm in arm with a handsome young man. Goldie blinked. What was her photo doing there—on the set of a game show? And who was that in the photo with her? Was that Joe? Coffee Guy Joe?

The announcer's voice boomed again. "Our next item up for bid is a new life for Goldie Jensen."

The audience oohed and aahed while the announcer went on to explain that this wonderful new life included a fulfilling job, an up-to-the-minute fashionable wardrobe, loads of exciting experiences, a doting boyfriend and all sorts of fabulousness she had never before imagined.

Goldie stared at the giant picture. It was her, but at the same time wasn't her. The photo-Goldie glowed somehow. She looked the same, but happier. Blissful, even. And the way photo-Joe looked at photo-Goldie, with such tenderness and longing in his gaze, made regular Goldie's throat go bone dry. This was a man who wanted to do more than just attend dog training classes together.

"Goldie Jensen!" Her name rolled off Cary's tongue with dramatic flair. He waved his note cards at the smiling couple in the enormous picture. "That looks like quite a prize. Tell us, what price tag do you put on this thrilling new life?"

Goldie stared at the photo again, transfixed, and found she couldn't speak. She was physically incapable of uttering a single word.

"C'mon now Goldie," Cary urged. "You must name a price. What's it going to be?"

She struggled to say something, anything at all. Cary, the audience, even the model with the graceful wrists waited for her to come to her senses. Finally, she managed to squeak out two words. "Too high."

It was too much. The stakes were too high. More than mere dollars, the price included such intangible things as her pride, humiliation, hope. And perhaps most importantly, faith. Faith in a God who she'd given up on in recent days.

No, it was too much. Too much for her to even dream about.

Cary stood before her, squinting behind his black-rimmed glasses. He wasn't smiling anymore. In fact, he looked pretty grim. "Goldie, time is running out. We need you to name your price."

"Too high. I can't," was all she said.

ॐ◌ॐ

Goldie blinked at the television screen, confused by what she saw. No orange shag carpeting. No skinny models showing off fancy items. No bonus round. No showroom shootout.

"What is going on?" she muttered.

At the sound of her voice, the orange and white ball of fur in her lap twitched to life. Goldie squinted at the television screen again while Bliss's tail thumped against her thigh. The spaniel looked up at her with sleepy eyes.

Dramatic music pulsed from the T.V. speakers in a familiar one-two beat that could only mean one thing: *Law & Order*.

Goldie flew off the sofa, sending Bliss tumbling to her feet, all flailing paws and flying ears.

"Sorry, puppy." Goldie scooped the dog up in her arms as she scurried to the bedroom. "But, we're late. Late, late, late."

If *Law & Order* was already on, that meant it was past time for the beginning of Care Group. How had she zoned out on the sofa for an entire day? Goldie readily admitted to watching too much television, but this was excessive, even for her. Where had the time gone? And what was that bizarre daydream all about?

Goldie shook her head in an effort to clear the cobwebs and snap herself into the present. Obviously, the daydream was about yesterday and her walk with Joe. It was about dog training class and their *non*-date.

She was suddenly very glad it was Care Group night. Maybe it was time to start talking to God again. Clearly, she was making a mess of things trying to handle them on her own. She glanced at herself in the mirror hanging above the dresser in her pink bedroom.

"Ugh," Goldie groaned at her reflection. "Still in your pajamas. How pathetic is that?"

Bliss pranced in circles around Goldie's feet, her paws making little pitter-patter noises on the hard wood floor.

"Don't worry. I'm not leaving you behind." Goldie picked her up and set her in the new dog carrier she'd picked up yesterday before her fateful trip to Joe's Coffee Shop. It looked like a handbag, so her older friends probably wouldn't ever know a dog was hidden inside. But it made Goldie feel good to know Bliss was near.

"You don't even care if I'm still in my pajamas, do you?"

Bliss cocked her head and pawed at the air. Goldie laughed. "That's what I thought."

The spaniel snuggled into the soft, faux lambskin lining and Goldie slid her arm through the leather handles. She took a peek in the mirror again.

It was quite a fashion statement. A plush, amethyst velvet "handbag" paired with Sponge Bob pajamas and pink slippers. But she was already late and she was only going next door. Besides, the members of Care Group were her friends. They wouldn't care if she sneaked next door in her p.j.'s. Hadn't Peggy herself worn pajamas to Care Group one night right after her gall bladder surgery?

No biggie.

"Let's go," Goldie whispered into the pet carrier as she closed the front door behind her.

She nearly tripped on the large paper cup sitting squarely in the middle of the top step on her porch.

Joe's Coffee Shop, Turtle Beach, North Carolina the lid of the paper cup screamed at her. Goldie nudged it out of the way with her fuzz-clad foot and marched to Peggy's house.

When she reached Peggy's front door, Goldie debated whether she should ring the bell or just try to sneak inside. She hated the thought of disrupting prayer requests, if they were still in progress. At the same time, she also hated to barge right in. She might frighten someone, and since giving one of the other members of the group a heart attack seemed like a very real possibility, she decided to knock softly instead.

After a shuffling noise on the other side of the door, it swung open and Goldie found herself face-to-face with her dear friend.

"Hi, Peggy. Sorry I'm late." Goldie made a move

toward the threshold.

Peggy shifted so that she blocked Goldie from entering the house. She shut the door behind her until only a sliver of light poured out from inside. "Um, hello dear. What a surprise."

"Surprise? What do you mean? It's Thursday, right? Care Group night?" Goldie may have lost track of the time, but she was pretty sure she still knew what day it was. She struggled to get a peek inside. Sure enough, she spied George Brown sitting in his usual spot. He gave her a sheepish grin and a tiny wave.

"Yes, that's right." Peggy shifted her weight from one foot to the other and planted herself more firmly in front of the entrance. "We just weren't expecting you. That's all."

What was Peggy's problem? She was acting awfully strange. If Goldie didn't know better, she would think she was still stuck in that crazy daydream. "I know I'm late. I'm sorry. But I'm here now."

"Maybe you shouldn't be." Peggy's gaze swept the length of her pajama bottoms and lingered on her slippers. Unlike Joe, Peggy wasn't smiling at the slippers.

Goldie felt the blood begin to drain slowly from her face. "Uh, I-I'm sorry about the way I'm dressed. It's just been one of those days, and I didn't want to be any later than I already was. So, can I please come in now?"

Peggy folded her arms across her chest. "I'm afraid not."

What? When had Peggy changed from her sweet neighbor into a bouncer for Bible Study?

Goldie stared at her and waited for her to come to her senses. Or at least move out of the way.

But she didn't budge. "As you know, Care Group is a gathering for senior adults. And you are a young woman, Goldie. We loved having you here with your Grandpa. But he's gone now. Don't you think it's time for you to fellowship with a group of believers your own age?"

Goldie held the velvet dog carrier closer to her chest, close enough to feel the warm lump of spaniel nestled inside. "Are you serious? Are you actually telling me I can't come to Care Group any more?"

Peggy patted her shoulder and offered a serene smile. You would never know by looking at her that she was the type of person capable of kicking someone out of Bible Study. "We just think it would be best, dear. You need to...um, how should I put it? Get a life."

Goldie stiffened beneath the touch of Peggy's fingers. *Get a life? Get a life!* She opened her mouth to object, to tell her that she had a life, thank you very much. Sure, she didn't have a job. But she would get one. Maybe she would even tell her how close she'd come to having an actual date. But instead of saying anything, she stood there on the porch, slack-jawed, remembering that she was still in her pajamas. It was difficult to retain any kind of dignity when she was dressed like a five-year old.

And then there was the matter of Bliss, who chose this precise moment to let out a pitiful whine.

Peggy lifted a brow at the velvet pet carrier. "Is your dog in your purse?"

"It's a pet carrier, not a purse," Goldie retorted. She tried to forget how she was dressed, pushed her shoulders back and stood a little straighter. "And yes, Bliss is inside. I didn't want her to get lonely."

"Is she really the one who's lonely?"

Goldie blinked furiously to keep the tears at bay. The last thing she wanted to do was cry and make her humiliation all the more complete. "Look, forget about the dog. If you think I'm so lonely, why are you kicking me out of Care Group?"

"Oh, Goldie. Don't think of it as being 'kicked out.' Think of it rather as being pushed out of the nest. Like a sweet baby bird. We love you and want what's best for you."

That was it. Goldie needed to get out of here. Now. She shot the meanest look she could muster at George Brown through the crack in the door then tried her best to gather her dignity. "Fine. Have a good evening."

Then she spun on her heel and sauntered back home, praying Peggy wouldn't notice the telltale shake of her shoulders as the tears finally spilled down her cheeks.

❧

"No. Way." Eve punctuated the two words on the other end of the phone for added emphasis.

Goldie laughed. A little. As much as she could manage a mere twenty-four hours after the incident. "Really. I'm officially no longer welcome at Care Group."

"How did the others react when she told you to leave?"

"She wouldn't even let me in the door. I never saw anyone else." Goldie shuddered as she remembered craning her neck to see inside Peggy's living room. "Well, I guess I did get a glimpse of your boyfriend.

You know…George."

Eve's tinkling laughter traveled through the phone line. "I can't believe he didn't come to your rescue. Honestly, I may have to break up with him."

Despite the flush of embarrassment that coursed through her every time she thought about trying to force her way into Bible study, Goldie smiled. She always could depend on Eve to take her side and to make her feel better. "I think he might be afraid of Peggy, too."

"Of course he is, *mon ami*. We all are." Goldie could imagine Eve trembling with mock fear. "He still should have done something. And here I thought he was the perfect gentleman."

"I guess your search for a husband must go on."

"I'm afraid you're right." Eve lowered her voice. "So, in all seriousness, are you OK?"

"Yeah. I'm OK. Actually," Goldie paused for dramatic effect. "I have news."

"What kind of news?" Eve's voice bubbled on the other end of the line, but quickly turned skeptical. "By any chance does this have anything to do with that coffee guy?"

Goldie considered telling her about the dog training class and how it was the very next day. She thought for the briefest of moments of telling her about their walk on the beach, and how the sand had dusted the tips of his chestnut hair, but thought better of it. So, she stuck to her less controversial news. "I have a job now."

"Really? Oh, Goldie, I'm thrilled for you. See, this is the beginning of a whole new life."

Her reaction brought back the fantastical *Name that Price* daydream and Goldie suddenly imagined the telephone receiver as a slender microphone. It all came back to her. Cary's nerdy glasses. The lithe models. The photo of her, wrapped in Joe's arms.

The shag carpeting.

"Helloooo? Goldie? Are you still there?" Eve nearly shouted.

"I'm here. Sorry. I zoned out for a minute." She really needed to stop that. It was becoming a dreadful habit.

"I'm thrilled you found a job. Tell me all about it. Where is it? The mall? A fancy boutique? Oh, I know, a day spa! We can get discount mani's and pedi's!"

OK, now Eve was the one lost in a dream world. "Actually, no. Even better."

"Better than a day spa?" Eve sounded doubtful.

"Yes." Goldie paused, letting the news linger on the tip of her tongue. She may as well enjoy the moment. It was so much better than getting kicked out of Bible Study. Get a life? Ha. She'd show them. She'd already gotten a job at a place she adored. Now she could check that off the list. "I'll give you a hint. Where have I gone every week since I was a little kid?"

"I'm sticking with the mall."

Goldie sighed in exasperation. "We're talking about me, not you."

"I give up. Spill."

"The library. My favorite place in Turtle Beach."

Besides Joe's Coffee Shop.

Goldie rubbed her temples. *Good grief. Focus.*

"The *library*?" Eve spat out the word as if it left a terrible taste on her tongue.

"Yes, the library. You know how much I love the library. I went this morning to check out some books about dogs and dog training and before I knew what was happening, they offered me a job." Goldie could scarcely believe her luck. No, not luck. It was a blessing, pure and simple. Maybe she would have to start talking to God again. "Isn't it perfect?"

There was a long silence on the other end of the phone. With every quiet, passing moment, Goldie found herself getting more and more irritated. Everyone had been telling her to get a life, and now she finally was. Was she asking too much to get a more supportive reaction?

At last, Eve said something. "Well, maybe it will do until you find something better."

"Better? What do you mean? I think this is perfect. I start on Monday. Mrs. Simpson, the head librarian, is even letting me take charge of the children's hour. She said I could bring Bliss if I like, and the kids can pet her while I read aloud fun, doggy books to them. I can't wait." Goldie had already scanned the shelves, stunned at the sheer amount of canine-themed books for youngsters. There was *Clifford the Big Red Dog*, *Martha Speaks*, *The Bookshop Dog* and countless others she'd never heard of before. After flipping through more than a dozen picture books, she'd picked an adorable story about a mixed breed dog that was "part hound, part fraidy-cat" to read at children's hour on Monday.

"Honey, how does Mrs. Simpson know about Bliss? You've only had her for a couple of days." Eve's question was laced with disbelief.

"Oh, I had her with me when I went to the library. In her new pet carrier. It's like a handbag." What was with all the questions? Goldie was still waiting for Eve to join in her excitement about her new job.

"No," Eve moaned. "You did not take that dog

with you to the library."

"Um, yes I did. It was no big deal. Everyone there loved her." Mrs. Simpson had fawned all over Bliss, and the Cavalier had wagged her tail until it became nothing but an orange-and-white blur.

"Goldie, I'm going to say something, and I don't want you to take it the wrong way because I'm saying it for your own good." Eve took an audible deep breath which caused Goldie to brace herself for whatever was coming next. She knew without a doubt it couldn't be good. "If Bliss were a cat, you would be in serious danger of becoming a crazy, old maid cat lady."

Goldie paused to wonder if there was possibly a right way to interpret that comment. Ultimately, she decided no. It was an insult, plain and simple. "I'm going to try to forget you just said that."

"I'm not trying to hurt your feelings. Honestly. But look at the facts—you're a pretty, young woman, and you've spent your whole life around old people. No offense to the big guy." She took a breath and continued, "But now is your chance to start over. You can do anything. *Anything*. And you get a job as a librarian and drag your dog around in your purse everywhere you go."

"It's not a purse. It's a pet carrier." Goldie was starting to feel like a broken record. And worse, she was getting the urge to climb back into the Sponge Bob pants.

"Whatever. All I'm saying is if you start wearing your hair in a bun I'm going to schedule an intervention."

Despite her disappointment in her friend's reaction to her big news, Goldie had to suppress a laugh at the bun comment. "No bun. I promise. But could you try to be a little more enthusiastic about my new job? I really am excited about it. Even if you think it's lame. Look on the bright side—I'll be spending a lot of time with kids. Technically, they are the complete and total opposite of elderly people. You should be thrilled."

Eve giggled. "Hmm. I hadn't thought about it that way. You do have a point. But no buns!"

"No buns."

"Or orthopedic shoes."

Goldie glanced down at her sock feet. At least she wasn't wearing slippers. That was progress, right? "No orthopedic shoes. I can't promise high heels, though."

"Can you promise me one more thing?" Eve switched her tone and suddenly sounded way more syrupy sweet than bossy.

The sudden change made Goldie's head spin. And scared her more than a little bit. "What is it?"

"I want you to come to church with me on Sunday. Please. You need somewhere new to worship, so why not give it a chance?"

Ugh. She should have known this was coming. Eve had been hounding her for years to go to church with her on Sunday mornings. Goldie resisted every time. There was nothing wrong with Eve's church—but she felt beyond awkward walking into a Sunday school class for "young singles." Yes, she was young. Younger than everyone at her regular Bible Study, at least. And clearly she was single. But did she really need to broadcast it to everyone at church? She'd always used the fact that Care Group was her Christian home as an excuse, but now how could she say no?

As if sensing her reluctance, Eve continued begging. "Pleeease. Just once. If you don't like it, you don't have to come back. You *are* planning on going to church services somewhere, right?"

"Of course." Although in all honesty, she hadn't given it much thought. But, naturally, she had to keep going to worship. She may be giving God the cold shoulder at the moment, but she would never completely turn her back on Him.

"Then, come with me this Sunday. It will be your second step in getting a life."

Third, actually. If dog training class with Joe counted. Which, in Goldie's mind, it most certainly did. Even if it wasn't a date. Somehow, she sensed now was not the time to mention it to Eve, though. "OK. I'll go."

Eve let out a squeal that caused Goldie to hold the phone a full foot away from her ear. Bliss awoke from her nap with a start and pricked her ears at the sound. "Super! Meet me there at 9:30. You know where it is, right?"

How could she not? It was the most popular Christian singles spot in town. "Yes. I'll be there."

"Great!" Eve gushed.

Goldie couldn't help but wish Eve had had the same reaction to the news about her new job at the library.

Then, as if her friend could read her mind, she continued, "And Goldie, I'm sorry I wasn't more supportive about the library thing. You'll be really good at it, and if it makes you happy that's all that matters. We all love you Goldie, and we simply want what's best for you."

"Thanks. I know," Goldie said, silently wondering just what that might be. What...and who.

Chapter Six

Joe paced back and forth in the parking lot of the Turtle Beach Community Center, Java watching every step with his mismatched eyes.

"Sorry, boy," he murmured as he cupped the Husky underneath the chin and gave him a nice scratch.

Java was picking up on his nerves. That much was obvious. He took a deep breath, resisted the urge to pace and instead, glanced at his watch. Class didn't start for another fifteen minutes. Of course, she wasn't here yet.

Joe raked a hand through his hair and wondered for the thousandth time why he hadn't told Goldie he would stop by her house and pick her up on the way to class. Why, oh why, had he suggested that they meet here? He presumed it was because at the time he was so intent on even getting her to agree to come to class, that he hadn't given any thought to the travel arrangements. The fact that she'd said yes had been a victory in and of itself. He wasn't about to push his luck.

Now, of course, he wished he had. Both for his own sake and that of his dog.

Java let out a pitiful *woo-woo* and hung his tail

between his legs. Without even realizing it, Joe had started pacing again.

"OK, I'll stop. I promise." Joe sat on the curb and put Java in a down-stay. "See, we're relaxed now."

As if he could really, truly relax. He hadn't seen Goldie since that day on the beach. That glorious afternoon she'd appeared in his coffee shop when he'd least expected it. Now, he sometimes wondered if it had all been a dream, if none of it had really happened after all. Had the Goldie with the windswept curls tied back in the wispy silk scarf been a figment of his imagination?

Surely not. He never could have imagined a smile so sweet, porcelain skin so lovely or the delectable fragrance he breathed in as he walked beside her. She smelled of caramel and salty ocean air—a combination he would forever associate with her. It made his chest ache deep inside even now as he remembered it.

Then, just as his panic was about to reach a fever pitch, she was there. With the afternoon sun shining pale pink behind her, she seemed to shimmer to life before him. Soft rays of sunlight bounced off her blonde curls, making her appear almost gilded.

Oddly enough, his nerves settled down the minute he laid eyes on her. He didn't worry about what to say or how to act. She was here. With him. That was all that mattered.

He rose from the curb, released Java from his down and sought Goldie's gaze. "You made it."

"Of course we did." She nodded toward Bliss, who was scrambling at the end of her leash in an effort to greet Java. "I told you we would be here. We've even been practicing."

"Really?" Joe asked, noticing that she seemed

different somehow. Her face more relaxed than in recent days, brimming with something bordering on confidence. The change brought a smile to his lips. And gave him a warm sensation deep inside.

"Yes. Watch this." Goldie took a small treat from her pocket and held it over her dog's head. "Bliss, sit."

Immediately, the spaniel plopped her tiny, orange-spotted rump on the concrete. Goldie cooed and called her a good girl, offering her the treat from the palm of her hand.

"Well, look at you," Joe said in a voice he hoped brimmed with encouragement. "You're a natural."

"Well, I did sort of cheat," she confessed. "I did a little reading so we would know what to expect at class."

"That's not cheating. It's..." he paused, and then grinned. "Preparation."

"Preparation. I like that. Kind of like homework, in advance."

"Exactly. I only wish you would have told me before you went out and bought any books. I have plenty of training books I could have loaned you, if I'd known."

"Thanks for the offer, but don't worry. I didn't buy anything. I checked out some books from the library." At the mention of the library, her blue eyes sparkled, piquing Joe's curiosity.

"The library, huh? I loved going to that place when I was a kid." Some of his fondest childhood memories took place sitting cross-legged on the Turtle Beach library floor, listening to the singsong voice of the librarian reading aloud stories that transported him to other worlds far away from his small Carolina beach town. "Do you go there often?"

"All the time." Goldie beamed, and her eyes positively danced beneath her thick lashes. "In fact, I'll be going there a lot more often. Nearly every day."

"My, my. It sounds like someone has a secret." Joe bumped his shoulder against hers and grinned.

Goldie shook her head. "It's no secret. They offered me a job. I'll be working there starting Monday."

Joe could scarcely believe his ears. This was wonderful news—exactly what Goldie needed. Watching her make the slow, steady climb out of her grief touched his heart as nothing had before. He felt as if she were coming back to life before his very eyes. Slowly, but surely. "No kidding?"

"Really. I'm going to help out behind the counter and do the read-aloud every afternoon to the children. I've already chosen the first book." She grinned at Bliss. "It's about a dog. And Bliss is going to come, too."

"That's fantastic, Goldie. I think that's great." Without even thinking, he wrapped his arms around her in a congratulatory hug. At first, he felt her stiffen slightly at his touch. Then, her fingers wrapped around the muscles in his back and she melted into his embrace.

"You really think so, don't you?" Her words were but a whisper, dancing a soft waltz against his skin.

Reluctantly, he let her go. What had they even been talking about? He'd lost track of anything and everything in the brief moment he held her in his arms. "Um, what?"

The corner of Goldie's lips lifted into a grin and her cheeks flushed rosy pink. "You really think it's a good idea—my job at the library?"

"Of course I do. I think you'll be great. Bliss will, too, of course." He gave the Cavalier a little pat on the head. She promptly rolled on her back for a belly scratch.

"Well, I'm excited about it."

He could tell. So this is what her newfound air of confidence was all about. He desperately wanted to reinforce it, as he knew she was still fragile. Grief as deep as hers wasn't conquered overnight. So, he said the words he hoped would mean the most to her. "He would be proud of you, you know."

Even though Joe didn't say so specifically, they both knew he meant her grandfather.

"Thank you," Goldie murmured, breaking his gaze and looking down at the dogs. "I hope so."

"I'm sure of it." Joe glanced at his watch again, almost disappointed when he realized class was due to start any minute. "Shall we go inside?"

"Sure. We're ready to show off our sitting skills." She gave a gentle tug on Bliss's leash and the spaniel trotted alongside her while she followed Joe toward the community center building.

Part-time reception hall, part-time boat dock, the Turtle Beach Community Center sat right on the water's edge. Throughout the small town's history, it had been used for many purposes, most notably as a location for the Underground Railroad during Civil War times. A sense of pride in his town's heritage always swelled in Joe's chest when he came here and this time was no exception. He glanced over at Goldie and noticed her gaze land on the historical marker surrounded by the purple and gold petunias flanking the walkway.

"I've always loved this place," she said.

"Me, too."

They stopped for a moment in front of the marker and listened to the waves lap against the bulkhead.

"I guess we should go inside." Goldie turned to face him, her eyes bluer than the sea on a clear summer day.

"Yes, it's about that time." Joe swung open the door for her and placed the hand that held Java's leash in the small of her back to guide her inside. When she walked past him, the turquoise scarf wound through the belt loops of her jeans grazed his arm with a whisper-touch. His skin instantly felt alive, covered with a million tiny prickles.

Then, he smiled and said, "Here we are."

❧

Goldie felt like she was on a date.

She wasn't kidding herself. They were in a large room surrounded by panting dogs, not in some darkened restaurant sharing a candlelight dinner.

Yet somehow, it still felt like a date.

She couldn't put her finger on exactly what it was—perhaps the warmth of his hand in the small of her back as he steered her through the crowd, or the way the other class members looked at her with knowing smiles—but it was a feeling she couldn't shake for the rest of the evening.

A feeling she rather liked.

Goldie tried to remember why she was there while Bliss pawed at her own shins and danced on her hind legs. *Oh yeah. Dog training class.*

Goldie tore her attention away from Joe and glanced around the room. With its confusing labyrinth of orange traffic cones and strange signs with arrows pointing all different directions, it looked more like a maze than a classroom. She'd been in the Community Center countless times since she was a little girl, but had never seen it like this. "What are all the cones for?"

Joe leaned toward her to explain. "Our training club is preparing for an upcoming dog show where we'll complete in an event called Rally Obedience. Have you heard of it before?"

"No, I haven't. It looks awfully complicated." Goldie fidgeted with the end of Bliss's leash, suddenly feeling embarrassed about her pride in teaching the dog to sit. From the looks of things, this was a whole different level of dog training.

"It's a relatively new type of dog obedience. And it's not nearly as difficult as it looks. At the beginning level, called *novice*, your dog only needs to know how to sit, down, and walk next to you without pulling on the leash. The rest is just knowing how to read the signs and figuring out where to go." Joe must have sensed her uneasiness because he reached over, took her free hand in his and gave it a little squeeze. "Don't worry about a thing. This is all just for fun."

Then he winked.

Yep. Definitely still feels like a date.

"Come with me. I'll introduce you to the instructor." He laced his fingers through hers and guided her to the middle of the cone-maze where an older man with white hair and kind eyes stood next to a jet-black poodle. "Goldie, this is Harold, our teacher."

Her breath caught in her throat as she introduced herself to Harold, who reminded her at once of her grandfather. When he shook her hand and then bent down to greet Bliss, a sense of comfort overcame her, and her earlier nerves slipped away.

"We're so glad you're here, Goldie." Harold gestured to the myriad of signs and cones while the poodle at his feet watched his every move with keen interest. "Please don't be intimidated by all this. We're all here to learn something new and have fun with our dogs."

Date or not, Goldie was increasingly glad she'd come. Everyone was so nice, and she had to admit she was fascinated to see what all the arrows and squiggly lines meant. Bliss bounced at the end of her leash, pawing Goldie's leg to capture her attention. When Goldie glanced down at her, Bliss plunked into a sit position. Obviously, the little spaniel shared Goldie's enthusiasm for training class.

Goldie slipped a treat into Bliss's mouth and watched Harold and his poodle work their way through the course. Despite Harold's teasing comment that he'd named his dog Bugsy because she "bugged the heck out of him," the two of them moved with perfect precision. At each sign, Harold stopped to explain the symbols to the students. Once she learned what the different shapes and arrows meant, Goldie agreed that it didn't seem quite as difficult as it originally appeared. Every time a stop sign appeared, the dog was supposed to sit. The arrows pointed out any change of direction the dog and handler were required to maneuver.

Goldie gathered Bliss in her arms, moved closer to Joe and whispered in his ear. "I think we might be able to do this."

"Of course you can." He gave Bliss a pat on the head. "I believe in you, Goldie. You can do whatever you want."

Before she even had a chance to digest that comment, Harold called her name.

"Goldie, why don't you bring Bliss out here and give it a try?" He waved her toward the center of the room while Bugsy once again sat and trained her eyes on him, as if waiting for another command.

Joe's low voice tickled Goldie's neck. "Go ahead. Give it a try."

She kissed Bliss on top of the head and then put her back down on the floor. As she walked toward the training course, Goldie was careful not to glance back at Joe. She could feel his gaze on her, consciously aware of the fact he was watching her every move. If she thought too much about it, she would never be able to concentrate on what she was doing.

"Are you ready?" Harold asked as she stood next to the cone with the sign that read *Start*.

"Yes." Goldie answered, reaching in her pocket for a doggy treat. She waved it in front of Bliss to get her undivided attention. "We are."

"OK, let me know if you need any help. Forward," Harold called and stood back to watch.

Goldie walked from cone to cone, the orange and white spaniel never straying far from her side. Every time she gave the *sit* command Bliss obeyed right away. She plunked her little bottom on the floor and waited for her treat. The sparkle in her dog's eyes was infectious, and Goldie soon forgot there was an entire room full of people and their own dogs watching her. She was simply having fun with her dog. She followed Harold's instructions, giving her commands in an upbeat, cheerful tone and walking at a brisk pace. To her utter delight, the Cavalier basked in the attention and fell all over herself to do whatever Goldie asked.

Before she knew it, they had reached the final cone. Goldie guided Bliss past the *Finish* sign and lavished her with praise.

"Very good," Harold said. "With a little more work, you'll be ready for the show in a couple weeks."

Goldie furrowed her brows. "Show? What?"

But by the time the words left her mouth, another student had entered the ring and Harold turned away to watch their performance.

She made her way back to where Joe stood beaming at her, his hand absently stroking Java behind the ears. "You did great. See? I knew you were a natural."

Heat rose to Goldie's cheeks, and her stomach gave that familiar clench at his words of encouragement. "Thanks."

"You looked like you were having fun out there."

"Actually, I was. Thank you so much for inviting me." *Whether it was a date or not.* But, oh how she wished she knew if it were.

"So, does this mean you're coming back next week?" Joe lifted his brows, his face full of hopeful expectation. "If you like, I could pick you up and we could ride together."

Goldie's heart rose all the way to her throat. "Thank you. I'd like that very much."

❧☙

The look on Goldie's face was one of sheer terror. "Harold can't be serious. I can't possibly be in a dog show."

Joe couldn't help the chuckle that escaped his mouth.

"You're laughing?" She jammed her hands on her hips, but her lips curved into a smile. "It's not funny."

"Actually, it is." Joe slid closer to her on the curb where they sat watching their dogs tumble and play on the lawn beside the Community Center. He reached over and gave her knee a squeeze. "You look terrified. This is all for fun, remember?"

She glanced at the dogs, then back at him with a look that stole the very breath from his lungs. "Well, *this* is fun."

He couldn't agree more. "I'm glad."

"But a show is a whole different story. I can't do that."

"Of course you can. Although, technically, Bliss would be the one entered in the show," Joe teased. "Not you."

"What? You don't think the judge would be impressed if I walked around the cones and sat cross-legged at each stop sign?" Goldie broke into lilting laughter, and Joe wondered if he had ever heard such a beautiful sound. It tore at his heart and filled him with gratitude.

Thank you, Lord. Thank you for letting me be a part of her healing.

"Don't forget about the down signs. You'd have to stretch out on the floor." He curled into a fetal position in the grass and pretended to snore.

Goldie stopped giggling long enough to reply, "Hey, maybe I could wear my Sponge Bob pajamas."

They collapsed into one another with laughter until their shoulders bumped against each other. Soon the dogs bounded over to see what all the fuss was about. Bliss climbed into Goldie's lap and Java's plumed tail beat against Joe's cheek.

"Thanks for the mouthful of hair, you stinker," he muttered to the Siberian Husky, which sent Goldie into another fit of laughter.

Joe sent up another silent prayer of thanks. He always knew it could be good between the two of them. How many times had he imagined moments such as this one? The two of them laughing and enjoying one another's company? More times than he could count. And there would be many, many more as far as he was concerned.

He hoped with every fiber of his being that Cinnamon would show up at church tomorrow. If it hadn't been for their impromptu agreement, he would ask Goldie out on a proper date right here and now. He toyed with the idea of forgetting about Cinnamon and asking her out anyway. The memory of the tender fit of Goldie's hand cradled in his, beckoned to him. The smooth, soft feel of her fingers laced through his.

But, no. He couldn't do it. He'd reached out to Cinnamon and talked to her about Jesus. She was on the verge of coming to church and learning more, perhaps even giving her heart to God. What if he went ahead and asked Goldie out on a date? Cinnamon would be thrilled for him, no doubt. But, would she still come to church?

Somehow, he doubted it. It was a risk he couldn't take. Not when Cinnamon's relationship with the Lord might depend on it.

He would have to wait it out. He'd waited this long. What was a little while longer?

Too long!

He ignored the voice in his head and concentrated instead on Goldie's mass of blonde curls and her pink, bow-shaped lips. "Seriously, you should enter the show. It would be fun."

And it would mean I could see more of you.

"That's easy for you to say. You and Java did the entire course with perfect precision. Off lead!"

"Well, you have to remember that we've been working at this a little longer than you and Bliss. You'll get there someday. But you're already almost ready for the Novice class." They weren't empty words. Goldie had a knack for training and Bliss was happy to do whatever she asked. "Just think, if Bliss won a ribbon you could bring it to the library and show it off to her legions of fans."

Goldie rolled her eyes. "She doesn't have any fans yet. I haven't even started. The kids might not even like her. Or me, for that matter."

"Surely you don't believe that." Joe fixed his gaze with hers, intent on making sure she knew he was serious. "I meant what I said earlier. You can do anything you set out to do. You are a warm, caring woman. I've seen how you nurture people, take care of those around you. Of course, those kids will love you. How could they not?"

How could I not?

The air stood still between them, and it was all he could do not to take her in his arms and kiss her. To tell her how he felt about her all this time. Goldie's eyes grew wide, like glistening pools of cool, clear water. And Joe panicked, suddenly afraid he'd said too much, too soon. What was he doing?

"Well, um," Goldie stammered, "I hope you're right."

He wanted to assure her, to tell her whatever would take away her doubts. He would promise her anything—the sun, the stars, the moon—if he thought she was ready to hear it. But, he couldn't push her. Wouldn't.

"I am. You'll see." He winked. "Maybe I'll stop by Monday morning with a special cup of coffee to kick-start your first day. Would that be OK?"

"Maybe. It depends." She peeked at him demurely from behind the fringe of her lashes. "Could I have whipped cream on top?"

His thoughts screamed *whatever your heart desires.* But instead, he said, "I think that could be arranged."

"And could it be caramel flavored?"

"Of course. Unless you'd like to try something new."

"No." Goldie's gaze settled over him, full of unspoken emotion that left him breathless. "New things can be nice, but sometimes the very best things are the ones that have been around all along."

Chapter Seven

The next morning something near miraculous happened. Goldie woke up to a persistent, furry paw poking her in the face. The miraculous part wasn't so much the paw as the fact that she woke up at all. Because, as everyone knows, waking up means there was actual sleep going on.

Sleep. The one thing that had eluded her night after night since living in the house alone.

Somewhere between curling up in bed, her head swirling with thoughts of Joe, and waking up with her mind a fuzzy haze of dogs and signs with crazy arrows, she'd fallen into a deep, peaceful sleep. Yet still, upon waking, he was there. Joe. The memory of his kind words of encouragement, his strong arms wrapped around her when she'd told him about her new job and the way his hair curled up at the ends where it grazed his collar. Most of all, she remembered the way his gaze lighted on her lips when they sat side by side on the curb, and she'd wondered what he was thinking. Were his thoughts the same as hers? Did he, too, wonder what it might be like if their lips came together in a kiss?

Goldie sighed with contentment and stretched

beneath her squishy down comforter. As strange and intriguing as her time spent with Joe felt, at the same time it brought her a deep sense of comfort. She'd returned home from dog training class feeling as though her heart itself was wrapped in a tight, peaceful hug.

"Thank you, Lord. Thank you for sleep. Thank you for yesterday. Thank you for Joe."

Goldie froze after she mumbled the words aloud in the direction of the ceiling. Bliss darted her head to and fro searching for the cause of Goldie's alarm.

She had just spoken to God for the first time since Grandpa's death. All these days she'd been resisting, holding back from any sort of eternal conversation. Even at the funeral, she'd remained stoic, refusing to seek His presence. And now, here she was, shooting up a causal prayer of thanksgiving.

Could it really be that simple? All this time she'd been afraid to talk to Him. She dreaded having the Big Conversation. The one about her Grandpa and how it felt now that she was alone. So, she'd remained silent, ignoring the God who she'd been so close to since she was a small child.

Of course, she knew He was there all along. Now maybe she could talk to Him again, as she did before. Maybe they didn't even need to have the Big Conversation.

She hoped so.

In any case, she supposed it was a relief she could at least utter a few words to Him since she was about to try out a new church.

Goldie groaned aloud at the mere thought of walking into Eve's Sunday school class, and resisted the temptation to pull the covers over her head. She didn't belong there. She wasn't a "young single." Not in the same sense as all the other people there were. What could she possibly have in common with them? She was willing to bet none of them had watched *Name that Price* in the last month. Or sat down and played an old-fashioned board game.

Deep down, she knew she could be wrong. But she couldn't shake the nagging feeling that she had more in common with the members of her Care Group than the young singles. She supposed it didn't really matter in the long run. She couldn't go back to Care Group anyway. At least not until her 65th birthday.

Goldie climbed out of bed.

"Time to face the music," she muttered to Bliss. "But I promise you one thing. If I walk into that classroom and see a disco ball hanging from the ceiling I am turning right around and coming back home."

There was no disco ball. And there was no chance of chickening out and running anywhere. Eve swooped down, squealing with glee, the second Goldie walked in the door.

"You came." Eve threw her arms around her and lifted a perfectly groomed eyebrow at the amethyst velvet bag hanging from her shoulder. "Cute purse. Is it new?"

Oh no. No, no, no. Goldie fought to keep herself between Eve and the dog carrier. "Um, no. It's old. Older than the hills."

Eve shimmied from side to side, trying to peek around Goldie and get a good glimpse of the bag. "Are you sure? I don't think I've ever seen it before."

What Goldie did next was hardly the smartest move. But, gripped with panic at the possibility of Eve finding Bliss nestled inside the purple velvet bag, she wasn't thinking straight. So, she did the only thing she knew for a fact would divert Eve's attention from the fancy pet carrier.

She turned on her brightest smile and cooed in Eve's ear. "Wow, who is that guy over there? Isn't he dreamy?"

The minute the words left her mouth, she regretted them. Eve would never, ever let this go.

Sure enough. Her eyes widened in surprise, then a look came over her face that made the contestants who were invited to "come name that price" look downright sedate. "Oh, my gosh! I knew this was going to happen. You've already found someone you're interested in. Aren't you *so* glad you came?"

No, as a matter of fact I'm not. I've been here less than a minute, and it's already turned into a complete, unmitigated disaster.

Eve's head swiveled around at an alarming rate. "Who? Who is it? Which one is he?"

Goldie just stood there, trying in desperation to figure out some way to start the entire day over again. What she wouldn't give to be back in her bed, pale sunlight filtering through her eyelet curtains, tender memories of Joe and dog-training class playing on her mind.

But Eve's matchmaking freight train had already left the station, and there was no stopping it. "Point him out to me." She clutched Goldie's forearm with a finely manicured death grip. "But try not to be too obvious. Be cool."

If there was ever a testament to the fact that Goldie didn't have a single *cool* bone in her body it was this precise moment. What had possessed her to say such a thing? It must have been the disco balls dancing in her head.

"Uh, ahem," she stammered while she looked around for some, poor guy to play the role of *cute guy* in this ridiculous little drama. "Him. Over there."

Goldie jerked her head toward a rather large, blonde surfer-dude type standing near the room's only window. He seemed nice looking, in a sandy sort of way, but the reason she chose him had more to do with the fact that he was engaged in a serious looking conversation with another woman. A woman who bore a striking resemblance to Heidi Klum in all her long-legged glory. Goldie figured this guy would be a harmless choice. No matter what Eve did to try to push them together, she'd be safe. He would never choose her over Heidi.

"Perfect."

Before Goldie knew what was happening, Eve had dragged her across the room and shoved her between Heidi and Surfer-guy.

"Hey Josh," Eve purred. "Have you met my friend Goldie? She's new here."

"No. Er, no I haven't. Hi Goldie. It's nice to meet you." Josh gestured toward Heidi, who seemed surprisingly unperturbed at the interruption. But, then again, when you look like a supermodel, does anything ever get you down? "And this is my sister, Jill."

"Hey Goldie. We're glad to have you here," Heidi/Jill said.

His sister. *Great.*

Goldie pasted on a smile and said as few words as possible. "Hi."

She searched the walls of the Sunday school room for a clock and offered up her second prayer of the day.

Dear Lord, please, please get this show on the road

before I can get myself into any more trouble.

"Good morning and God bless everyone," the pastor's voice boomed from behind a podium at the front of the room. "Shall we get started? Everyone find a seat."

At last. Divine intervention.

Thank you, Lord.

"You don't mind if we sit with you, do you Josh?" Eve batted her eyelashes at the poor guy and then shoved Goldie into the folding chair next to his.

Goldie let out a weary sigh and clutched the purple bag close to her heart, seeking the security and familiarity of Bliss's warmth. Of course, if she'd left the dog at home like a normal person, she wouldn't be in this mess right now, would she?

"Let's open with a prayer, shall we?" The pastor smiled at all the young singles lined up in their chairs, pausing for a moment when his gaze lighted on Goldie. He winked at her, the newcomer, before closing his eyes and beginning the opening prayer.

Goldie shut her eyes and tried to concentrate on the prayer. This was church after all. She let the pastor's words wash over her and bring the slightest bit of peace to her soul. When she opened her eyes, she did so with a new attitude. So what if Eve thought she found Josh attractive? Nothing would come of it. As soon as Sunday school was over, she would drag Eve off to a nice lunch somewhere and tell her all about her afternoon at the dog training class. She would fess up and admit to her friend that she thought she was developing feelings for Joe. Eve might be disappointed at first, since she didn't think he was dating material for some ridiculous reason. But, in the end, she would accept it and be happy for Goldie. Heck, she might even be excited. She was doing it—moving on. In her own way.

All she had to do was survive the next hour and everything would be fine.

That would have been easy.

If not for the crinkly bag.

At dog training class, Goldie had heard some of the other handlers joking around about the dreaded "crinkly bag." She had looked in question at Joe who was more than happy to explain.

"Ah yes, the crinkly bag." His eyes had danced when he'd said it, and Goldie had had to concentrate really hard to absorb what he was saying. "A dog handler's worst nightmare."

"Why is that?" she'd asked.

"Well, above all, dogs are creatures of habit. And they're smart. Much smarter than we give them credit for." At this point, Joe had run his hand casually over Java's pointy ears. "Like most dogs, Java loves food. It didn't take long for him to learn the sound of dog biscuits shaking in a cardboard box or the hum of a can opener prying open a can of wet dog food."

"Ahh," Goldie had said, having an inkling where this story was going. "I know what you mean. Bliss already comes running when she hears the refrigerator door open."

"Then let me ask you—has Bliss ever tasted a potato chip?"

Goldie shook her head. "No. I don't eat that junk."

Joe's lips twitched as he tried not to smile. "Never, ever?"

"Nope. Never. No chips." Then Goldie lowered her voice into a whisper. "Maybe the occasional cheese puff, but definitely no potato chips."

Joe laughed. "Too late then. You're doomed. She knows what sorts of treasure lie in those crinkly bags."

"You mean chip bags?"

"Mmm hmm. Even if you never let her eat one, she can smell them. And what dog could resist the smell of a tasty cheese ball?"

"OK. I think I get it. She probably knows that the sound of a crinkly bag means yummy food."

"Bingo!" Joe winked at her, sending her stomach into a tumbling riot. "Just wait until you're at a dog show and someone nearby picks that moment to open up a bag of chips while you're in the obedience ring."

Or church.

As it turned out, the crinkly bag wasn't her downfall at a dog show. No, Goldie's crinkly bag experience took place in a much more humiliating setting.

Everything had been going so well. She'd managed to forget she was sandwiched between surfer-Josh and Eve, even though Eve kept poking her in the ribs and trying to get her attention. She stayed focused on the pastor's message and flipped through the wispy pages of her Bible, propped up on the top of the velvet bag, still sitting innocently in her lap.

Then, somewhere down her row of folding chairs, she heard it. The crinkly bag.

So did Bliss.

At the very first rustle of cellophane, the purple bag shifted sideways with a sudden jolt.

Goldie tightened her grip on the bag and wondered who in the world would eat chips in the middle of a Sunday school class.

Maybe it's not chips. It could be cheese balls. Or those dried onion circles. They're pretty popular. I've never like them much, though.

Goldie shook her head. What was she doing, sitting here ranking her junk food preferences? She had to make a plan or at the next crinkle, her purple bag just might fly off her lap altogether.

Eve was already looking at her with a strange expression on her face. It was time to think of something. Fast.

"Um," she murmured barely loud enough for Eve to hear. "This is a great message, huh? Fascinating stuff. I need to get a pen. Gotta write some of this down."

Goldie looked at Bliss through the mesh flap in the dog carrier, trying to send her an urgent message with her eyes. *Stay. Do not move. Do not make a sound. Stay. Staaaaaay.*

The Cavalier's ears perked to attention, but she didn't move. Not even when another loud rustle of crinkly bag came from somewhere down the row of chairs. Still, Goldie wasn't taking any chances. She unzipped the bag just far enough to stick her hand inside in search of the nonexistent pen.

"Hmm, I know I have a pen inside here somewhere," she whispered, just to keep up her charade.

Bliss flinched when Goldie placed a firm hand on her back. But she stayed put. And Goldie breathed a sigh of relief.

Until the bag crinkled again. And the chip eater bit into the chip—or cheese ball, or onion thing…whatever—with a resounding crunch.

Bliss's wiggly form slipped through Goldie's fingers, and before she knew what was happening, the spaniel bounded out of the fancy pet carrier and landed with a pounce square in the center of Josh's lap.

"What in the …?" Josh, visibly stunned to find a live creature plop in his lap seemingly from out of nowhere, stood up, his arms flailing at the air.

The poor pastor froze behind the podium as complete mayhem broke out all around him. Confused screams filled the air as Bliss—by now a squirming orange and white streak—bounded from one lap to the next.

"Oh, my gosh! I'm so sorry." Mortified, Goldie sprung from her seat and followed the furry ball of Bliss's form as she dashed across the laps of each and every "young single." Everything around her seemed to move in slow motion. Yet, somehow, she still couldn't seem to catch up with the little dog.

Until the Cavalier found what she was looking for.

"There you are! Come here, you bad girl." Goldie knelt on the floor where Bliss was buried up to her little furry shoulders in a bag of corn chips.

Ugh. Goldie had always hated corn chips. They were even worse than the dried onion things.

"Bad girl," she whispered in the dog's silky, copper ear. "Bad, bad, bad girl."

Goldie scooped Bliss into the crook of her elbow, being careful to pick the corn chip crumbs out of her fuzzy coat.

"I'm, uh, so sorry for the disruption. I think we'll be going now." She pretended to scold Bliss as she gathered the purple velvet bag and her upturned Bible together. In reality, she was too humiliated to meet anyone's gaze.

But right before she turned to slink away, as the pastor tried to gain control over the room full of giggling singles, she stole a quick look at Eve.

Bad idea.

Eve wasn't giggling. Or smiling. In fact, she looked downright angry.

"I'm sorry. It was the crinkly bag," Goldie mouthed. Then she offered a meager grin and whispered, "I don't suppose you'll forgive me since I didn't wear my hair in a bun?"

❧

Joe heaved his guitar strap over his shoulder and strummed the first few chords of the opening worship song. He tried his best to open his heart to the Lord in praise, to feel the hymn flow through him as he played along with the other members of the Turtle Beach Christian Church worship team. Before him, the voices of the congregation rose. The ocean roared at his back, a powerful reminder of the Creator's presence, but for once, it failed to keep his thoughts on track.

Turtle Beach Christian Church started its special beach service over three years ago. At first, it was intended to be a seasonal venture, designed as an outreach to summer tourists and beachgoers. But God had other plans. As the months passed, more and more local residents began to show up, lawn chairs in hand and smelling of the sweet, tropical scent of sunscreen. So, the elders decided to keep the beach service and make it a year-round affair. It was a huge success, drawing nearly a hundred worshippers, happy to let their toes sink in the sand while they listened to God's word, even in the dead of winter.

Joe had been with the worship team since day one. All his life, he'd worked in the coffee shop mere yards from the foamy ebb and flow of the tide. Back when the shop belonged to his father, and Joe himself was just a child, he'd begun to think of the beach as his backyard. It was as much a part of his life as his childhood bedroom and Spot, the first dog he'd ever called friend. And coffee, of course. For Joe, there was nothing more comforting than the rich scent of freshly ground coffee beans mixed with the briny fragrance of the sea. When he first heard about the beachside church service, he'd signed right up.

Who wouldn't love it—standing under the rising sun, surrounded by nothing but crashing waves and the wind blowing off the ocean like the very breath of God? It soothed his soul and brought him peace every Sunday morning.

Except this one. Try as he might, he just couldn't concentrate on worship at all. He kept glancing up and scanning the crowd for a glimpse of Cinnamon. So far, he hadn't spotted her. But, he could have missed her. There were quite a few people at church, and she could be lost in the crowd of flip-flops and beach hats.

Joe struck the wrong chord, and the other guitar player shot him a questioning glance.

"Sorry," Joe muttered and got his fingers back on the correct strings.

Who was he kidding? When was the last time Cinnamon actually blended in with a crowd? Her flaming red hair alone stuck out like a sore thumb. Not to mention the nose ring.

She wasn't here.

Yet. She's not here yet. *She could still show up. Plenty of people drift into the crowd after worship has started.*

The first song turned into the second, the second into the third and then it was time for Joe to pack up his guitar and listen to the sermon along with everyone else. The message swirled in and out of his ears until the pastor's closing prayer. As he snapped the closures on his guitar case, he resisted the urge to crane his neck toward the back of the crowd for a glimpse of his wayward barista.

"Great worship today, Joe. Thanks for your service." Pastor Paul slapped him on the back and grinned. "I don't know what we'd do without you around here."

Joe immediately felt horribly guilty. Had he even absorbed one word of the pastor's message? No. He'd been too wrapped up in his own world, anxious for Cinnamon to show up so he could ask Goldie out on a date.

"Thanks, Pastor," he managed to mumble.

"Are you OK? You look a little green in the gills."

Joe laughed at the expression, and Pastor Paul added, "Lame, I know. Just a little beach humor."

"Thanks. I could actually use a laugh." Joe sighed. "I was hoping a friend of mine would show up today, and she's not here…"

"Well, don't worry. She'll show up eventually. Everything in the Lord's timing, remember?"

The Lord's timing. Something about that sounded familiar.

Oh yeah. The sermon had something to do with the Lord's timing, didn't it?

Joe squeezed the handle of his guitar case so hard his knuckles turned white. He rubbed his temples with the other hand, frustration gathering behind his eyes in the form of a raging headache. What was wrong with him? He always enjoyed Pastor Paul's sermons, and now he couldn't even recall a single word of the one he'd given less than five minutes ago.

"He has made everything beautiful in its time." Pastor Paul winked as he recited the words to Ecclesiastes 3:11. "Be patient. He knows what He's doing."

He has made everything beautiful in its time.

The Pastor's words settled over Joe's soul as he strolled back to the coffee shop to stow his guitar in his office. The shop was always closed on Sundays, so it was quiet and empty except for Java's *woo-woo* greeting and the click of his doggy toenails on the scuffed tile floor.

"Hey, boy. Let me put up this guitar and we'll head for home."

As Joe made his way to his office, his gaze found its way to the soft curves of Goldie's name spelled out in chalk on the menu board. *Goldie's Latte Macchiato.*

He felt a familiar ache in his heart when he saw the words. Even the letters of her name were beautiful.

Beautiful.

He has made everything beautiful in its time.

Joe dropped his guitar case on the floor with a thud. All at once, he realized God was doing exactly that. He was turning Joe's relationship with Goldie into a beautiful thing. She looked at him differently now. Her eyes sparkled to life when she saw him instead of looking through him as she'd done for so many months. Each glance sent a surge of longing through him so strong he had to clench his teeth to push it down.

And they talked to each other when they were together. About silly things and serious things too, like her grandfather. Their time together no longer included awkward silences or trivial chitchat.

Best of all was the fit of her hand in his—and what

it meant for the two of them. They fit together. They belonged together. He wanted it now more strongly than ever.

And, unbelievably, he was beginning to think Goldie just might want it too. After all this time, he could hardly believe it.

Yes, God was making their time together a beautiful thing. And He was faithful. He wasn't finished with Joe and Goldie. He would make them beautiful.

Together.

In His perfect timing.

Java nudged Joe's hand with his snout and prodded his leg with a big paw.

"OK, OK, we're going home." Joe picked up his guitar and propped it in the corner of his office. As he and Java locked up, Joe searched for Goldie's name on the menu once more through the window. He whispered her name and the letters tasted warm and sweet on his tongue, just like caramel.

Chapter Eight

"Here are your books, Mrs. Watson. I hope Joey enjoys them." Goldie slid the stack of picture books toward the harried looking young mother on the opposite side of the library counter.

"Oh, he will. And he's really excited about children's hour today." Mrs. Watson hoisted the books into her enormous handbag and grabbed the little boy by the hand. "We'll be back this afternoon."

"Great. I'll see you both then!" Goldie tried to infuse her voice with as much enthusiasm as possible, but the words caught in her throat, and she very nearly had to choke them out. She'd been so looking forward to children's hour, but now that she was actually here at the library it seemed rather intimidating.

She tried to remind herself of the pep talk Joe had given her at dog training class. Everything was going to be fine. The kids would love Bliss, who waited patiently in her carrier sitting near Goldie's feet. What could possibly go wrong?

Goldie cringed. It seemed a lot was going wrong lately. Since her grandfather died, she'd been kicked out of Care Group and been forced to slink out of a Sunday school class with her tail between her legs. If she wasn't careful, she would wind up banned from every church activity in Turtle Beach. Was God trying to tell her something? Maybe she'd been wrong about the Big Conversation. Maybe it wasn't something that could be avoided after all.

"Goldie, you have a phone call," Mrs. Simpson, the librarian, looked at her over the top of her bifocals and waved the telephone receiver in the air.

"Oh, thank you." Goldie couldn't imagine who could possibly be calling her here. "I'm sorry. I'm sure it will only take a minute."

"Don't worry. Take your time. We're always slow on Monday mornings." Mrs. Simpson beamed at her. "But there are sure to be lots of eager children around lunchtime, anxious for you to read them a story."

Goldie gulped and squeaked into the phone, "Hello?"

The voice on the other end was succinct and to the point. "So, I've decided to forgive you."

"Eve?"

"Of course it's me. Who else needs to forgive you? When you left my Sunday school class yesterday did you run off and terrorize another church somewhere?"

Goldie breathed a sigh of relief. At least Eve was joking about it now. She'd looked so angry after the dreaded crinkly bag episode that Goldie had wondered when she would hear from her friend again. "I'm so sorry. It was the crinkly bag."

After a considerable pause, Eve responded, "That's what you said yesterday, and it still makes no sense. I've no idea what you're talking about. It's like you're speaking a foreign language or something."

Goldie couldn't help but say, "You mean like when you speak French to me?"

"Whatever." Goldie could practically hear Eve wave her hand in the air with a flick of her wrist. "I'm forgiving you. What's done is done. How is your first day of work going?"

"Great. My hair is in a bun." Goldie struggled to keep any hint of humor out of her voice.

It didn't work. "I don't believe you."

"Really, it is."

"It better not be." Eve's tone suddenly changed, and a teasing lilt strung her words together. "You never know when you might have a visitor there at the library."

How did Eve know Joe was planning to bring coffee this morning? Goldie was certain she hadn't mentioned it. Or had she, without even realizing it?

While Goldie desperately tried to remember what she could have possibly said, Eve kept on talking in the background. "...so Josh said he might come see you today. I told him you worked at the library, and he actually thought it was cool. Who knew? I guess some guys think it's a turn-on or something."

Wait. What did she just say? "Who?"

Eve blew a heavy sigh into the phone. "Josh."

The name rang a bell, and not in a good way. "Who's Josh?"

"Goldie! *Josh.* You know. The guy you were crushing on at Sunday school. Personally, I thought you had completely blown it after your dog went berserk. But after you left, he was asking me all sorts of questions about you." Questions Eve, no doubt, was all too happy to answer. "I think he might like you."

Oh. No. "Eve, Josh cannot come here this morning."

"Sure he can. You won't get in trouble. It's a public

place. That's why it's called the Turtle Beach *Public* Library." Shuffling noises came from the other end of the phone, and Goldie could hear Eve talking to someone else. "Look, I've got to go. My next class starts in less than a minute. I just wanted to give you a quick heads up about Josh. You can thank me later. *Au revoir, mon ami!*"

The line went dead and Goldie stood, frozen to the spot, unable to move.

Thank her? Hardly.

How in the world had this happened? She should have known better than to pretend she was attracted to Josh. Or, at the very least, she should have admitted to Eve that she'd made up the story about Josh just so she wouldn't notice Bliss in the "handbag."

In all honesty, Goldie had forgotten all about Josh once Bliss had whirled around the room like a little orange and white tornado. Come to think of it, what kind of nutcase was this guy that he wanted to see her again after she'd made such a spectacle out of herself?

Goldie plunked the phone back on the hook. It didn't matter what kind of guy he was. He wasn't what she wanted. He wasn't Joe.

"Morning, Goldie." Suddenly, as if she'd dreamed him into existence, Joe was standing right in front of her.

She smiled and took in the sight of him standing at the library counter holding a steaming paper cup with the familiar *Joe's Coffee Shop* logo. She'd just seen him Saturday afternoon at dog training class, but seeing him here felt different somehow—as though she hadn't seen him a long time. It was a giddy feeling, and yet somehow comfortable, all at the same time.

"Good morning, Joe," she whispered. It was a

library, after all.

"This is for you." He held the paper cup toward her with a wink. "So, how is it? Your first day?"

Goldie wrapped her fingers around the warm coffee cup, grateful she now had something to do with her hands besides fidget like a nervous wreck. She couldn't help but wonder if there was a caramel G drizzled on top of her drink underneath the plastic lid. It seemed like a ridiculous notion. Who would go to the trouble to decorate a drink when it was hidden in a take-out container?

Joe would. If anyone would do something that sweet, it would be him.

"Everything is going great so far." Goldie glanced at the clock that hung on the wall above a beautiful painting of Turtle Beach from the 1950's. It was remarkable how similar the town still looked today, which is one of the things Goldie loved so much about living here. Even the library interior hadn't changed at all since Goldie was a child. Except now, everything seemed so much smaller. Especially now that Joe was here. The way he towered over her, with his broad shoulders and muscular chest, made the smooth maple desks and chairs near the library counter shrink before her very eyes. "I'll read to the children in less than two hours."

"Don't worry. They'll love you. Just like I told you at class the other day." His gaze flitted to her hands, still wrapped around her macchiato. Goldie wondered if he would have given them a comforting squeeze if they'd been free. She liked to think so.

"Speaking of training class, Bliss and I have been practicing."

Joe's eyebrows rose, and a look of delight came

over his features. "You have?"

"Yes." Goldie nodded and tipped her head toward the pet carrier resting behind the counter near her feet. "We had an unfortunate incident at church yesterday, and then we went home and got to work."

At the mention of the word *church*, a strange, wistful look came over Joe's face. It vanished as quickly as it came, leaving Goldie wondering if she'd merely imagined it.

"You took Bliss to church?"

A burning sensation crawled up Goldie's neck and settled in her cheeks. She hadn't meant to let that part slip. "Um, well, kind of. Yes."

But Joe didn't seem horrified. At least not in any way resembling Eve's disturbed reaction. "I was just asking because sometimes I bring Java to church myself."

"Really?" Goldie's heart quickened its pace. Joe didn't think she was crazy for sneaking Bliss into church at all. He even took his own dog to church, too. She could scarcely believe it. "But how? He's too big to fit in a handbag."

Joe knit his brows in obvious confusion, but the corner of his lips lifted into a bemused grin. "That's true. He won't fit in a handbag. Or even a suitcase for that matter. But he can still go to church."

"I don't get it. He just walks right into the sanctuary?"

Joe nodded and let out a little laugh. "I guess you could put it that way. I go to Turtle Beach Christian Church's early morning service on the beach. We worship right there in the sand. It does seem like a sanctuary, perhaps the most beautiful one of all because it was created by God."

"Wow. That sounds incredible." Now that he mentioned it, she remembered hearing about the beach service a while back. It was always advertised pretty heavily during tourist season, but she hadn't even realized it continued during the winter months. "And people bring their dogs?"

"Sure." He shrugged. "It's very laid back. Everyone is welcome. Even those with four legs and a tail."

Everyone is welcome. Goldie wondered fleetingly if that meant she was guaranteed not to get kicked out. Given her recent track record, it gave Joe's church great appeal. "I might have to give that a try sometime."

"You should. I'd like that very much." His smile broadened and Goldie thought she just might melt on the spot. "And bring Bliss."

At the sound of her name, Bliss let out a little woof from her pet carrier. Goldie jumped with a start, and then giggled. She looked over her shoulder at Mrs. Simpson and mouthed, "I'm sorry."

Mrs. Simpson just waved her hand in the air. "Don't worry about a thing, Goldie. Like I said earlier, we're really slow. And you're right where you need to be anyway. Right there behind the counter."

Goldie couldn't be sure, but then it seemed as if Mrs. Simpson's eyes sparkled behind her bifocals as her gaze moved back and forth between Goldie and Joe. The knowing look on the woman's face left Goldie feeling a little breathless.

"I should go. You need to get to work." Joe leaned closer. "But before I leave, you've got to tell me what you meant when you said you and Bliss had an unfortunate encounter at church. Please don't leave me in suspense."

"Oh. That." Goldie cleared her throat and did her best to sound clever, even a bit flirty. "Let's just say it involved Bliss being smuggled inside, and a run-in with a crinkly bag."

"No!" He drew the word out in his charming Southern drawl. "The crinkly bag strikes again."

"That's right. It was really bad. Trust me; you don't want to know the details."

And at that moment, Goldie's very own crinkly bag walked through the door of the Turtle Beach Public Library. She watched, a sick feeling gathering deep in the pit of her stomach, as Josh flashed her a lazy smile and headed toward the counter.

Oh no. No, no, no.

Goldie tried to gather herself together. There still seemed to be so many things she wanted to say to Joe before he left. Things she wanted to say to him in private, certainly not with Josh, her fake love interest, hovering nearby. But faced with the surreal vision of the two men standing nearly side-by-side she couldn't find the words.

"Thank you, Joe." She gazed down at her cup, still warm in her hands. "For the coffee."

This was a painful understatement. She'd meant to thank him for so much more.

"You're welcome." Joe's gaze flitted to Josh, approaching the counter in a much brisker fashion than Goldie would have expected, given his laid back surfer boy image.

Surely, he would see she was busy with Joe. He wouldn't just barge right in on their conversation, would he? Joe could be a library patron for all Josh knew. If he had any manners at all, he would linger in the background while she struggled to give Joe a proper goodbye.

But, apparently, Josh didn't have any manners. He strode right up next to Joe and leaned against the counter on his elbows. Goldie resisted the strong urge to ask him if he was raised in a barn. This was the South, after all. He should know better than to interrupt.

Oblivious to the mental scolding she was giving him, Josh nodded his head toward Joe and then focused solely on Goldie. "Hey, Goldie."

Goldie's heart twisted in a knot when she saw a flicker of worry pass through Joe's warm, brown eyes. It felt as though someone were physically wringing it out, like a dishrag. She placed a hand on her chest in a gesture of protection. Or, perhaps, self-preservation.

Then, to her astonishment, at the sound of Josh's voice, a low, rumbling growl came from the pet carrier at her feet.

Josh's eyebrows rose, and he peered over the counter. "Don't tell me that's your crazy dog. You bring it to work with you, too?"

"Um…" Goldie stammered, a bit perturbed that he would call her dog crazy. Granted, she had misbehaved in Sunday school. But still. Crazy? Wasn't that a bit harsh?

"Excuse me," Joe chimed in. "I don't believe we've met. I'm Joe."

There was a certain edge to Joe's voice that she'd never heard before. When she turned to look at him, she noticed his square jaw was clenched. His usual calm demeanor was gone. He looked…ruffled. Discontent.

"Hey man, I'm Josh." He slapped Joe on the back. "Have you seen her dog? It's a wild thing."

"She," Joe said, the edge in his voice becoming even more pronounced. "The dog is a *she*, not an *it*."

Goldie was quickly becoming fascinated by this strange, new side of Joe. But she couldn't just stand there with her mouth gaping open. She cleared her throat and intervened. "Actually Josh, her name is Bliss. And she was a gift to me from Joe."

"Oh, is that right?" Josh's grin turned a bit sheepish. "Uh, sorry about the crazy comment. It's just, well, you should have seen her at church on Sunday."

Goldie slid her gaze toward Joe. "Remember? The crinkly bag incident I told you about?"

Thankfully, his jaw relaxed slightly, and his eyes sparkled with humor. "That's right. The dreaded crinkly bag."

Josh looked back and forth between the two of them, his own jaw beginning to clench.

"Well, I really should start preparing for children's hour. Thank you so much for stopping by." Goldie plastered a smile on her face and silently prayed that Josh would take the hint and leave, too. All crazy comments aside, he seemed nice enough, but still not what she wanted. Still not Joe. So, she added for good measure, "Both of you."

"OK," Joe focused solely on her for a long moment, and she wondered if he was trying to pretend that Josh didn't even exist. If so, he was doing a startlingly good job. "You're going to have a wonderful first day, Goldie. Bliss, too. I promise."

Goldie sighed. It would have been the perfect moment if only they were alone. "Thank you. And thanks again for the coffee."

Joe winked. "Who knows? Maybe I'll stop by tomorrow for another delivery."

And as he turned to leave, Josh stopped him and asked, "Hey, you're that Joe? The one from the coffee shop? I didn't know you guys deliver."

"We don't," Joe answered in a monotone voice. Then he walked away, leaving Josh alone with Goldie, a bewildered expression on his sunburned face.

"Huh," he muttered. Then louder, he said, "Well, it doesn't really matter anyway. I'm not even sure why I asked him about it. I don't even like coffee."

Goldie tore her gaze away from where Joe had disappeared through the double doors of the library only moments earlier. She crossed her arms in front of her and shook her head from side to side. "Don't be silly. Everyone likes coffee."

Chapter Nine

Joe's hands shook as he walked back to the coffee shop. By the time he'd traveled the three blocks from the library to his front door, he had to jam them in his pockets to hide the trembling.

"Hey, boss," Cinnamon chirped when he walked across the threshold. "How was the..."

"I'm going for a walk." He cut her off mid-sentence as he headed for Java's leash hanging on a hook in his office.

His voice had more of an edge to it than he'd intended, which was exactly why he needed to get out of here. He struggled to remind himself that none of this was Cinnamon's fault. As far as he knew, she certainly hadn't pushed that horrid Josh fellow through the double doors of the Turtle Beach Public Library.

Still, if she had just come to church yesterday he could have already asked Goldie out on a date. Perhaps they would even have plans for this evening. Goldie would at least have an inkling about how he felt about her. As it was, he had no idea if she saw him as just a friend or something more.

And who in the world was this Josh guy? Where

did he fit into all this?

"OK." Cinnamon's voice interrupted his thoughts. "Do you, um, want anything to take with you?"

She sounded uncharacteristically hesitant, and Joe knew he needed to calm down. "Yes. Coffee. Black."

To match my mood.

Then, in an effort to be tolerable, he added, "Please."

Java danced around at Joe's feet, toenails clicking on the tile floor. Joe stroked the Husky between the ears and peered into his mismatched blue and brown eyes. He saw his own reflection staring back at him, tiny and distorted. It was exactly the way he felt right now.

"Here you go." Cinnamon pushed his coffee toward him from the other side of the counter. "Um, is everything OK?"

He clenched his jaw and shot her a look meant to say *Please don't ask me any questions right now*, but the way Cinnamon flinched, made him think perhaps his look had said something more.

Before he could further intimidate her and guarantee that she never darkened the door of any church, much less his own, he grabbed his black coffee and headed outside.

Java tucked himself right next to Joe, as close to him as possible. With every step, Joe felt the dog's warmth brush against the side of his leg. He looked down at Java and the way his furry dog eyebrows knit together, causing the silver fur to gather in furrows on his forehead.

"I'm sorry, boy." Joe scratched Java between his ears and over his muzzle, as if he were trying to rub the worry lines off his face. "I'm just in a mood. That's all."

Java woofed softly, and Joe gave a half-hearted smile. He sipped his coffee and winced. He never drank it black, but it seemed appropriate now.

And through it all—the reassuring pats he gave Java and the bitter sips of coffee—Joe walked.

And walked.

He didn't have any particular destination in mind, but his footsteps carried him to the place he always went.

Gulls cried overhead and Java slowed as his paws sank in the pale, soft sand. Joe kept on walking, all the way to where the water met the shore. The ocean roared in his ears, and he stood there with the sea spray hitting him full in the face until he could hear nothing else around him.

He wanted to scream. Scream until his voice became lost in the cry of the tide. But he didn't. Instead he sank to his knees.

Right there in the sand, he dropped before God in the place where he'd always felt closest to Him. Waves lapped at his knees, soaking his jeans. The cold water should have been a shock to his system, but he barely noticed it. All he could think about was Goldie.

Yesterday he'd been so confident that God was really bringing them together. All it had taken was that brief encounter at the library to shake his confidence. It wasn't right, and he knew it. Either he trusted God or he didn't.

He bowed his head.

God I want to trust you.

What was holding him back?

He stayed there, on his knees in submission to his Lord, and did his best to listen. A stirring in his heart made him believe if he listened closely enough, perhaps he could hear God's voice in the crash of the ocean waves.

Lord, help me trust you more.

God knew how long Joe had loved Goldie. He knew every moment of Joe's silent longing. He'd heard every prayer Joe had uttered for Goldie. Each plea on her behalf. For her happiness, for the healing of her grief. And now, when he finally felt as though he were a real part of her life, Joe was gripped with panic. Why?

Slowly, realization dawned on him and left a chill in his bones that had nothing to do with the frigid sea water. He trusted God to heal Goldie and to make her happy. But deep down, part of him was afraid God's plans for her future didn't include him in the way he so desired.

Yes. God was making his relationship with Goldie a beautiful thing. But, what if all the Lord had planned for Goldie and Joe was a beautiful friendship? It was a thought that hadn't really occurred to him until he'd seen the way Josh looked at Goldie.

If he really, truly loved Goldie, what he needed to want for her was God's best—His plan for her future. Whether it was as his wife... or only his friend.

His next prayer, he spoke aloud. "Lord, help me. Help me love her in the way you desire, whatever that may be."

As soon as the words left his lips, his anger lifted away. He felt drained, empty even, but strangely at peace.

Java nudged him with a wet nose, as if he understood whatever divine conversation Joe had been having was over.

"You ready to head back?"

Java leapt up from the indention he'd made in the sand and spun in a circle.

"OK, let's go."

Joe lifted himself up from his knees and looked at his watch.

One o'clock.

He smiled to himself. Right now, just three blocks away, Goldie was surrounded by a circle of children. When he closed his eyes, he could see her sitting cross-legged on the floor of the library holding the picture book open for all the kids to see, Bliss snuggled in her lap. He could hear her singsong voice reading the words aloud. Best of all, he could imagine the faces of all the children, enraptured with her story.

She would be great. He knew it in his heart. After watching her care for her grandfather for so long, he knew she had that special nurturing touch children would adore. He couldn't think of a job that would suit her better. And he just knew working with children would fill her soul with joy.

Just what he'd been praying for.

The thought brought the familiar ache of unrequited love to his chest. But this time it was different. It was still there—the yearning so palpable he felt at times he could reach out and touch it—but now it held a certain tenderness that had been missing before. He carried it within him like a precious seashell, a treasure from his time spent on the beach.

When he walked back into the coffee shop, Cinnamon immediately looked up, her eyes widening at the sight of him. "What happened?"

"Nothing. I just had some things to work out."

Joe noticed that at the sound of his calm voice,

Cinnamon's shoulders dropped and she became visibly more relaxed. "Did they require you to roll around in the sand?"

He looked down at his knees, coated in wet sand, and laughed. The bottom half of his jeans were soaked and left a little puddle at his feet. "Not exactly. I guess this does look a little strange."

"It's OK," Cinnamon said. "We were crowded for the lunch hour, but everyone's gone now. Don't worry. No one's here to see you."

"That's OK. There are worse things than getting caught on your knees praying."

Cinnamon's gaze darted to his sandy knees and she bit her lip. "Is that what you were doing?"

Joe unsnapped Java's leash and wiped sand from the big dog's face with a gentle movement. "Yep."

"It seems like it helped." Color rose to her cheeks. "I mean, you seemed upset before, and now you seem better."

Unsure exactly what to say, Joe just nodded as he hung Java's leash on its hook.

"Joe?" Cinnamon's voice was small and quiet, like a little girl's.

"Yes?"

"I'm sorry I didn't come to church yesterday." She didn't offer an explanation, simply an apology.

Joe answered her with a genuine smile. "It's OK. You'll come when you're ready."

And, for perhaps the first time since they made their deal, Joe wanted her to come for reasons that had nothing to do with him and Goldie. He wanted her to come simply so she could meet Jesus on the beach, just as he had.

Chapter Ten

Hi, Goldie. This is Josh. It was great to see you at the library today. I was, um, just wondering if you'd like to get together sometime this weekend. Maybe we could go the beach together on Saturday afternoon or something? I'll try and call you back later or maybe I'll swing by the library again. See ya.

Goldie stood, rooted to the spot, and stared at the answering machine in horror. With every blink of the dancing red light, and every rise and fall of Josh's recorded voice, she felt the giddy energy drain from her body. Walking home from the library, with Bliss bouncing alongside her, she'd felt so carefree. Happy even. The memory of reading to the children during story hour, and how they'd delighted in the tale of the part-puppy, part-fraidy cat character, warmed her heart and made her feel as though she floated home on clouds. She couldn't remember the last time she'd felt so filled with purpose.

Then she'd drifted into the house, stealthily avoiding her grandfather's bedroom behind its firmly shut door, and listened to the answering machine.

She wasn't floating anymore. Or drifting. In fact, she was doing pretty good just to remain upright.

Goldie looked at the sofa with longing. It would be so easy to plop right down and stay there for the rest of the night. She and Bliss could curl up into a ball and forget all about Josh. Maybe she could even step back into the Sponge Bob pants.

Goldie forced herself to look away from the couch.

No. I'm not going there. What good would it do? Josh might just saunter back into the library next time Joe's there.

And then what? She didn't think she could take another awkward moment like this morning.

No. This had to stop. Now.

Goldie picked up the phone, but her finger lingered over the keys. What was she doing? He hadn't even left his number.

I'll bet Eve has it.

Surely, there was some sort of Sunday school roster with everyone's telephone number in it. Her stomach churned at the thought of calling Eve, though. Asking her for Josh's number would send the worst kind of message. She would jump to the conclusion that Goldie was still very much interested in him and that just wouldn't do.

No, it wouldn't do at all.

In fact, the more she thought about it, before she even talked to Josh, she really needed to get this whole thing straightened out with her friend. After all, what if she called Josh, told him she wasn't interested in being anything more than friends, and then he told Eve all about it at Sunday school? Goldie couldn't imagine a worse scenario.

But if she was going to break the news to Eve, Goldie needed some backup. Someone who could help her fend off Eve if she blew a gasket over this whole thing. And she knew the perfect person for the job.

After calling Eve to invite her over for an impromptu dinner, and rushing to get off the phone before Josh's name could be uttered, Goldie marched across the front yard and knocked on Peggy's front door. Goldie gulped while she waited for Peggy to answer the door and tried not to think about the last time she'd stood here in her Sponge Bob pants begging to be let into Care Group. No, it was definitely best not to go there.

Peggy swung open the door and greeted her with a cheerful smile as though the unfortunate Care Group incident had never happened. "Hi there, Goldie."

Goldie cleared her throat, preparing to sound every bit like a person who was getting on with her life. "Hi," she chirped, in an octave a tad too high.

"How are you doing, dear?" Goldie noticed the corner of Peggy's mouth lift a bit as she took in the sight of Goldie standing there in a soft pink sweater and jeans. It was pretty pathetic when you could impress someone merely by wearing a pair of pants that didn't have goofy sponges cartwheeling up and down the legs.

"Good." For some reason, Goldie's throat tightened as she answered.

Get it together. You cannot break down in front of Peggy or she'll never let you back in Care Group.

This was harder than she thought it would be. Why? She'd known Peggy for years. "I started my new job today."

Peggy enveloped her in a tight hug. "Oh, honey. I'm so proud of you. That's wonderful."

In the warmth of the older woman's embrace, the tightness in Goldie's throat subsided. "Eve's coming over for dinner, and I was hoping you could come, too."

"That sounds fun. Just let me clean up for a minute, and I'll be right over. What are we having?"

Goldie suppressed a grin. "Why, casserole of course. Take your pick. I've got King Ranch Chicken casserole, chilimac casserole, and tuna noodle casserole. In fact, I think I might even have casserole casserole."

Peggy laughed, sending her white curls bouncing. "Sounds great. I'll be right over."

By the time Goldie fed Bliss her dinner and defrosted one of the many casseroles still packed in her freezer, both Eve and Peggy had arrived. While they ate, Bliss curled up in a ball on top of Goldie's feet and Goldie filled her friends in on her first day of work at the library.

"Tell us everything. Spare no details," Peggy urged, her eyes sparking with enthusiasm.

So, she told them all about story hour and how she'd poured over books all afternoon in an effort to choose just the right one for the next time she was supposed to read to the children.

"Are you bringing the dog with you to work again tomorrow?" Eve pointed her fork at Bliss and frowned.

As if she could understand, Bliss peered up from underneath the table with sad puppy dog eyes. Goldie sighed. Eve may have forgiven her, but it was obvious Bliss was another matter entirely. "She has a name, you know."

Eve rolled her eyes while Peggy suppressed a snort of laughter. "I know. Bliss. Are you taking her royal highness, Bliss, to work with you again tomorrow?"

Goldie decided to ignore the royal highness

remark because, after all, she had bigger battles to fight with Eve. Namely, Josh vs. Joe. "Yes." She inhaled a shaky breath before adding, "In fact, Joe is coming by tomorrow to set up an exercise pen in my office so she'll have her own little area out of the way."

There. She'd brought up Joe. That was sure to start the ball rolling.

Peggy laid her hand on her heart and sighed. "What a sweetheart."

"Are you talking about the dog or the man?" Eve's tone of voice told Goldie her friend didn't think either of them fit the description.

"The man." Peggy winked suggestively.

"He brought me coffee this morning," Goldie added, her voice turning breathy and dreamy.

Oops. She hadn't really meant to say it out loud.

Eve huffed in frustration. "By any chance, did any one else come visit you today?"

"Actually, yes." Goldie paused, gathering every last bit of confidence within her before she continued. She had a feeling she would need it. "Josh came by. And he left a message on my answering machine, too."

Eve gasped, so obviously thrilled she dropped her fork on her plate with a clatter. From her spot underneath the table, Bliss let out a little growl.

Peggy just looked back and forth between Goldie and Eve, confusion clouding her features. "Who's Josh?"

"Goldie's dream guy. She met him at church last Sunday."

"Is this true?" Peggy raised her brows at Goldie. "You went to a new church last weekend and met someone?"

"Yes. I mean…no."

"What do you mean 'no'? That's exactly what happened. I should know. I was there." A smug smile played on Eve's lips.

"That's not exactly how it went. Yes, I did attend a new church." Goldie wanted to place special emphasis on this point, for Peggy's benefit. "And I met someone named Josh. But it wasn't at all like it sounds."

"Yes it was. You said you thought he was handsome. You practically begged me to introduce you." Eve's voice bordered on whiny.

Great. Now she's hurt. I would actually prefer anger.

Goldie had to get it over with before it got any worse. "Well, I may have exaggerated the tiniest bit."

Eve's green eyes flashed and Peggy leaned closer, her jaw hanging open. Goldie offered a weak smile and continued, "I really wasn't so eager to meet Josh. The truth is…I just made all that up."

"Oh, this is getting good." Peggy propped her elbows on the table and rested her chin on her hands.

Eve threw her napkin on the table, narrowly missing her plate of casserole. "What? Why would you do something like that?"

"Well, I knew you would be upset if you discovered Bliss in my handbag. I mean, carrier." Because really, it wasn't a handbag. "So, I said those things as a diversionary tactic. I never imagined it would lead to all this."

"I cannot believe you, Goldie." Eve shook her head, then stopped and remained eerily still.

Goldie and Peggy stared at her, wide-eyed, and waited for her to move. Or say something. Anything.

"But wait," Eve said in such a calm manner that Goldie instantly felt chills rise on the back of her neck. "Let's just wait a minute. So you weren't as, er, enamored with him at first as you led me to believe. But surely, now that you've gotten to know him, you like him. You do, right?"

This was the moment. It was now or never. "Not in that way. No."

Eve's face fell. "But why? He's such a great guy. And he's a Christian, too. I don't get it."

"I know why." Peggy drummed her fingers on the table and wiggled her eyebrows.

"What do you mean? How could you possibly know? You hadn't even heard of Josh until about two seconds ago."

"It's obvious." Peggy fixed her gaze on Goldie and lifted a brow. "Are you going to tell her or should I?"

Goldie took a deep breath and thanked God for Peggy. But as helpful as she was, Goldie just couldn't let her do the dirty work. She bit her lip and glanced solemnly at Eve. "Because of Joe."

For a second, Eve looked uncharacteristically disoriented, as if she didn't have a clue who Joe was. This, of course, irritated Goldie to no end. She was determined to smooth things over with Eve, however, so she offered a prompt. "Remember? Coffee guy?"

"Oh, I know very well who he is. I just hadn't realized you were dating him. How many times have you gone out?" Eve crossed her arms and cocked her head.

Goldie swallowed and twisted the napkin in her lap. "Well, we haven't exactly gone out on a date."

"Yet," Peggy chimed in. "They haven't gone out on a date *yet*."

"But he has asked you out, right?" Eve waited for an answer, her French manicure drumming a beat on the tablecloth.

"Um." Goldie felt heat rise to her cheeks as she remembered that day outside the coffee shop when she'd been so sure Joe was about to ask her out on a date.

OK, so maybe he hadn't asked her out yet, but he would. She was sure of it. "No. But I'm sure he will. We're still getting to know each other."

The burning in Goldie's face only grew worse when she heard how small and pitiful her voice sounded. She cleared her throat and sat up a little straighter. She had nothing to be ashamed of. If she closed her eyes, she could feel the warmth of Joe's hand in the center of her back and the shivers that ran up and down her spine when he'd laced his fingers through hers at dog training class. No, they had not gone on a real date yet, but that was only a minor detail.

"For goodness' sake, Eve. Leave her alone." Peggy wagged a scolding finger in Eve's direction.

"What?" Eve shrugged her shoulders. "I was just getting the facts straight."

"Well, it doesn't really matter if they've gone out on an official date. Sheesh, you young people. Always trying to rush things." Peggy shook her head and made clucking noises. Goldie noticed Eve squirming in her chair under Peggy's scrutinizing gaze. "He's bringing her coffee every day. They're going to dog training class together. With the dog he *gave* her."

Goldie scooped Bliss into her arms and kissed the orange spot in the center of her furry head. She shot a glance toward Eve, who just rolled her eyes at the spaniel.

"He's courting her, plain and simple." Peggy nodded and scooped another forkful of casserole into her mouth.

"*Courting* her?" Eve spat out. "This isn't the eighteen hundreds, you know."

"Courting, wooing, flirting. It's all the same thing. He's taking things slowly." Peggy winked in Goldie's direction. "If you ask me, it's sweet. He's quite a gentleman."

Courting. Goldie turned the word over in her mind and decided she liked the sound of it. Quite a bit, actually.

"OK, OK. So he's a gentleman and all." Eve's lips curved into a sweet smile, which was somehow more than a little unsettling. "I just don't see why this means Goldie can't go out with Josh. I mean, she and Joe aren't even dating. What's wrong with her getting to know Josh, too? Is there some rule that says you can't *court* more than one person at a time?"

"Hello? I'm still sitting right here." Goldie waved her napkin in the air and Bliss lunged at it, catching the corner with a snap of her teeth. "I'll tell you what's wrong with it."

Eve's eyes widened but, thankfully, she sat back to listen to what Goldie had to say.

"It's not fair to Josh. I don't want to lead him on when I know that my heart already belongs to Joe. I like him, Eve. A lot. I may even be falling in love with him."

No one at the table uttered a word or dared to move. Besides Bliss, who gnawed on the napkin and batted it around with her paws.

After what felt like an eternity, Eve finally spoke. "I didn't know you felt that way, Goldie."

"I know. That's why I needed to explain." Goldie smiled weakly. This whole ordeal had been even more emotionally draining than she had imagined. "And who knows? Maybe nothing will ever come of Joe and me. But right now, I'm happy spending time with him. And I don't mind taking things slowly. I kind of like it. I guess I'm old-fashioned that way."

Eve smirked. "That's one thing you two have in common."

Peggy picked up her fork again. Before she dug in, she added, "You know who else was that way? Your Grandpa. I think he would be very happy if you and Joe ended up together. Very happy indeed."

The thought gave Goldie a warm glow all over. She had to agree.

Apparently, so did Eve. "I see what you mean. And I, for one, wouldn't want to argue with the big guy."

రావ

"Thanks so much for coming over tonight." Goldie handed Peggy a steaming cup of hot tea as they headed toward the sofa. Eve had left soon after dinner to attend a special event at her church, but Peggy stayed to help clean up. "As you can see I needed some back-up."

Peggy chuckled while she stirred a spoonful of sugar into her mug. "That Eve. She's really something. She loves you like a sister, though. You may not know this, being an only child and all, but sisters can be bossy."

"Yea, I've actually picked up on that." Goldie patted the cushion on the sofa next to her, and Bliss hopped up, snuggling between the two women. "What in the world do you think she's going to say to Josh?"

"I have no idea, but it was nice of her to offer to talk to him and explain the situation."

"You do think she's going to tell him the truth, right?" Goldie frowned, suddenly wondering if Josh would waltz through the library door again tomorrow morning. Maybe she should have been more insistent about talking to him herself.

Peggy waved a hand in the air. "Don't worry. She gets it now."

While she appreciated Peggy's confidence, Goldie wasn't quite so sure. "You really think so?"

Peggy reached over and squeezed her free hand. "Yes, dear, I do. Anyone could see your feelings for Joe when you talked about him earlier at dinner. It was written all over your face, child."

Embarrassed, Goldie stared at her tea, and then realized she wished it were coffee.

Thankfully, Peggy changed the subject. "So, do you think you'll be going back to Eve's church this Sunday?"

"No!" Goldie blurted out, a tad too quickly. "It would be awkward, with Josh there and all. Besides, it's not the right place for me. I think I might try Joe's church. They have a service right on the beach. Doesn't that sound nice?"

Peggy nodded thoughtfully. "It does."

Goldie gripped her mug tighter. She hadn't planned to talk to Peggy about Care Group tonight, but she'd already confessed to Eve and admitted her feelings for Joe to everyone. She may as well keep on putting herself out there. "Unless…"

"Unless what, dear?"

"Unless you would let me come back to Care Group." She took a breath and kept talking, before

Peggy could answer. "I've started a new job at the library. I told you how much I care for Joe. You wanted me to get a life. Well, mission accomplished. I think you should let me come back. I'll even wear real clothes."

Peggy looked at her with solemn eyes over her cup of tea.

"Please," Goldie added, this time nearly choking on her emotions. "I won't bring Bliss, either."

Peggy sighed and Goldie's heart sank. Sighing was not good. Not good at all.

"Yes, you certainly have accomplished a great deal in the short time since we last talked about Care Group." Peggy sipped her tea and Goldie couldn't help but notice the older woman's gaze turn in the direction of the closed door to her Grandpa's bedroom.

Goldie had to suppress the strong urge to stomp her foot and argue that they never really talked about Care Group. If memory served, Peggy had done the talking and Goldie just stood on the outside of the house begging to get in. She didn't recall having a say in the matter at all. But, acting like a child and throwing a fit was no way to prove she had moved on and gotten a life.

Also, what did Peggy mean by *short time*? It hadn't seemed short to Goldie at all. In fact, it seemed more like an eternity since she'd laughed and prayed with her older friends in the comfort of Peggy's warm living room. The stinging humiliation of peering inside the barely open crack of Peggy's front door and finding out she wasn't welcome was still fresh in her mind, however.

"Don't forget I also went to visit another church," Goldie added, wanting to emphasize the most spiritual aspect of her *moving on* status. Never mind that it was a complete and utter disaster. Some things were better left unsaid.

"Honey," Peggy tore her gaze from Grandpa's door and looked at Goldie, her eyes filled with sympathy. It was an expression Goldie had grown accustomed to seeing in recent weeks. "There's more to *moving on* than actual movement. Sometimes the best way to move on is by sitting completely still."

Sitting still? You mean I could have stayed right here on the sofa watching television? She must be crazy. That made no sense at all. "Peggy, I'm not at all sure what you mean."

Peggy closed her eyes and held one palm up toward the heavens, as Goldie had seen her do many times before at Care Group. "Be still and know that He is God."

"Psalm 46?"

"That's right."

"I still don't get it."

"Goldie, with all this moving on that you've been doing, have you taken the time to talk to God? To really hash things out and let him know how you feel?"

How did she know? Was Goldie wearing some sort of sign around her neck that advertised the fact she was barely on speaking terms with God at the moment? "He's God. He already knows how I feel."

"Yes, yes He does." Peggy nodded. "But He wants to hear about it from you."

Goldie knew she was right. They'd discussed this exact fact in Care Group many times before. She knew God wanted to be in a relationship with her. He knew all about her cares, her hurts, her deepest desires without her ever saying a word. But as her Heavenly Father, He wanted her to come to Him with these feelings. This could only mean one thing—the Big Conversation. The one she'd been avoiding as best she could. The mere thought of it caused a sick feeling in the pit of her stomach.

Goldie's voice cracked with emotion, and she instinctively plunged her hand in the softness of Bliss's fur. "It's just so…hard."

"I know, dear." Peggy laid a comforting hand on top of Goldie's.

Goldie felt Bliss's soft heartbeat pumping beneath her palm and the warmth of Peggy's hand resting on hers. The feeling brought her great comfort, and she closed her eyes, wishing she could stay there as long as possible.

"You'll get there. When the time is right, you'll pour your heart out to Him." Peggy squeezed her hand and then rose from the sofa, preparing to leave and walk back to her house next door.

Goldie stood and carried the teacups to the kitchen before walking Peggy to the door. When she found herself wrapped in Peggy's arms for a goodbye hug, she didn't bother asking again if she could come back to Care Group. She knew the answer already.

Chapter Eleven

Goldie wrapped a silky lavender polka dot scarf around her ponytail and tied it in a loose bow. There. She was ready. All of Bliss's training items were packed in a small backpack by the front door—treats, her Rally Obedience rule book, a collapsible water bowl with bottled water. She was dressed in soft, faded jeans, a comfy violet sweater and sneakers. Harold had a strict rule about all the students in obedience class wearing sneakers. He didn't want any of the handlers to accidentally step on a dog's foot in hard-soled shoes. As soon as Joe got there, she'd be ready to fly out the door. Goldie glanced at her watch.

Yep, he should be here any minute.

She took in an excited, shaky breath and checked herself in the mirror one last time. Even though she'd seen Joe every day this week, when he'd kindly brought her a nice, warm *Goldie's Latte Macchiato* to the library, she still felt a nervous thrill while she waited for him to arrive. They were going to dog training class, just like last Saturday. Only this time, he was picking her up so they could ride together. Which made it seem more like a date than ever!

Even though she'd been expecting it, the sound of

Joe's knuckles knocking on the front door startled her so badly she nearly jumped out of her skin.

Calm down.

She took a deep breath, smoothed her ponytail and swung open the door.

"Hi Joe," she said, rather breathlessly.

"Hi." Joe's voice carried a hint of gruffness and Goldie noticed his gaze dart to her polka dot scarf.

"Is that what I think it is?" She pointed to the paper cup in his hand.

He grinned. "No, Miss Smarty-pants. As a matter of fact, it's not."

Goldie's stomach flipped a little at the sound of his flirty tone. "You mean that's not a *Goldie's Latte Macchiato* you have there?"

"Nope." He shook his head. "This is the weekend. I thought I'd bring something a little more..." He paused, and then finished with, "playful."

"Oooh. That sounds intriguing."

"Here." He held the cup toward her. "Try it and let me know what you think."

Goldie took a tentative sip from the cup's straw. A rush of ice-cold, whipped sweetness filled her mouth, with just a hint of coffee. The chill tickled her nose and she rubbed it with the tip of her finger.

Joe's grin grew wider. "Did the cold catch you by surprise?"

"It did." She took another sip, this time prepared for the icy tingle on the tip of her tongue. "But this is delicious. Absolutely wonderful, almost like a milkshake. What is it?"

"A whippaccino." He shoved his hands in the pockets of his jeans and his grin wavered, a sheepish expression washing over his features. "A *Blissful*

Whippaccino, to be precise."

Oh, wow. Goldie suddenly had trouble swallowing the cool, creamy drink. She couldn't help feeling the tiniest bit exhilarated.

It's one thing to have a yummy coffee drink named after you. It's quite another to also have one named after your dog. Quick. Think of something clever and cute to say.

"Um, that's so, so…nice." Ugh. Goldie could have cringed at her tragic lack of skills in the flirting department.

Fortunately, Joe didn't seem to mind at all. In fact, he practically beamed at her pleasant response. "I'm just glad you like it."

"I do. Very much." She took another sip from her straw.

"So, are you about ready for class?" Joe nodded toward the car, where Java waited with his head poking out the back window.

"I sure am." Goldie slung her backpack over her shoulder and pulled the door shut behind her.

She skipped down the front steps, but when she was about halfway to the curb where Joe's car was parked, she realized Joe wasn't beside her. "Joe?" She turned around and saw him still standing by the door, his soft, brown eyes sparkling with amusement.

"Aren't you forgetting something?" he asked, his lips twitching at the corners.

"I don't think so." Goldie unzipped her backpack and took a quick inventory. Everything appeared to be in order. She even had extra treats in case anyone in class ran out.

Joe walked over to where she stood, still peering inside the backpack. With a gentle touch, he moved her silky bow to the side so he could whisper in her ear.

His breath danced on the sensitive skin of her neck and he said only two words, "Your dog."

"Oh!" Goldie shrieked and dropped her backpack on the ground with a thud. She ran back to the house, a distinct burning sensation crawling up her neck and settling in her cheeks. She could hear Bliss scratching at the other side of the door. "I'm coming, Bliss."

The Cavalier launched herself into Goldie's arms as soon as the door opened. Goldie gave her a kiss on top of the head. "I can't believe I forgot you. I'm so sorry."

Mortified to her very core, Goldie turned and walked back toward Joe, who stood holding her backpack and whippaccino. His expression bordered on one of immense pain. She could tell he was doing everything in his power not to burst out laughing. Goldie had to hand it to him. He was doing a good job. His lips sat in a mostly-straight line, but his warm brown eyes danced with mischief. "All set now?"

"Um, yes." Goldie peeked at him through the fringe of her lashes. If she looked him straight in the face, her cheeks just might spontaneously combust. "I think I have everything now."

"Then, shall we?" He made a sweeping gesture toward his car and, as if they'd rehearsed it, Java woofed from the backseat.

Goldie and Joe laughed at the big Husky while they climbed into the car. Thankful for the diversion, Goldie took a deep breath and tried to relax. Her growing feelings for Joe were sending her into a tailspin.

Dear Lord, please. Don't let me do anything stupid.

It was a simple prayer, but she figured God would understand.

დიოდი

Joe drove the short distance to dog training class, wishing somehow he could make the trip take longer. He didn't want the drive to end. How many times had he dreamt about having Goldie here by his side, her sweet-smelling perfume filling the air? The inside of the car suddenly seemed smaller, and Goldie was so close. Close enough for him to hear the rise and fall of her breath and to feel the heat of her embarrassment over forgetting her dog.

The memory of her startled gasp when he whispered in her ear made him smile. She'd been nervous. Otherwise, she never would have left Bliss behind. He wondered what it meant. Hope lingered in his thoughts, buoyed by the realization that he'd seen none of Josh since that first day at the library. Not only had Josh failed to show up again, but Joe could tell Goldie wasn't even expecting him to waltz back through the door. Every morning when he'd delivered her coffee, her gaze had remained focused squarely on him. It never wavered. Her blue eyes took him in. Him alone.

So, did that penetrating gaze have anything to do with her nerves this afternoon? Could it be possible she felt the same skittering thrill deep in her bones that he knew so well? *Lovesick*, some people called it. Yes, it was an affliction he'd grown accustomed to in recent months. Hoping to gather enough information to make a similar diagnosis in Goldie, he stole a glance at her sitting quietly beside him.

It was hopeless. In the fleeting glimpse, all his attention was drawn to the tiny white dots on the violet scarf wound around her hair. They danced in time with the hum of the car engine and, all at once, Joe could once again feel the smooth silk of the fabric against his fingers like when he'd moved her bow to the side so he could whisper in her ear.

He clenched his fist and dug his nails into the palm of his hand. Perhaps he should spend less time worrying about Goldie's nerves and more time keeping his own in check.

"Are you OK?" Goldie's gaze landed on his fist.

Joe relaxed his grip on the steering wheel and cleared his throat. "I'm great."

And it was true. With her sitting beside him, he couldn't be better.

❧❦

Bliss tugged at the end of her leash, dragging Goldie toward the door of the Community Center. Goldie shook her head in amazement. "It's incredible how much strength a twelve-pound dog can muster when she's anxious to get somewhere."

Joe chuckled. "Yea, it looks like Bliss is excited to be back at class."

She's not the only one.

Goldie's heart swelled as they walked into the Community Center together and were met with friendly greetings from Harold and all the other students. As much as she enjoyed working with Bliss, she had to admit part of the appeal of training class was the way everyone looked at her and Joe. As though they were a couple. Like they belonged together.

"I know you've been busy with your new job this

week. Have you had a chance to practice?" Joe asked as he stuffed Java's treats into the pocket of his jeans.

"Oh, yes." Goldie untangled Bliss's leash and wound the excess length carefully around her left hand. "We've been working hard. We wouldn't want to disappoint you."

He winked at her, causing her knees to quake. "Impossible."

"OK class," Harold's voice boomed from the center of the room. "Let's get to work. Why don't you put your dogs in their crates and come walk the course?"

Goldie zipped Bliss into her portable crate and set her leash on top. "You be a good girl. I'll be right back."

Bliss just peered through the mesh door of the crate as Goldie turned to follow Joe and the other students to the center of the room. Behind the white lattice ring gates, Harold had set up another course made up of a jumble of signs and orange traffic cones. Only this time, Goldie knew what it all meant. In addition to practicing obedience skills with Bliss, she'd also been studying the rule book Harold had given her. She found it to be somewhat easier than it looked. Once she'd learned what most of the symbols meant, like the stop and the curving arrows, the signs were rather easy to decipher.

As she and Joe moved closer to the *Start* sign, he placed his hand in the center of her back in that protective gesture that she loved so much. "Ladies first," Joe murmured with a flash of his pearly white teeth.

Goldie slipped in front of him and tried to concentrate on reading and practicing the signs. She moved her hands in the proper motions for each command, as if an imaginary little spaniel pranced alongside her and did exactly as she said. Joe's presence behind her was more than mildly distracting, but she did her best to focus. After all, she'd worked hard this week, and she was eager to get a chance in the ring with Bliss.

So eager, in fact, that when Harold asked if anyone wanted to go first she raised her hand and called out, "I will."

Joe glanced at her, his brows raised in surprise. Goldie gave him a tiny nod. "We're ready. You'll see."

"OK then," Harold smiled pleasantly at her. His ever-present companion, Bugsy, stood by his side. "Go get Bliss, and let's see how you do."

While Goldie bent down to let Bliss out of the crate and fasten the leash in place, she found herself once again struck by how much Harold reminded her of Grandpa. Naturally, they were similar in age. But there was something else, too. Something Goldie couldn't quite put her finger on that almost made her feel as though her grandfather was the one standing in the Rally ring.

She shivered as she stood and strode back to the center of the room, trying to shake the strange sensation that came over her when she looked at Harold again. At first, she'd found his similarity to her grandfather comforting, but the more he reminded her of Grandpa, the more unsettling it became. She wondered why. With a pang, she realized that Peggy would say it had something to do with the closed door to her grandfather's room.

This is ridiculous. He's an older man. Of course, he reminds me of Grandpa. And it doesn't matter that I still haven't gone in his room. I'll be ready eventually. Someday.

Goldie approached the *Start* sign and settled Bliss into a sit-at-heel position, close to her left foot. She just needed to focus on her dog and making her way through the Rally course. That's all.

"Are you ready?" Harold asked.

Goldie didn't want to take the chance of looking at him and forgetting everything she'd been practicing all week, so she focused her gaze on Joe instead. He nodded at her and gave her a thumbs-up sign. Goldie smiled in return. "Yes, we're ready."

She expected Harold to call out, "Forward," to send her on her way through the course. But, he didn't. Instead, he gave her a few last minute reminders. "Don't forget to give Bliss signals with your left hand only; otherwise, you'll get a crooked sit. Each crooked sit is a one-point deduction. You want to avoid that, if possible. And talk to her as much as you can. Keep her engaged and interested in you."

"OK," Goldie replied and automatically glanced over at him. He had his arms crossed as he spoke, and she noticed that the pinky finger on his right hand was curled tightly closed. Her heart skipped a beat. Grandpa's pinky finger had looked like that. Since he injured it in a printing press accident years ago, he couldn't straighten it if he tried. She'd never seen him without the bent pinky. It had been that way for as long as she could remember.

Goldie's throat grew dry as she stared at Harold's finger. He kept talking, saying things that didn't register in her consciousness, as she waited for the pinky to unfold.

"Goldie? Are you listening?" Harold uncrossed his arms and held out his palms. Two outstretched, perfectly normal looking palms.

Goldie relaxed and took a breath. "Y-yes. Go on."

His hands are fine. Just fine. That's Harold, not Grandpa. What is wrong with me?

She longed to look at Joe and bask in the comforting glow of his gaze, but she didn't dare. Harold already thought she wasn't paying attention, and she didn't want to appear rude. So, she nodded in all the right places and tried her best to appear eager, even though Bliss's leash shook like a leaf in her trembling hands.

"Look how nicely Bliss is sitting there, waiting for you to start," Harold cooed. Even Bugsy looked as though she approved. "I'll stop talking now so you can get going. One last thing, though—remember to loosen up on the leash. At the dog show, each time the leash is pulled taut you'll get a one-point deduction, just like a crooked sit. Capeesh?"

All at once, the blood drained from Goldie's head. Her ears throbbed with a deafening whooshing noise. What had he just said? *Capeesh*? That was her Grandpa's word. She'd never once heard any one else say it, except for Joe that day they walked on the beach together. "I-I-I beg your pardon?"

"Capeesh. It's an Italian slang word." Harold furrowed his brows. "Are you all right, Goldie? You don't look well."

"No," Goldie answered, her voice taking on an eerie, distant quality. "I'm not OK. I'm not OK at all."

Suddenly, it was all too much. All the memories of her grandfather came crashing down on her at once—things she hadn't dared think about since he passed away. His bent pinky finger, his favorite slang word, the way he sometimes cheated at checkers just to let her win. Standing there at the *Start* sign in the Rally practice ring, she realized she couldn't avoid the memories any longer.

She was vaguely aware of the other students' worried glances in her direction. Harold was saying something—she wasn't sure what. The sound of his voice made her want to clamp her hands over her ears.

"Goldie."

The voice in her ear wasn't Harold's. This one was softer and full of emotion. Disoriented, she blinked at its source. "Joe?"

He stood right near her, his arm wrapped around her shoulder. With his free hand, he ran his thumb over her cheek. "It's me. I'm right here."

Part of her wanted nothing more than to melt in his arms, but she couldn't. It was time. Time to face everything. Time for the Big Conversation. "I need to go home now."

"OK. Come on." She let him guide her, like a small child, out of the ring. "Let's get you home."

Somehow, she ended up sitting in the front seat of Joe's car. Bliss and Java were safely tucked in the back, along with the collapsible crates and all the other training equipment. Goldie had no idea how any of it happened. Of course, Joe must have packed up everything. But even though the world around her swirled in a slow-motion fog, she had no recollection of lowering herself into the warm leather seat, of Joe carrying all her things or even buckling her seatbelt.

Yet here she sat, alongside Joe, on the way back to her house.

"I'm worried about you, Goldie." Joe eyes searched hers for a moment before he looked back at the road.

When he faced forward once more, Goldie watched the vein in his temple throb and swell. She tried to force herself to respond. "I-I just need to get home. It's time."

"Time for what?" His voice was gentle, yet urgent.

"The conversation. The big one."

Joe shook his head. "I don't understand."

Goldie sat in silence. She wished she could tell him what was happening, but she couldn't bring herself to put it into words.

Joe reached over and took her hand in his. He ran his thumb over her knuckles in slow, easy circles. "It's OK. Everything is going to be OK." He lifted their interlocked fingers and pressed his lips against the back of her hand. The kiss was slow, deliberate. When it was over, he held her hand against his cheek for a long moment before letting go.

Goldie wondered why he returned her hand, empty, to her lap.

Then, he spoke again. "We're here."

"Oh." She looked out the window at the only home she had ever known, and sighed. "We are."

"Can I come inside with you?" Joe's gaze was pleading. "I don't think you should be alone right now."

Goldie shook her head. "No. I wish you could. But I can only do this alone."

"Isn't there anything at all I can do to help? It's killing me seeing you in pain like this."

"I'll be OK," Goldie murmured, but the words came out all wobbly and disjointed.

Joe took his time climbing out of the car and unloading all of her things. The whole time, she sat motionless in the passenger seat. Even though she knew she needed to go inside, to finally have it out with God and face all the painful memories, weariness penetrated her bones. She honestly didn't know how she would make it from the car to the front door.

"Are you ready to go in?" Joe held her door open and offered his hand. Bliss stood panting at his feet, her head swiveling as she looked back and forth between Goldie and Joe.

Goldie nodded and placed her hand in his. When he helped lift her out of the car, he placed a firm arm around her waist and walked her to the front door. Goldie fumbled with her keys, her hands still trembling. Agitated, Bliss stood on her hind legs and pawed at Goldie shins.

"Here, let me." Joe slipped the keys out of her fingers, and Goldie was struck by how natural and familiar the warmth of his skin felt against her own.

As soon as the door opened, Bliss charged inside, spinning in excited circles. Usually such antics brought a smile to Goldie's lips, but this time, she felt nothing.

"If you need anything, Goldie. Anything at all…" Joe's voice trailed off, but the message was clear.

"I'll be OK," Goldie managed to say. "Really. Thanks for everything."

Joe jammed his hand through his hair and exhaled a sharp puff of breath. "But I haven't done anything."

"Yes you have." This time Goldie was the one to reach out to him. She placed her palm on his chest, right where she could feel the steady beat of his heart. "Just being there for me is more than I could ask."

The look on his face was more than she could bear. It would be so easy to stay out here on the porch and try to forget all about the closed door to Grandpa's room. If she didn't turn around and go inside immediately, she knew she might never deal with her grief. And then, what would happen? Where would she be the next time it hit her? In the grocery store? At the library?

Without another word, Goldie turned and walked inside. She didn't even turn around when she closed the door, but instead just shut it behind her back so she wouldn't have to see him at all.

Chapter Twelve

Joe had never felt so powerless in all his life. The very moment Harold had used that word—capeesh—the hair on the back of Joe's neck stood still. If it affected him like that, what must it have been like for Goldie?

Completely devastating, by the looks of things. Watching her stand there in the center of the room at dog training class had been like witnessing the very life drain right of her. Before he could even cross the room, leap over the white lattice ring guards and reach her side, she'd all but disappeared. His Goldie was gone. Replaced by this broken girl who he had no idea how to fix.

He paced back and forth the small length of the front porch. If only she would let him inside. Surely, there was something he could do to help. She was barely coherent. He didn't see how in the world she would be safe alone like that. All the way home, she was hardly responsive. She just kept mumbling something about a conversation. He didn't even know who she needed to talk to.

Joe sank to the ground, frustrated beyond belief. He tried praying, but could barely concentrate. Even worse, he wasn't sure exactly what to pray for. After several failed attempts, the best he could come up with was simply, "Lord, please take care of Goldie."

Only six small words.

They seemed painfully inadequate.

When he was finished praying, he tried to make himself as still and quiet as possible so perhaps he could get some sort of sense of what was going on inside Goldie's home. He leaned his back against the heavy wooden doorframe and took shallow, quiet breaths. Nothing. He couldn't hear a thing. Then he realized that that was probably for the best. He knew he shouldn't be spying on Goldie. The temptation was almost too much to bear. For a brief flicker of a moment, he actually considered trying to peek inside one of her windows.

No. I can't. She doesn't want me in there. I've got to respect her privacy, even if being out here is tearing me up inside.

So, instead, he busied himself trying to imagine Goldie, alone in the silent house. Had she loosened her ponytail from the silky scarf? He closed his eyes and pictured her thick, blonde curls tumbling over her shoulders in gilded waves. For once, he couldn't take pleasure in such a vision. Every time he conjured her in his mind, her eyes stole his focus from all else. Sometimes he saw them bright and shiny, brimming with unshed tears. Even worse, other times he saw them dull and lifeless, like they'd been all the way home in the car. Try as he might, he couldn't bring the image of Goldie, happy and whole, back to his mind's eye.

Java, still situated in the back seat of the car, hung his head out the backseat window and whined pitifully. The mournful noise beckoned to Joe and took him out of his reverie.

"Sorry, boy," Joe muttered as he lifted himself off the porch and walked to the car. His footsteps were careful, slow and deliberate. They became more hesitant with each step he took.

Java whined again, as if urging him forward. The poor dog furrowed his brows and cocked his head in concern.

"Don't worry. I'm coming," he whispered toward the Husky. "We'll be home before you know it."

But as the words left his mouth, he knew at once they were untrue. What was he saying? He couldn't go anywhere. Not now.

When at last he closed the distance between himself and the car, he reached for the handle of the back door instead of the driver's seat. He gave Java a shush command before letting him bound out of the car. As soon as his paws hit the pavement, the Husky shook his body from the cold tip of his black nose to the end of his tail. He stood for a few moments, taking in his surroundings. Then he sat politely and woofed in a very soft voice at Joe. Everything about his posture seemed to say, "Now what?"

If Joe hadn't been so worried about Goldie, he would have chuckled. Instead, he shrugged his shoulders at Java. "I don't know. I haven't the first clue what to do now. I just know I can't leave."

The two of them lingered there, side by side. Finally, Java yawned a big, squeaky dog yawn and started to curl up in a ball at Joe's feet.

"No, no. We can't just stay here at the curb." Joe ran both hands through his hair and gripped his temples. "Come on, get up."

At Joe's urging, Java scrambled to his feet again. Joe reached inside the car and brought out Java's travel bowl and a bottle of water from his dog training supplies. Without thinking, he also grabbed the remains of Goldie's whippaccino.

"Come on." Joe nodded backward toward Goldie's porch and Java trotted toward him. "Let's go sit over here for a while."

With the big dog on his heels, he made his way back to the porch. He filled up Java's water bowl and once the dog had had a drink, Joe patted the top step and urged him to lie down. With a heavy sigh, the Husky folded his legs beneath him. When he was all settled, he curled his tail around his body in a tight hug, the white hair on the very tip delicately covering his nose.

Joe gave the dog a wistful smile and then realized he was still holding Goldie's whippaccino. He didn't know what he was even doing with it. Somehow, he must have supposed if he had it ready, waiting for her, she might possibly step out onto the porch any minute.

She didn't.

Joe finally set down the cup with a careful hand, right next to the front door. Then, he sat next to his dog and held his head in his hands, emotionally spent. As the hours passed, the radiant light of the afternoon slipped away and was replaced with the cool tranquility of twilight. Tiny white petals from the cherry trees in Goldie's yard floated on the evening breeze. In the distance, Joe could hear the rush of high tide bubbling at the shore. Tomorrow was Sunday, and he was expected to stand on that very beach and lead worship at his church.

Joe exhaled heavily. Tomorrow morning seemed

so far away, yet he knew he would need to be there no matter what else—if anything—happened here tonight. He took another, long look over his shoulder at Goldie's front door. Then he rested against its frame, finally allowing his eyes to close. The darkness of night wrapped around him and Java like a heavy blanket. Joe's last thought before drifting off to sleep was that sitting here, keeping this strange vigil, seemed almost like the ultimate act of faith. It would have been far easier to bang on the door and insist Goldie let him in. Instead, he could do nothing but wait and trust that whatever Goldie was going through, God would be right there by her side.

۞o

The first thing Goldie did when she was finally inside was untie the scarf wound around her ponytail. As she walked into the living room, she let the lavender dotted silk slip through her fingers and flutter to the floor. After shooting a glance in the direction of the sofa, she stepped out of her clothes on the way to the bedroom. The jeans remained pooled in a pile on the floor while she slid into the familiar Sponge Bob pajamas. Goldie supposed it was OK to wear them for the Big Conversation. There wasn't a rulebook for this sort of thing, so she hoped it wasn't inappropriate. The thought of facing God wearing them sent a hysterical bubble of laughter from her lips, which turned into a strangled sob. She wasn't thinking clearly. That much she knew. But she had to get out of those clothes—the ones she'd worn to class. She couldn't get them off fast enough. She was like a snake shedding its skin. She needed a fresh start. A new beginning.

"We're going to do this, Lord. Whatever it takes, I'm ready."

For once, she spoke the words aloud. Her voice sounded strange, foreign. Even Bliss noticed. The little spaniel froze in place, her tail tucked between her legs, as she eyed Goldie with curiosity. Goldie didn't even respond. No words of reassurance. Nothing.

Instead, she turned and headed for the sofa, plopped down cross-legged in the center, and closed her eyes. She tried to formulate the words for what had happened at class. She supposed that was the best place to start. She would just tell God about Harold, the bent finger, everything… finishing with her complete breakdown in front of everyone.

"Dear Lo-rd"

Before she could finish His Name, she choked on a sob. This time, instead of pushing it down, holding it back, as she'd been doing for so long, she let it out. That's what this was all about, right? Finally letting God know the depths of her pain and asking Him for healing. The sob wracked her body with a horrendous shudder and turned into a horrible groan. Its intensity frightened Goldie, and somewhere in her consciousness, she noticed Bliss dive under the bed in the pink room.

In the long moments that followed, Goldie truly understood Paul's words in the book of Romans, "We do not know what we ought to pray for, but the Spirit Himself intercedes for us with groans that words cannot express." It was a familiar verse. She'd heard it countless times, but never grasped the true meaning of it until this very instant. She had no idea what to pray for anymore, but she needed God more than ever. Strange choking sounds came from deep inside her throat, and she just gave into them. She let all the ugliness and grief pour out of her, all the while trusting that somehow God was there. That he knew all the feelings she was struggling with that she couldn't manage to put into words. In some way, her prayers reached His ears when she couldn't articulate them.

And, somehow, through all the tears and pain, she felt His presence. For the first time since her grandfather died, she was showing Him how she felt. It wasn't pretty. But it was honest. It was her truth. And Jesus—the way, the truth and the life—was all about truth, wasn't He?

Goldie had no idea how long she poured her heart and soul out to God that afternoon. Long enough to leave the sofa cushions damp beneath her tearstained face. And long enough that the late afternoon sun no longer peeked through the curtains. By the time she at last lifted her head and took in her surroundings, night had fallen.

But, strangely enough, her soul felt as if it were finally emerging from the darkness.

Goldie clutched her chest, as though she were testing the condition of her heart. She braced herself for the familiar tightness that had been there for weeks now. Sometimes it pressed down like an anvil, and others, like when she was around Joe, it was barely noticeable. It was always there, though. A constant reminder of what she had lost. Just in case she forgot that she was all alone in the world.

Not anymore.

She inhaled a deep breath, so deep she almost choked. Then the choking turned to hesitant laughter.

I can breathe. I can really breathe.

The pressure was gone, lifted away by an angel or more likely, God Himself.

Thank you, Lord.

Goldie rose from the sofa, surprised by how buoyant her body felt. She imagined that if she really tried, she could probably float into the pink room. She had never been so exhausted in her life, but it was a good kind of tired. She felt as though she had been poured out, but miraculously filled back up. It was quite a heady feeling. She suppressed a smile when she realized just how tense she'd been for so long without ever realizing what a toll it had taken on her.

I guess Peggy was right, after all. The thought brought a smile to her lips. *That probably shouldn't come as a surprise.*

Goldie had the sudden urge to cram her feet in her fuzzy slippers and run next door. If only it wasn't so late. The sleepy hands of the mantle clock told her it was past midnight. She couldn't wait to tell Peggy she'd finally done it. She'd had the Big Conversation and lived to tell about it. Better than that, she no longer had to live in fear she might lose it at any given moment. She didn't know why she'd pushed God away. Well, she guessed it was because she was angry. Angry at being left alone. But now she knew the truth. She wasn't alone. She never had been. God was there all along.

And with this knowledge, Goldie had a revelation.

Joe had been there all along, too.

Her breath hitched in her throat at the thought of him, and her heart thudded with greater intensity than when she'd last seen him. She loved him. She'd known it for a while now. But this was different. Now, she was ready to act on that knowledge. To take a chance on a future with Joe.

Goldie's eyes flitted to the quiet television and she remembered her silly dream about being on the game show. She giggled aloud thinking about Cary asking her to put a price tag on a fabulous new life with Joe by her side. At the time, she couldn't bring herself to respond. The price, the risk of heartbreak was too high. She clamped her eyes closed tight, picturing the emcee in her mind, thrusting his microphone toward her, watching, waiting for her to name that price. This time she would do it. She would take a chance.

A strange, snuffling sound broke her dreamy connection to Cary, and Goldie's eyes flew open.

What was that?

She stood very still in the silent house, wondering at first if she'd only imagined the strange noise. Then it happened again. Goldie turned her head, the hair on the back of her neck standing on end.

"Hello?" she called.

A mournful whine was the only response.

Goldie let out a ragged breath. "Bliss? Is that you?"

She padded to the pink room and looked under the bed. No Bliss.

The poor thing. Goldie realized her hysterics had probably frightened the life out of the little dog. "Bliss, where are you, sweetheart?"

The spaniel whined again and then started digging on the hardwood floor. Goldie followed the sound to the entry way and found Bliss frantically pawing at the front door.

"What in the world are you doing?" Goldie stood with her hands on her hips and furrowed her brows at the little dog. Good grief. She'd ignored Bliss for a few short hours to get things right with God, and the poor dog had gone crazy.

Goldie bent to pick her up, but Bliss would have none of it. She flailed about in Goldie's arms, all four legs pawing furiously at the air.

"What has gotten into you?"

Goldie tightened her grip and tried to nestle the spaniel close to her chest, but Bliss sprung out of her arms and flung herself at the threshold. Once on the ground, she pushed her black nose into the tiny crevice between the door and the frame. She sniffed, snorted and scratched at the floor.

Goldie watched with mounting curiosity. "Is something out there?"

Bliss looked up long enough to woof and then went back to sniffing.

Goldie leaned toward the peephole. She couldn't see a thing, but perhaps Peggy's cat had taken up residence on her porch. That would certainly explain Bliss's sudden agitation. If that was the case, she needed to shoo the kitty back home or they would never get any sleep.

With a firm hand, she scooped up Bliss off the floor. This time, when the dog tried to wiggle free, Goldie was prepared. "Oh no you don't," she scolded. "Why don't we put you in your crate for a minute?"

Once Bliss was safely confined to her crate, Goldie hurried back to the front door. She peered through the peephole once again, but it was like looking into a black hole. She couldn't see a thing. As she reached for the doorknob, she hesitated, her stomach twisting into a nervous knot.

She took a deep breath and told herself not to be silly. There was nothing frightening out there. It was

Peggy's cat. That's all. Before she could change her mind, she twisted the doorknob and yanked open the door.

What she found there wasn't a cat. Not by a long shot.

Goldie gasped and her heart skidded to a stop at the sight of Joe and Java sleeping quietly on her front doorstep. She had to brace herself against the doorframe to keep from falling down in utter shock. What was he doing here? It didn't make any sense.

While she stood gaping at them, Java opened his sleepy eyes and blinked up at Goldie. Goldie made the shush motion she'd seen Joe use before to keep the Husky quiet. Java sighed and closed his eyes once more, curling his tail more snugly around his body. Goldie wasn't quite sure why, but she didn't want to disturb Joe. Even though he was slumped against her porch, he looked so peaceful. She couldn't take her eyes off him.

Willing herself not to make a sound, she knelt beside him. Her knee bumped against something and she realized it was her damp cup of melted whippaccino. Goldie picked it up, her gaze flitting back and forth between the paper cup and Joe's sleeping form.

My whippaccino. Does this mean he's been out here this whole time?

At this thought, guilt and delight both swirled within her, warring with one another. He must have been terribly worried about her to stay out here all afternoon and into the night, watching over her like a guardian angel. She felt awful for causing him so much concern. Yet, she couldn't suppress the bubble of joy that rose up in her soul knowing that he cared for her to such an extent. This was much more than bringing her coffee every day, or even giving her a puppy. The man had camped out on her porch all afternoon and fallen asleep sitting up.

Goldie supposed she really should wake him. That was her intention when she leaned toward him. But as the distance between them closed, her heart beat faster and more furious. She was honestly stunned that he couldn't hear it, that it didn't wake him with a start.

When she was close enough to whisper in his ear, she said simply, "Joe."

He didn't move. A lock of his chocolate hair rippled under her breath, but he remained perfectly still. Sitting this close to him, Goldie noticed for the first time the impossible length of his dark eyelashes. With her gaze, she traced his strong jaw line and the gentle curve of his bottom lip and had the sudden urge to wake him, not with a whisper, but with a kiss.

The very thought of kissing Joe made her dizzy. She backed away and sat on her heels, unable to look away from him.

She couldn't wake him. Who knew what would happen if she did. She couldn't very well throw herself into his arms and kiss him without warning. If he'd been worried about her before, he would likely think she'd gone completely off the deep end.

No, it was better to leave him here. There was, however, one thing she could do for him.

After taking one more lingering look at those long eyelashes, she rose and sneaked quietly back into the house. Without any hint of hesitation, she went straight toward her grandfather's room. The closed door greeted her. Goldie clenched her fists and braced herself to enter.

I can do this. After all, that's what tonight was all about, right? Opening doors.

The door opened with a lazy creak. Goldie stepped over the threshold, noting that the room hadn't changed a bit. That fact surprised her, although she wasn't sure why. No one had been inside, so why wouldn't it look the same? She let her gaze sweep over her Grandpa's glasses, still sitting on the bedside table, only now covered with a fine layer of dust, the pillow still with a faint depression in the center, and his favorite afghan folded neatly at the foot of the bed. She ran her hand over the knotted yarn. Like Goldie's afghan, this one had been crocheted by her grandmother's nimble hands years ago. It felt soft and soothing between Goldie's fingers as she lifted it gently off the bed.

She held it up to her face and inhaled, closing her eyes. The blanket still smelled vaguely of her grandfather—a familiar combination of coffee and buttered, cinnamon raisin toast—the scents of her childhood. A soft smile played on her lips as she realized the coffee smell now reminded her of Joe.

Joe, who still lay sleeping on her porch.

Snuggling the afghan close to her chest, Goldie walked back out of the bedroom. This time, she left the door propped open behind her. Her shoulders lifted slightly. It felt like she had just shrugged off a bulky winter coat.

When she reached the porch, Joe remained still as stone. White cherry blossoms dusted his shoulders and swirled around the moonlit night. She knelt beside him again and resisted the urge to reach out and stroke his face, to brush the rumpled hair off his brow. Maybe if she touched him, and felt his warm flesh beneath her fingers, she would believe he was real. No, she couldn't. Instead, she unfolded the blanket, pausing to admire the careful loops of interwoven yarn. With a touch lighter than a hummingbird, she spread the afghan over Joe, praying she wouldn't wake him. He stirred slightly, his eyelids fluttering while Goldie held her breath with anticipation. The damp sea breeze seemed to stop blowing around her as she waited for him to sit up and open his eyes.

But he didn't. He breathed out a long sigh, burrowed under the blanket and murmured something that sounded oddly like her name as he drifted back to sleep. Goldie sat and watched him for several long moments waiting for him to say her name again. Then, she slowly rose, said a silent prayer over him and whispered, "Good night, Joe. Sleep well."

She felt Java's gaze on her back as she slipped away.

Chapter Thirteen

Joe wasn't quite sure what woke him first. It was a toss up between Java's enormous paw batting him square in the face and the ferocious crick in his neck. Every time he moved his head, even a fraction of an inch, pain shot through him from his jaw-line clear to his shoulder.

I suppose that's what happens when you sleep against a wooden doorjamb.

After spending the better part of an evening and an entire night here on Goldie's front porch, the doorjamb seemed more solid than ever. He needn't worry about her safety. That door could have been made of lead.

"Woo woo," Java howled and he poked Joe with a sharp jab of his muzzle. Clearly, the Husky had had his fill of the vigil himself.

"Take it easy, there." Joe struggled to sit up straight and then rubbed his ribs, which had absorbed much of the impact of Java's impatience. He glanced at his watch and realized he needed to head home and change clothes almost immediately if he was going to make it to church in time to lead worship. "We'll be on our way in just a second."

Joe winced at the words. Although they were true, he hated that he meant them. He didn't want to leave. Not now. Not without seeing Goldie first. Even in his woozy, half-asleep state, he knew that much was true.

He rubbed his eyes and cleared his throat. What he wouldn't give for a cup of coffee right now. Instinctively, he glanced over to the spot where he'd left Goldie's melted whippaccino the day before. It wasn't there. He blinked. Where could it have gone?

It was in that puzzled moment that Joe recognized the comforting sensation of a blanket wrapped around his shoulders. He looked down. Sure enough, there it was. Robert Jensen's favorite afghan draped loosely over his body. He would recognize it anywhere. For the last few months of Bob's life, it had been a constant presence—usually spread over his lap while he rested on the sofa.

And now, here it was. There was no doubt how he'd come to find himself huddled beneath Goldie's grandfather's beloved blanket. Goldie must have been here sometime during the night and left it for him. His gaze swept instantly to the front door. It looked the same as it had the day before when he sat out here waiting in agony for some sign of life beyond its carved wooden grooves. But today, instead of filling his soul with dread, the sight of it gave him a strange feeling in his bones. The same stab of longing lingered, only this time, it was tinged with a fine layer of hope.

Goldie had been out here, in this very spot.

Joe stood and folded the afghan as carefully as possible. Frustration fueled his movements. She had been here, and he'd slept through the whole thing. He jammed his feet back into his sneakers while Java shimmied around his legs.

Joe shot the Husky a pained glance. "At any point when Goldie was out here did you even consider waking me up? Did it cross your mind at all?"

Java's pointy ears pricked and swiveled at the sound of his voice.

"You know, you're supposed to have my back. Man's best friend and all. Sound familiar?"

Java just stared, his thick, plumed tail sweeping back and forth in a low arc. Joe cupped the dog's muzzle in the palm of his hand and winked. "It's OK. I forgive you."

His kind words sent Java into a frenzy of delight, his nails clicking on the wooden steps of Goldie's home. Joe ran his hand over Java's head and paused, trying to imagine Goldie standing over him while he slept. He wondered what had made her come outside. Had she been surprised to find him there?

Well, most likely she had. Camping out outside someone's home wasn't exactly on the normal end of the behavioral spectrum. In fact, if he took the time to think about it, it was rather stalker-like. So, he chose not to think about it.

Instead, he tried to conjure an image of his beautiful Goldie, bathed in moonlight, spreading a blanket over him with her delicate ivory hands. His gut clenched at the mental picture. Had her face been awash with tears when she'd been so close to him? Did he miss his chance to comfort her when she needed him the most?

Blankets and late night visits aside, he still had no idea what was going on behind that closed door. But surely, the afghan was a good sign. If Goldie had been in the same near-catatonic state as yesterday, she couldn't have made the conscious decision to tuck him in for the night. And he couldn't help but wonder about the significance of the fact that she'd chosen to cover him, not with just any blanket, but this particular one. Her grandfather's blanket. Perhaps he was reading too much into it, but for him the gesture carried with it a certain poetic beauty he couldn't seem to shake.

Joe sighed, and with great reluctance, whistled to Java and strode away from the porch. He didn't dare look back, knowing that if he did, he might not be able to resist the urge to run back and beat the door down. It was a fortuitous decision, for halfway down the sidewalk he heard his name.

"Joe?"

He stopped. Java plunked into an automatic sit.

"It is Joe, isn't it?" A kind woman with a grandmotherly face smiled up at him.

"Yes." Joe raked a hand through his unkempt hair, trying to gather his wits about him. "I'm sorry. You startled me."

"Yes, it seems I did." The older woman's gaze shot to the blanket folded into a tidy square on the threshold and then back to him. "I'm Peggy, Goldie's next door neighbor."

"Yes, of course. We met at the funeral." Joe was uncomfortably conscious of his wrinkled clothes and the dark shadow that undoubtedly covered his jaw line. Goldie had enough to deal with right now without her neighbors making any inappropriate assumptions.

"I'm glad I bumped into you, Joe. I wanted to thank you for all the wonderful things you've done for Goldie. She thinks the world of you, you know." Peggy's face broke into a broad grin.

The sentiment caught Joe off guard. His chest tightened, and his voice turned gruff. "Hmm, er, thank you. The pleasure is really all mine. I would do anything for her."

Peggy's eyes sparkled behind her glasses. "She's a special girl."

"Very special." Joe nodded, the tightening his chest becoming almost unbearable.

"I can see you think so." Peggy narrowed her gaze, and for a brief moment, Joe felt as if she could see clear into his heart. Then she smiled again, and the eerie mood lifted. "I'll let you get going. I'm sure you have somewhere to go."

"As a matter of fact, I do need to get going." Joe checked the time on his watch. It was even later than he'd thought. He'd lingered on Goldie's doorstep as long as he possibly could. "I've got to run home and then off to church."

"Church? How nice." Peggy patted him on the arm. "Don't let this old lady keep you."

"It was a pleasure seeing you again." Before Joe led Java to the car, he had the sudden urge to wrap his arms around her in a big bear hug.

"Oh." The move must have caught her off guard because she gave a little start in his embrace.

Before he let her go, Joe whispered in her ear, "If you see Goldie, tell her..." He paused. What did he want to tell her? It was too much to put into words. He struggled to come up with something, but instead stood there strangely silent.

Peggy patted him on the back and he released her without finishing his thought.

"Don't worry." She winked. "I'll tell her you were here."

❧❧❧

If Goldie had been fully awake when the knocking on the door started, she would have realized it wasn't the familiar steady rhythm of Joe's knock at once. As it happened, she wasn't fully awake. In fact, she was sound asleep. The kind of perfect, dreamless sleep she hadn't experienced in a very long time.

So, when Bliss scurried to the door in a frenzy of barks and spinning circles, Goldie assumed at once that Joe was awake. Awake and waiting for her right on the other side of that door. She bolted upright in bed, pausing only long enough to make sure the healthy, whole feeling from the night before hadn't somehow slipped away in the night.

I'm still here. Still here, all in one piece and actually happy. Thank you, Lord.

The banging on the door resumed.

"Coming! I'll be right there." Goldie tried to sound remotely coherent. Not an easy task with a mouthful of peppermint Scope.

She sprinted to the door, running a hasty hand through her hair, and scooped up Bliss. She gave the Cavalier a quick kiss on the nose and opened the door, a smile of heavenly anticipation dancing on her lips.

"Good morning." The words were out of her mouth, in a breathy whisper, before she realized the person standing on the threshold was not Joe at all.

"Were you expecting someone else?" Peggy's eyes danced with humor, and in her arms, she held Grandpa's afghan, once again folded into a rectangle as if it had never left the foot of the bed.

Goldie blinked at the afghan as her cheeks burned

with tiny invisible flames. "Um, well, no. Of course not. Come on in." She waved Peggy inside, willing herself not to crane her neck outside in search of Joe.

"Good grief." Peggy rolled her eyes as she stepped inside. "Save it, Goldie. I know he was here. The whole neighborhood knows he was here."

The flames intensified. "The whole neighborhood?" She gulped.

Peggy laid the blanket on the back of the sofa and then plucked Bliss from Goldie's arms. "Of course. You had a man camped out on your front porch. A rather handsome man at that. Did you really think no one would notice?"

Goldie shrugged her shoulders. "I didn't know he was there."

Peggy's gaze darted to the afghan.

"Not the whole time, any way. I found him there asleep in the middle of the night." Goldie skirted around Peggy and headed to the kitchen to get Bliss her morning biscuit.

Peggy, naturally, was hot on Goldie's heels. She stopped when Goldie disappeared inside the pantry in search of dog treats. "So, what exactly…"

Her voice trailed off, and Goldie immediately popped out of the pantry. It was a rare occasion when Peggy was rendered speechless, so naturally Goldie was curious. She found her older friend frozen in place in the kitchen, a strange look on her face. Then, Peggy's mouth curved into a sly smile as Goldie followed Peggy's gaze to the open door of Grandfather's bedroom. She dropped Bliss to the floor and the spaniel scampered to Goldie for a biscuit.

"It looks like something big really did happen here last night," was all Peggy said.

"Oh, Peggy," Goldie sighed dreamily. "I finally did it. I talked to God about the whole thing."

She launched into a detailed explanation of the entire experience, from the bend of Harold's pinky finger all the way to discovering Joe on her porch. Peggy stumbled to the sofa, and sat, mesmerized, hanging on her every word until she was finished.

"I'm so proud of you, dear," she said when Goldie had revealed everything. "I should have noticed something was different right away. You have a newfound peace about you. You even look different."

"I feel alive again." Goldie shook her head, still in disbelief. "I'm sure there will still be tough times ahead. I miss him. And I will for a long time. But when the bad times come, I won't wait so long to talk to God about everything. Never again. He's been here for me the whole time. When I look back over the past few weeks, I can see His grace in everything around me. My friends, my new job." She paused, the air between them swirling with meaning. "Joe."

Peggy reached over and squeezed her hand. "Good for you. I knew you had it in you. And, now that you've got things with the Lord all sorted out, it's time."

"Time for what?" Goldie knit her brows. Was there no pleasing this woman? What could she possibly have up her sleeve now?

Peggy beamed. "To deal with the Joe situation."

Goldie gulped. "There's a situation?"

Peggy opened her mouth to answer, but Goldie stopped her with an open palm—not only the universal sign for halt, but also the sign for stay, at least in dog training circles. "I think we may need some coffee for this conversation."

"Since when do you drink coffee?" Peggy's tone was full of mock-seriousness.

Goldie's heart skipped a beat. "It's a taste I've acquired in recent weeks."

It didn't take long for Goldie to locate her grandfather's coffee maker and get it going. Once both women were settled on the sofa with steaming mugs of coffee—Goldie's with generous spoonfuls of cream and sugar—and Bliss was happily chomping on a rawhide chew, she was ready to hear what Peggy had to say. "OK. So there's a situation? With Joe?"

Peggy nodded, her eyes ablaze with some untold secret.

Goldie struggled to sit still. She would have liked to blame the caffeine for her restlessness, but she was sure it had more to do with the knowing look in Peggy's gaze. "Do you care to elaborate?"

"Sure." Peggy took a long, slow sip of coffee. Goldie wanted to scream. The suspense was killing her. Peggy had always been such a dear friend, but right now Goldie felt more like her torture victim. Something about that look in her eyes made Goldie's stomach churn.

Then Peggy said something that made the bottom drop right out of it. "He wants to marry you."

Goldie choked on her coffee, nearly spewing it all over Peggy, the sofa, everything. And Peggy had the nerve to sit there and laugh. "That's not something you should joke about, Peggy."

"Oh, I'm not joking. I'm dead serious." There was the look again, this time with a fierce edge of determination, as if she were daring Goldie to disagree with her.

Despite the voice in her head that told her to calm

down and not get ahead of herself, a thrill of delight ran up Goldie's spine. She shivered, and her heart thumped with alarming speed. "And how would you know something like that?"

"Easy." Peggy took another excruciatingly slow sip from her cup. "Your grandfather told me."

Goldie wasn't sure what she expected Peggy to say, but this was far out of the realm of possibilities. Her heart pounded so out of control she was forced to plunk her coffee cup onto the end table. Caffeine suddenly seemed like a very bad idea. "M-my grandfather?"

"Yes." Peggy reached over and took Goldie's trembling hand. "He sat right here on this very couch and said 'Joe from the coffee shop wants to marry my Goldie.'"

My Goldie. It sounded exactly like something Grandpa would say. As much as she yearned to believe it, there was no way it was possible. She barely knew Joe back then. Her grandfather must have been confused. He got that way a lot toward the end. Her heart slowed down somewhat, and she asked, "When did he tell you this?"

"Three days before he died."

Goldie took a sharp intake of breath at the word *died* and silently asked God to give her strength. "Go on."

Peggy sighed and rubbed her temples, as if trying to remember everything. "I had come over to bring him a chocolate milkshake. Remember how much he loved those?" Of course Goldie remembered. In those last weeks, he'd consumed little else. Peggy nodded in silent agreement, her expression wistful, and continued. "And while he was drinking it, I asked him about the checkerboard still out on the coffee table. He said Joe had come over, but they never got around to playing. When I asked him why, he said Joe had wanted to talk to him about something. Something very important."

Goldie tried with all her might to tamp down the hope stirring in her soul. "Then what happened?"

"He grinned. A really big happy grin. Now that I think about it, it was probably the last time I ever saw him smile like that." Peggy dabbed at the corners of her eyes with her napkin. "I asked him why he was so pleased if he'd missed his chance to beat Joe at checkers. And he said, 'Joe wanted to come over today to make me a promise. He said he didn't want me to worry about a thing. He wants to watch over Goldie and make sure she's happy after I'm gone.'"

Goldie bit her bottom lip to prevent the inevitable flow of tears. Her head was swimming as she recalled Joe's stubborn persistence in those early days after her Grandpa's death. All those coffee cups lined up on the steps.

Peggy spread her napkin back over her lap. Goldie couldn't understand how Peggy could be so calm when her own skin tingled with the sudden prick of goose bumps. Was this normal for her? Did she go around doing this sort of thing all the time? "I told him that was wonderful and that Joe sounded like a very fine young man. And Bob said, 'There's more. He loves her. Can you believe it? Joe from the coffee shop wants to marry my Goldie.'"

Hearing it for a third time did nothing to lesson the shock. "Are you sure? Absolutely sure that's what he said?"

Peggy reached out and cradled Goldie's cheek in

the palm of her hand. "Dear Goldie, is it so difficult to believe? You should have seen Joe this morning. He's worried sick about you. He loves you. It's written all over his face."

Goldie blinked back her tears. She refused to cry, even tears of joy. She'd done enough crying to last a lifetime. "Do you really think so?"

"I do." Peggy nodded solemnly.

Despite Peggy's conviction and the growing sense of elation swelling in Goldie's heart, the smallest hint of doubt flitted into Goldie's thoughts. "He left this morning without saying goodbye."

Peggy waved her hand in the air in a perfect gesture of nonchalance. "He was in a hurry to get to church. But let me tell you, he looked like he was in physical pain tearing himself away from here. I promised him I would tell you he was here."

Goldie shot off the sofa in a panic. "Oh my gosh, it's Sunday!"

With yesterday nothing but a blur, and last night one of the longest of her life, she'd completely lost track of the days of the week. She'd been planning to attend Joe's church this morning anyway, but now it seemed much more urgent. She'd run there if she had to.

"I've got to go," she shouted as she shed her clothing while fleeing to her bedroom. "I need to go to church. And I need to let Joe know I'm OK."

Peggy kept her remarkable sense of calm. "Don't worry about a thing. I'll clean up. You get going."

Goldie threw on a lightweight, pale pink, hand knit sweater and a pair of soft blue jeans, all the while sending up prayers of gratitude that Joe's church on the beach was laid-back and casual. With a quick glance at the clock, she decided she had enough time to sweep on some mascara, blush and lip gloss. Once she'd wrapped a hot pink scarf around her neck and run a brush through her hair, she was ready to go.

"Bliss?"

The spaniel came running at the sound of her name and Goldie snapped the leash in place.

"You're taking the dog to church?" Somehow, when Peggy said it, it sounded less like an accusation than it did coming from Eve's mouth.

"Yes. Joe suggested it. Sometimes he brings Java." Goldie's gaze swept the kitchen and living room. True to her word, Peggy had straightened up. Everything was neat as a pin.

"That's sweet." Peggy walked beside Goldie down the front sidewalk. "You have a good time at church."

"I'm sure we will." Goldie's stomach wavered ever so slightly. After last night, what would it be like seeing Joe? After all Peggy had told her? "And Peggy?"

"Yes, dear?"

"Thanks so much. For everything. I don't even know how to thank you…"

Peggy gave her a solid hug full of meaning, the kind Goldie would have avoided before the Big Conversation. "There is one thing you can do for me."

This came as a surprise. Peggy rarely asked anyone for help, but Goldie was happy to do whatever she needed. It was the least she could do. "Really? What?"

"I'd love it if you came to Care Group this Thursday."

Goldie gasped. "Don't tease me."

"I'm serious." Peggy planted her hands on her hips. "But you've got to promise me two things. First, keep talking to God. Don't shut Him out again."

"Yes ma'am. I promise." Goldie held her hand to her heart. She wouldn't make that mistake again. "What's the second thing?"

"You have to promise me you'll bring your young man." Peggy winked, a mischievous grin tugging at the corners of her lips. "Bring Joe."

Goldie felt the familiar flush return to her cheeks. "I'll see if that can be arranged."

Chapter Fourteen

Joe's fingers moved over the strings of his guitar, plucking and strumming songs of worship to his God. Unlike last Sunday, when he'd found himself distracted by the anticipated arrival of Cinnamon, he gave himself to the music with his whole heart. Nothing could tear his attention from worship this morning. He felt almost as if he were pouring himself out onto the sand, throwing himself at the feet of the Lord. All for her. For Goldie.

If he couldn't be with her, holding her hand, cradling her head on his shoulder, he would make every moment away from her count. And what better place to plead for God's grace for Goldie than here at church?

As the worship team began the opening phrases of the final hymn, Joe closed his eyes. His fingertips danced across the guitar strings by memory, perfectly in synch with the rise and fall of the melody. He didn't miss a single note. The song of praise flowed through him so smoothly that it was a jolt to his system when it ended.

Once he'd lifted the guitar strap from his shoulder and placed the instrument in its case, he sat in serene silence as Pastor Paul delivered the message. Joe recognized the familiar Bible passages, but he immersed himself in each one as if he'd never heard them before. He repeated the phrases in his mind, turning the words into prayers. When the service ended, his head was still bowed, his hands clasped together in a loose knot in his lap. He could hear the people around him milling about, but he finished his prayer before he dragged his eyelids open.

When he did, he found himself looking into a familiar face. It wasn't the one he so longed to see, but it was an astonishing turn of events nonetheless.

"Cinnamon?" He hoped his voice didn't give away the shock that skittered through him at the sight of her. For whatever reason, coming here wasn't easy for her. He didn't want to do anything to make her feel uncomfortable.

"Hi, Joe." She gave him a sheepish smile and fiddled with her hands behind her back. The shy gesture was so out of character for her that he had to fight to keep his jaw from dropping open.

"You came. That's wonderful." He rose from his seat and gave her a friendly pat on the back. "How did you like the service?"

"It was pretty cool." She nodded thoughtfully and Joe couldn't help but notice something was different about her. He couldn't quite put his finger on what it was. The thought nagged at him while she gestured toward the ocean. "I like being out here on the beach for the singing and the sermon and...stuff. It's really beautiful, you know? It kind of makes me want to believe."

"I know what you mean. It gets to me, too. I feel very close to God out here." Joe squinted at the sunlight bouncing off the water. "Lots of people struggle with doubt, Cinnamon. But I'll bet if you pray and ask God to help you believe, you'll find it gets easier."

Cinnamon's eyes widened, and she tilted her head. "Really? I can just tell Him I'm not sure if I believe He exists, and He won't get all mad and swallow me up in an earthquake or anything?"

Joe grinned. "No."

"You're sure I won't get struck by lightning?" She narrowed her gaze at him, her familiar spunk returning to her features.

"No lightning." Joe shook his head, resisting the urge to laugh. "The book of Mark tells the story of a man who asks Jesus to heal his son. Jesus tells the man, 'Everything is possible for him who believes.'"

Cinnamon's voice carried a note of hesitation. "Did the man believe?"

"That's the funny part. He immediately told Jesus, 'I do believe.' Then, right afterwards, he turned around and said, 'Help me overcome my unbelief.'"

Cinnamon breathed out a heavy sigh. "I don't get it. Did he believe or not?"

"I think he wanted to believe." Joe paused. "Sometimes that's half the battle."

Cinnamon was silent for a moment, and then asked thoughtfully, "What happened to the boy? The man's son? Did Jesus heal him?"

"Yes." Joe nodded. "Yes, He did."

Cinnamon's face broke into her familiar grin. Familiar, but not quite the same. "That's a nice story."

Joe wished he could figure out what was different about her. He tried to put the nagging thought out of his mind. "I think so, too."

"I think I'll come back next week." She nodded, a look of determination crossing her features. It was a look Joe had seen before at the coffee shop, and he knew she meant business.

"Great. Would you like me to introduce you to Pastor Paul?" Joe nodded toward the pastor mingling in the crowd. "I think you'll like him."

"Um. OK." Then, she jabbed her pointer finger at his chest. "Wait just a minute. We had a deal. Remember?"

Of course, he remembered. How could he forget? He cleared his throat and spoke in the quietest whisper he could manage. "Yes. Now that you've come to church, I'm supposed to ask Goldie out on a date. But..."

She cut him off mid-sentence. "No buts. We had a deal. You can't back out now. And there's no time like the present."

How was he going to explain to her that he couldn't ask her out now, even if he wanted to? Goldie was in no condition for any kind of romantic overture. "Be realistic, Cinnamon. I'm not going to call her right this minute."

Cinnamon rolled her eyes. "Why would you call her when she's standing right over there?"

"What?" It was impossible. Yet, hope burned deep in his soul. "Goldie's here?"

"You didn't know?" Cinnamon waved her hand toward the shoreline. "She's right over there. See? She even brought that cute little dog you gave her."

Joe turned and nearly had to brace himself against Cinnamon's shoulders to remain upright. It *was* Goldie.

He was in no way prepared for the sight of her standing right at the water's edge, the sunlight glimmering around her like a thousand tiny diamonds. Her hair whipped around her heart-shaped face in the ocean breeze, and from where he stood, he could just make out the sound of her laughter, tinkling like a bell. Bliss tumbled at her feet, spraying the bottoms of Goldie's jeans with clumps of sand.

Goldie is here. And she's laughing. How is that possible?

If Cinnamon hadn't seen her too, Joe would have thought he was having some sort of hallucination. He'd never seen Goldie look so beautiful, so free. Watching her twirl with Bliss in the surf on her graceful ballerina legs, he felt as if he were in some sort of surreal dream.

She turned and blew him a subtle kiss from the tips of fingers, and it nearly knocked the wind out of him. He heard his own sharp intake of breath, and it pulled him into action. Without tearing his gaze from Goldie, lest she vanish in a whirlwind back to his dreams, he tried to explain, "Cinnamon, I need to…"

"Go." She waved him off. "Go get her."

Joe smiled at her bluntness. "Are you sure you don't mind?"

"Of course not. This was part of our deal, after all." She winked. "I can introduce myself to the pastor. Don't worry about me."

"I'm so glad you came." He lowered his voice and leaned closer. "And not solely because of the reason you think."

"I know. And I'm glad I came, too. See you tomorrow, boss."

And, true to her word, she flitted through the thinning crowd toward Pastor Paul. Joe once again sensed something different about her, but couldn't concentrate long enough to figure out what it was. He supposed he should feel at least a little guilty. He'd invited her, so he really should have stuck by her long enough to introduce her to a few people. But he was being pulled toward Goldie like a powerful magnet. It was as if they were the only two people in the world, and nothing else around him existed.

He strode toward her, unable to look anywhere but straight into the clear crystal blue of her eyes. When he'd first spied her off in the distance, he'd wondered why she kept herself so far away. Now, whatever the reason, he was glad. They needed to be alone, so they could talk about what happened last night.

But when he finally reached her, the words caught in his throat. Nothing but stone cold relief washed through him as he realized she was OK. The puzzled, distraught girl from the night before had disappeared, and his Goldie was back. Better yet, this was a new Goldie, one he'd never seen before. He scarcely believed it when this enchanting woman balanced on her tiptoes and wrapped her arms around him in a tight embrace.

Joe never made the conscious decision to kiss her. If he'd thought about it, he supposed it never would have happened. It hardly seemed appropriate considering the state she'd been in the last time he'd seen her. But with her lithe arms wrapped around his neck, Goldie pressed her lips close to his ear and whispered, "Thank you for last night. Thank you for staying."

Then her lips, softer than rose petals, brushed against his cheek in the sweetest of kisses.

He couldn't think. Not with her this close, nestled

Teri Wilson

in his arms, as he'd desired for so long. He simply
reacted. With her warm lips lingering so near the
corner of his mouth, all he had to do was turn his head
the slightest bit and catch them with his own. Their
kiss began with her tiny gasp of surprise, but before
Joe could stop and apologize, Goldie was kissing him
back.

As their lips moved together, Joe wrapped one
arm around her waist and pulled her closer. He lifted
his other hand and cradled her face, ran his thumb
along the underside of her jaw, wanting to make sure
this was real. His Goldie was truly here, kissing him,
with her fingertips playing at the back of his hair. She
sighed—a perfectly sweet sigh of contentment—and he
thought he'd never heard such a delightful sound. He
kissed her one, two, three more times until the frenzied
yapping finally broke through his consciousness.

Bliss, plainly unhappy to relinquish her position as
the center of attention, tugged on Joe's shoelace and
barked her displeasure.

He and Goldie broke apart and, reluctant to
completely let her go, he wove her fingers through his.
"I think that took Bliss by surprise." He gave Goldie's
hand a squeeze.

Goldie's gaze flitted to the spaniel. "She's not the
only one." As she spoke, her cheeks glowed with a
pink flush, which only accentuated the aquamarine of
her sparkling eyes.

He reached out to touch her face, and then pulled
his hand back as foamy bubbles of seawater swirled
around their feet. What was he doing? They were at
the beach. Not fifty yards from his *church*. "Goldie, I'm
so sorry. I didn't think."

"Shh." She pressed her fingertip against his lips,

184

and he resisted the urge to plant a kiss on it. "Don't be sorry. I'm not."

"You're not?"

"No." She shook her head, causing a riot of blonde waves to cascade over her shoulders. "Surprised, not sorry."

Joe wished they could stay just like that forever. Hand in hand, basking in the warm afterglow of their first kiss. He hated to risk breaking their fragile connection, but he had to. The memory of her pale face, twisted in despair at dog training class, haunted him. He despised himself for making her talk about it, but he needed to know. "Goldie, what happened last night? Please tell me."

༒

Still reeling from the impact of Joe's kiss, Goldie blinked up at him. She found it beyond difficult to gather her thoughts when all she could seem to look at were those long, dark lashes of his. How in the world had she failed to notice them before? She knew she'd been depressed. But, good grief. She hadn't been temporarily blind, had she?

Focus, Goldie. Focus.

When she had at least partially recovered from her woozy, post-kiss fog, she was able to look beyond those incredible eyelashes and see the worry radiating in his gaze. Troubled lines creased his forehead. She struggled to find the right words. "Oh, Joe. Please forgive me. I didn't mean to worry you so."

He pulled her closer to him with his hand still interwoven with hers. "Don't fret about me. I just need to make sure you're OK."

"I'm fine. Really." She couldn't stop the flush from returning to her cheeks. "More than fine, actually. I didn't mean to frighten you yesterday. Everything happened so fast."

Joe squeezed her hand and nodded, urging her to continue.

Goldie glanced toward the area of the beach where the church service was held. "It had been a while since I talked to God about everything that happened with my grandfather. To be perfectly honest, I've pretty much been avoiding Him since before Grandpa even died. I was holding it all in, afraid to talk to Him about it. And something about the way Harold looked yesterday..."

Her voice trailed off, but still Joe remained silent, ever patient as always. How could she possibly put everything into words? This was much harder to explain than she had thought, but she wanted him to understand. She owed him that much, after all he had done for her.

"I imagined his pinky finger bent like Grandpa's." She ignored the painful wince cross Joe's features. "And then when he said capeesh."

She shrugged and shook her head from side to side. Before she could say another word, Joe scooped her back into his arms again and kissed her on top of her head. This kiss was different than the last one—gentle and protective—but it still left Goldie struggling to catch her breath.

"I saw it. As soon as the word left Harold's mouth, it was like the life drained right out of you. It was an arrow to my heart." Joe's voice cracked with emotion.

A sense of urgency overcame Goldie. As safe and warm as she felt in Joe's embrace, she pulled back so he could see her face. She wanted him to see her clearly, so he would know everything was fine now. "But then, I went home and finally had it out with God. The dam broke, and I let Him know exactly how I felt about everything. It was a tremendous release. And when it was all over, I felt free. Full of God's grace and free."

Joe watched her for a moment, his gaze never leaving her face, even when Bliss started digging a hole right at his feet.

Great. He thinks I'm going to lose it again.

"If you're waiting for me to have another breakdown, you're going to be here a while. It's not going to happen."

"Is that so?" His voice was serious, but the corner of his mouth hitched into a half-grin.

"Absolutely." Goldie nodded, and snuggled further into his arms.

"And how can you be so sure?" The question was a half-whisper. That's all that was necessary since her head was nestled securely underneath his chin.

"Because I'm not going to try to go it alone again. From here on out, I'm spilling my guts to God on a daily basis. More often, if that's what it takes." Joe's body shook with a wave of silent laughter. "Honestly, I'm great."

He inhaled a ragged breath. "I'm not going to argue with you. You certainly look great."

Goldie's heart quickened its pace and she squirmed a little in his arms, self-conscious at the effect he had on her.

"Where do you think you're going, Bashful?" He squeezed her into a tight hug. "You said I could stay here for a while and wait for you to break down.

Neither of us is going anywhere."

"Bashful?" Goldie suppressed a giggle. "I'm already named after a fairytale character. Now you're giving me the nickname of one as well?"

She tried to make light of the situation, but her ever-increasing heartbeat brought with it a flood of embarrassment. She ducked her head so he couldn't see her blush.

Joe lifted her chin in the most gentle of motions and forced her to look him squarely in his coffee-colored eyes. "I've waited an awfully long time for you to notice me, Goldie. Forgive me if I want to enjoy the moment."

In that instant, Goldie knew with the utmost certainty everything Peggy had told her that morning was true. All of it. A flood of emotions hit her so hard she would have collapsed if Joe hadn't been holding her up. She tried to speak, but it came out barely more audible than a breath. "Forgiven."

She tilted her mouth toward his. This time when he kissed her, she was ready. If anyone could truly be ready for such a kiss. Every subtle movement of his lips seemed to carry a new emotion, each one stronger than the last. Goldie lost herself in her response, trying to impart her answer to his unspoken question in the way she returned the kiss.

When they broke apart, Joe rested his forehead against hers and gave her a tiny kiss on the tip of her nose. "I think my heartbeat is giving yours a run for its money right about now."

"Maybe." Goldie rested her palm on his chest and felt a distinct thundering there. "Joe, can I ask you something?"

"Anything."

"Would you come to Care Group with me this Thursday? It's a Bible Study group that meets at Peggy's house."

"Are you asking me out on a date, Bashful?" Joe lifted his brows in mock astonishment. Clearly, he was still enjoying his moment.

"Actually, no." Goldie disentangled herself from his arms long enough to unravel Bliss's leash from around one of her legs. She scooped the dog into her arms and situated herself against Joe's chest, his arm slung over her shoulder. "Peggy invited you. I'm just passing along the invitation, smarty pants."

"Oh. Well, good," he said with a rather bashful smile of his own.

"Good?" Goldie frowned.

"Yes." He lowered his head so he could speak directly into her ear. "Because I was hoping to be the one to ask *you* out on our first date. Would you like to have dinner with me this Saturday?"

Goldie buried her trembling hands in Bliss's fur. This was the moment she'd been waiting for. "I'd love to."

"Wonderful. It's sure to be a special night." Something about his words and the way his eyes sparkled caused Goldie's stomach to tumble in a fit of nervous excitement.

Then, she remembered. "Wait," she gasped. "Saturday afternoon we have the dog show. Will we be finished in time to go home and get freshened up before dinner?"

Beside her, Joe stiffened. "You can't be serious." His tone became hard as stone. "You're not still planning on going to the dog show." It was a statement, not a question.

The intimate mood between them began to slip away. "What do you mean?" She nodded toward Bliss, who had settled quite comfortably in her arms. "Of course I am."

"No." Joe shook his head. "No, no, no."

Goldie wiggled out from under his arm and turned to face him straight on. "What do you mean 'no'?"

He paused. Goldie watched a vein throb in his temple while she waited for him to speak. After it had pulsed ten times, he rested his hands on her shoulders and smiled. It was weak effort, but at least he no longer looked angry. "I'm sorry. I didn't mean to sound as if I were telling you what to do."

He blew out a heavy sigh, and Goldie could tell he was choosing his words with great care. "I just don't think it's such a good idea for you to go to the dog show."

She had a pretty clear picture of what was going on, but still had to ask. "Why not?"

"Sweetheart," he breathed and Goldie instantly realized she preferred it when he called her Bashful. "You have to ask?"

Irritation pricked at her nerves. "I told you that wasn't going to happen again."

Joe cupped her face in his palms. "I know. But, wouldn't it be best not to take a chance?"

Take a chance on what? Me having another meltdown?

It was Goldie's turn to stiffen, but before she could say anything else, Joe fixed his melting gaze on hers, and she couldn't stay angry. All she saw there was worry and concern. And maybe a little exhaustion. He had slept on her porch, after all.

She tried to infuse her voice with a blend of

tenderness and confidence. "I'll be fine. I promise. Trust me."

"It's not that I don't trust you." He threw his head back and let out another sigh. "How can I explain this so that you understand? I can't see you in that kind of pain again. You weren't expecting it yesterday, and I know you've turned it over to the Lord, but I just want to protect you. Please don't go. Please come to dinner with me instead."

"Joe, I'm going to the show. I have to."

"You don't need to prove anything to me. My feelings for you have nothing to do with whether or not you can hold it together at dog training class."

Goldie bit her bottom lip and remembered the sensation of his kisses, each one more full of feeling than the last. Strong feelings. Love perhaps? She knew he was telling the truth. But she also knew, no matter how they felt about one another, they could never have a future if she hadn't dealt with the past. She wanted to go to the show and do well, to prove to both him and herself that she was dealing with the grief. That she was healthy and whole.

"I want to do this. It's important to me." She tugged on the front of his shirt. "And you're coming with me, right?"

Joe closed his eyes and took a deep breath. "Of course I'm coming with you. I'll be right there by your side. So will Java. And so long as you're up to it, we'll go on our special date afterward, but…"

"But what?"

The corner of his mouth lifted. "But I may have to start calling you Stubborn instead of Bashful."

Goldie swatted at his chest, and Bliss started in her arms. "Don't you dare."

"Don't worry." He pulled her close to him again, so close his lips brushed against hers when he spoke. "As long as your heart reacts like that when I hold you, I'll always call you Bashful."

Goldie could barely hear over the pounding of blood pumping through her veins. She had a feeling Joe would be calling her by her new nickname for quite a while.

Chapter Fifteen

Five days.

Joe shook his head.

Only five days until the dog show.

Despite the way his gut clenched whenever he thought about Goldie facing Harold again, an overwhelming sense of anticipation flooded his senses as well.

Five days until our date.

He tried to look at it that way. To forget all about Saturday afternoon and concentrate on their plans for the evening. But it was so difficult.

"Hey boss," Cinnamon's familiar voice sing-songed her greeting as she breezed in the door.

"Morning." He barely glanced up at her from his coffee, but it was long enough to register the change.

Cinnamon seemed to watch the awareness cross his features as it dawned on him what was different about her. How could he have not known before? The nose ring was gone, replaced with a tiny hint of a hole right next to her nostril.

Joe wanted to grab his guitar and sing a song of celebration at the sudden disappearance of the tiny rhinestone stud. But, if the way Cinnamon was looking at him was any indication, that would be a big mistake. Clearly, the topic was off limits.

Fine. He would pretend not to notice.

She narrowed her gaze at him. "What?" The word sounded almost like a threat.

Joe cleared his throat and focused all his attention on the swirl of cream in his coffee. "Nothing."

Cinnamon stood there for a moment, waiting for him to crack. Joe willed himself not to smile and busied himself with wiping down the counter. When at last she was satisfied that he wasn't going to mention the nose ring—or its mysterious absence—she put on her apron and prepared to get to work. Behind her back, Joe smiled at Java. He could have sworn the Husky smiled back at him.

"So, how did it go with Goldie yesterday?"

He turned to her. Cinnamon's eyes sparkled enough to make up for the missing nose ring, and Joe knew she must have witnessed their kiss on the beach. Thankfully, she was being uncharacteristically discreet. He was suddenly very glad he'd resisted making a crack about her ringless nose. "Good." In the history of the world, had there ever been a bigger understatement? "Really good."

Cinnamon rolled her eyes. "Well, don't keep me in suspense. We had a deal, remember? Did you ask her out or not?"

Joe held up his hands in a defensive gesture. "I did, I did."

"What did she say?" Cinnamon poured herself a cup of coffee without taking her eyes off him for a second.

"She said yes. We have a date on Saturday night." This time, when Joe answered her, he couldn't keep up the calm façade. His face split into an enormous grin. He could actually feel the joy radiating from his soul.

"Oh, boss. That's so great. I'm so happy for you." Cinnamon clapped her hands and jumped up and down. "I knew she would say yes."

Joe scanned the sidewalk out front for any potential customers. None, so far. Cinnamon could jump around all she wanted. "You did, huh?"

"Duh." She swatted him with a dishrag. "Please. Don't try and tell me you didn't know she would."

Joe paused, savoring the memory of Goldie's thundering pulse as he held her in his arms. "I suppose I had an inkling she'd say yes."

As the words left his mouth, he was overcome with a powerful longing deep inside. He couldn't help but wonder if Goldie would say yes to all the other questions he hoped to ask her.

"An inkling?" Cinnamon blew a puff of red hair from her forehead. "Boss, I'm going to level with you. I'm going to give it to you straight because you've done so much to help me…and, well, it just seems like the Christian thing to do."

Joe lifted his eyebrows and tried to keep the shock from showing on his face.

If Cinnamon noticed his surprise at her use of the word *Christian*, she hid it well. "Goldie is head over heels in love with you."

He didn't say anything at first. A month ago, even a week ago, his first impulse would have been to argue with her. He would have told her she was clearly mistaken and then gone on to list all the reasons why it was impossible that Goldie was in love with him.

But this wasn't a month ago, a week ago or even a day ago. This was today. And with a jolt, Joe realized he wasn't going to argue with Cinnamon at all.

"I think you may be right," was all he said.

Cinnamon's eyes popped open wide. "Yes!"

Joe grinned. Again. "Why do you look so surprised? You're the one who said it first."

"I was all ready to argue my case. I didn't think you'd believe me. You've always been so hesitant about Goldie. What's changed?" She cocked her head at him, and Joe flinched, waiting for the usual twinkle of the nose ring.

When he remembered it was gone, he grinned even wider. "Everything. Everything has changed."

The tinkle of the bell on the front door to the shop interrupted their conversation, and two of Joe's regular customers strolled in. Joe shot Cinnamon a warning glance. He figured she knew better than to continue talking about something so private, but it never hurt to be sure. In typical Cinnamon fashion, she responded by sticking her tongue out at him.

Joe just chuckled and disappeared into his office while she waited on the customers. Java shuffled behind him and peered up, his mismatched eyes full of devotion. Joe ran his hand over the spiky ridge of the dog's ears.

"Good boy," he said, and his thoughts took him back to that first day he'd brought Java with him to Goldie's house.

It had been the first time he'd seen Goldie smile since her grandfather died. Part of him wondered if that's when she first started falling in love with him. The other part of him didn't care. It was enough to know it was finally happening. God's perfect timing was here at last.

Joe dropped his head in his hands and his throat

clogged with emotion. It was almost too much for him to process. Not only had the Lord answered his prayers for Goldie's healing and happiness, now it appeared as though she may really love him the way he'd loved her for so long. He tried to form a coherent prayer in his mind, but failed. Merely saying thank you just wouldn't cut it. He wished there was some way to show God how profoundly grateful he was.

Java nudged him with a big paw, and he glanced down at the Husky again, thinking once more about that day on Goldie's front porch. The first smile. The first sip of coffee. He remembered with absolute clarity, crafting that first caramel G on her macchiato.

The idea struck him like a bolt of lightning. He shrank back in his chair from its force, and then sat up ramrod straight. It was perfect. A little daring maybe, but perfect.

He forced any trace of doubt from his mind and concentrated on what he needed to do. His date with Goldie was in only five days. Could he wait that long? And what if the dog show turned into a disaster? That would throw everything off course.

Joe shook his head, trying to physically rid himself of such thoughts. If Cinnamon, in all her fledgling belief, could be brave enough to change her life, surely he could do the same. He owed it to God to take a leap of faith.

He shoved his chair from his desk and all but sprinted into the shop. Cinnamon nearly dropped the pitcher of coffee she was carrying when he slid up next to her on the slick tile floor.

"You nearly scared me to death," she panted. "What's gotten you so fired up?"

"I need your help. Can you come up with a new

drink? It needs to be really special, your best one yet. Do you think you could come up with something by Saturday night?"

"Saturday night, huh?" Cinnamon raised her brows. "Interesting timing."

"I'll tell you all about it," he said with a wink. "So long as you make me a coffee drink that will knock Goldie's socks off."

"No problem, boss. It will be my pleasure."

꒰ঌ ໒꒱

"Bliss, down." Goldie stopped in her tracks as she gave the command and the little Cavalier King Charles Spaniel plopped into a down at her feet. Once Goldie had paused for a few seconds, she began walking again and Bliss scurried up on all fours and resumed prancing at her side.

"Bravo!"

"Yay Bliss!"

Goldie's informal audience hollered and whistled its approval. Bliss spun in manic circles, clearly pleased to inspire such a celebration.

Goldie wagged her finger at Peggy and Eve. "You guys can't do that at the show. It will completely distract her."

Peggy pretended to lock her lips with an invisible key. "Our lips are sealed."

"That's right," Eve chimed in. "We won't say a word."

"And no crinkly bags." Goldie clutched her chest. "That would be the death of me."

"No crinkly bags." Eve raised a pointed brow. "Although after her little performance at my Sunday school class, I would be completely justified to bring along a big bag of cheese curls."

Goldie gasped. "You wouldn't."

"Or, would I?" Eve laughed, doing her best impression of an evil villain.

"Oh, cut it out Eve." Peggy waved a knitting needle in her direction, and Eve abruptly clamped her mouth shut. "Don't you worry, Goldie. Eve will do no such thing. Right, Eve?"

Eve nodded meekly, her gaze fixed on the pointy knitting needle.

"We'll be there to support you. One hundred percent." Peggy nodded to emphasize her point.

Goldie sighed. "Good. I want Bliss to win a ribbon so badly. The children from reading hour at the library would be thrilled."

"I'll bring my camera. That way you can show the kids some pictures along with Bliss's ribbon," Eve promised, still shrinking away from Peggy's knitting needle.

"Thanks so much for watching us practice, you guys. I thought it would be a good idea for Bliss to work on her skills in front of an audience." Goldie knelt in the grass of her backyard and scratched Bliss on the belly. The spaniel writhed around in the lawn, nipping at Goldie's hand.

"Is Joe going to be there too? At the dog show?" Eve asked with a wry smile.

"Of course. He's entered in the advanced level with his dog, Java. Wait until you see them. They're incredible."

"Why don't we all go out to dinner or something afterward? That would be fun. I guess I should get to know Joe better since it looks like he's going to be sticking around a while." Eve looked back and forth from Peggy to Goldie, waiting for a response.

Goldie tried to stop the fierce blush she felt crawling up her neck toward her face. "Um, well…"

Peggy interrupted. "We can't. Goldie and Joe have a hot date Saturday night."

"Peggy!" Honestly, did she have to put it quite that way?

"What? It's true." Peggy shrugged, the perfect picture of nonchalance.

"Why does she know all about this and I don't?" Eve crossed her arms and hitched a thumb in Peggy's direction.

"Eve, I…" Goldie stammered until Peggy interjected again.

"Joe told me." Peggy shrugged her shoulders while Goldie and Eve both gasped in unison.

"What?" Peggy asked, her voice full of innocence.

Goldie narrowed her gaze at Peggy. "When did you talk to Joe?"

"Yesterday, I think. Let's see…today is Thursday. That would mean yesterday was Wednesday. Hmm." Peggy ticked off the days of the week on her fingers.

Eve snickered as Goldie struggled to resist the urge to shake her neighbor by the shoulders. She supposed that wouldn't be very neighborly. Or Christian, for that matter.

"So, it wasn't yesterday. It was Tuesday. Or maybe Monday." She shrugged her shoulders again. "Why, dear? Does it make a difference?"

"Well, I was just wondering how it came about." Goldie cleared her throat in an attempt to rid her voice of its telltale nervous tremor. "That's all."

"I stopped by his shop for a cup of coffee." Peggy

pursed her lips. "I was under the impression it was still a public place."

Eve, not Peggy's target, for once, burst out laughing. Goldie shot her a dirty look and then smiled sweetly back at Peggy. "Of course. Did you have a nice, er, chat?"

"Why, yes we did. I wanted to stop by and make sure he knew we wanted him to come to Care Group."

"Care Group. That's tonight, right?" Eve chimed in, her lips still twitching with laughter.

"Yes. And he's coming. I invited him at church on Sunday." Goldie focused all her attention on Bliss's soft, pink belly. She didn't trust herself to look either Peggy or Eve in the eye when she mentioned Sunday. Surely, they would see the passion lurking barely beneath the surface of her already-shaky exterior whenever she thought about their afternoon on the beach for even a moment.

"Yep, he mentioned that." Peggy went back to her knitting, needles flying with a blur through the yarn.

"Did he mention anything else?" *Like the fact that he kissed me? Not just any regular kiss, but the kind of kiss that sweeps a girl off her feet?*

Goldie's heart began to drum faster at the mere memory of being wrapped in Joe's arms.

Eve's eyes widened. "What is going on? You're blushing!"

The knitting needles froze, and Peggy and Eve both stared at Goldie, which only made her cheeks burn even hotter. "No I'm not."

"Yes, you are. Something happened." Eve plopped on the ground next to Goldie and Bliss. "You have to tell us."

Goldie shot a pleading glance at Peggy.

"I'm afraid you are indeed blushing, dear," was all she said.

Goldie took a deep breath and then blurted it out. "Joe kissed me."

"I knew it!" Eve clapped her hands. "What was it like?"

She must have really wanted to know because she didn't so much as flinch when Peggy gave her a gentle jab with one of the knitting needles and told her that Goldie might not want to talk about it. Of course, then the older woman added, "But if you want to talk about it, we'd love to hear all the details. I mean, if you want to tell us."

Goldie sighed dreamily. Even if she wanted to tell them, how could she possibly find the words? "It was the kind of kiss that could change my life."

No one said a word for a long moment, until Eve clutched her chest and mouthed, "Wow."

Peggy raised her eyebrows. "Well, no wonder."

"No wonder what?"

"No wonder he looked like the happiest man alive when I saw him at the coffee shop." Peggy winked at Goldie.

The burning in her cheeks returned with a vengeance. "He seemed happy?"

"That might be an understatement."

Goldie's insides tumbled with the now-familiar thrill, but one thought nagged at the back of her mind. "He told you about our date on Saturday. Did he mention the dog show at all?"

"No, I don't think so." Peggy shook her head. "Why?"

"He's not exactly thrilled that I'm going."

Eve planted a hand on her hip. "Why not? You

and Bliss are doing so well."

"It's not that. It's just that last time we were at obedience class I sort of had a breakdown." Goldie and Peggy shared a meaningful glance and then filled Eve in on the events of the previous Saturday. "Joe's been bringing me coffee to the library every morning this week and he hasn't mentioned the dog show once, but I know he's still worried about it."

"You mean he spent the entire night on your front porch?" Eve's jaw hung open.

Goldie nodded and Peggy shook her head. "You should have seen him the next morning. He was a wreck, worried sick about our dear Goldie."

"I can't believe I thought he was all wrong for you. What a great guy." Eve dabbed at her eyes and sniffed. For as long as Goldie had known her, Eve had always loved a good romantic story. "So, what are you going to do? You're still going to the dog show?"

Goldie sat up straighter, stiffening her spine. "Of course. Everything will be fine."

A fleeting look passed between Peggy and Eve.

"Well, Peggy and I will be there, too. In case you need us." Eve pat Goldie's hand, which was still nestled in the soft fur of Bliss's underside.

"There's nothing to worry about. Really, there's not."

And Goldie said a silent prayer that her words were true.

❧❧

"You brought coffee." When she opened the front door, Goldie could barely see Joe's cocoa eyes over the top of the enormous box in his arms. "Lots of coffee."

"Yep." His eyes crinkled in the corners, and Goldie could tell he was smiling, even though his lips remained hidden from view. "I thought the other members of Care Group might enjoy it."

"I'm sure they will. It smells wonderful." Indeed it did. The rich aroma of the coffee swirled around him, filling her senses. "Is there anything I can do to help you carry all that?"

"Do you mind grabbing my Bible?" He twisted so that his right side brushed against Goldie's elbow. "It's right there, tucked under my arm."

"Got it." Goldie slid the smooth leather into the palm of her hand, noticing at once the worn and battered condition of Joe's Bible. Apparently, he spent his fair share of time in God's Word. The thought made Goldie smile. "Are you ready to head over there?"

"Sure. Let's go."

The night was cool and the grass soft beneath their feet as Joe and Goldie made their way to Peggy's house next door. Cherry blossoms swirled around them in the evening breeze. As she walked in front of Joe, Goldie was aware of his gaze on her back. Or maybe it was her imagination. She couldn't be sure.

Until they reached Peggy's porch and Joe leaned forward to whisper in her ear.

"You know," he breathed. "If I weren't lugging around a couple gallons of steaming hot liquid, I'd kiss you silly right now."

With a galloping heart, Goldie pressed the doorbell and grinned up at him over her shoulder. For a fleeting moment, she wondered if her legs would always feel like noodles when she thought of kissing him. She still couldn't see much of his face other than his warm eyes dancing beneath his casually rumpled chestnut hair. "Is that so?"

Joe's voice grew huskier. "Oh, yes."

Only seconds before Peggy opened the door, Goldie hugged their two Bibles close to her chest and sighed, "I would kiss you right back."

A snickering sound came from behind the box of coffee as Peggy answered the door.

"Well, look who's here. Goldie and Joe." The older woman's white curls bounced as she looked back and forth between the two of them. Then, she added in a slightly lower voice, "Hmm. Don't you two look just like the cat who swallowed the canary?"

Unable to keep the grin off her face, Goldie pranced inside on her noodle legs, with Joe right on her heels. "I don't know what you're talking about."

"I may be old, but I'm not blind." Peggy held her hands out toward Joe and his super-sized box of coffee. "Aren't you so sweet to bring us coffee? Can I take that from you, Joe?"

"It's rather heavy." Joe heaved the box up higher so Goldie could only see his eyebrows. "Why don't you lead the way and I'll take it wherever you like?"

"OK. Come with me." Peggy grasped Joe's elbow and steered him through the living room.

Still clutching their two Bibles, Goldie watched Joe as he followed Peggy with his giant box of coffee. She rested her chin on the tattered leather cover of Joe's Bible as he set the coffee box in the middle of the dining room table, his every gesture perfectly fluid and graceful.

I can tell Joe's a musician just by the way he moves.

Somewhere in the room, a throat cleared. The sound was followed by quiet laughter. Goldie tore her gaze away from Joe and, for the first time, looked around the room. Every member of Care Group was already there, even George Brown. Some of the faces she hadn't seen since the day of her grandfather's funeral. And here they all were.

Watching her watch Joe Montgomery.

"Um, hello everybody." Goldie slunk into the nearest seat, wondering if it would be wrong to pray for some huge distraction like someone's dentures suddenly flying out of their mouth and tumbling onto the floor.

Yes, wrong. Very, very wrong. Oh God, please forgive me.

"Did I miss anything?" Joe slid into the seat next to her, still smelling faintly of coffee beans.

Oh nothing. Just me wishing bodily harm to a room full of elderly brothers and sisters in Christ. "No. Not a thing."

Peggy made a brief announcement about Joe's coffee and everyone darted out of their chairs—as fast as senior citizens can dart—to make a beeline for the dining room table.

Only Joe and Goldie remained in the room. Alone. Together.

"Goldie, what's wrong?" Joe was leaning toward her now, his eyes full of concern.

"Nothing."

Skepticism colored his features. "Are you sure?"

"Yes."

He lifted her hand, still resting on the cover of his Bible, and cradled it between his. "Then why are you talking in one-word sentences?"

This was never going to work. How could she possibly concentrate on Bible study with him right here? "I find your presence a bit…distracting."

Joe clamped his lips together, but Goldie could see

the laughter in his eyes. "Shall I leave, then?"

Goldie swatted him with his Bible, and then shoved it at his chest. "Not on your life."

It was exactly the sort of icebreaker she so desperately needed. As the others filed back in the room, mugs of fragrant coffee in their hands, she began to relax. By the time they had all fawned all over Joe and thanked him endlessly for the coffee, she felt a little bit less like everyone was staring at her. Why would they? Now, they were all in love with Joe themselves.

The thought gave Goldie a warm glow inside as Peggy started the prayer requests. She sneaked sideways glances at Joe every now and then, and saw him nod in all the right places. He even laughed at George Brown's corny jokes. But something about the way he flipped through the wispy pages of his Bible and the manner in which he freely offered his opinions throughout the discussion told her he was here with his whole heart. He wasn't merely going through the motions. He was truly enjoying himself. And not once had he even asked her why her Bible study group was filled with people half a century older than herself. What's more, he didn't seem to care. He fit right in here, just as she did.

Time passed in a whirl, and before Goldie knew what was happening, it was time for closing prayer. Suddenly, Goldie was sad to see the night come to an end. Sitting here next to Joe, among her oldest friends, she realized what life with him would be like. The two of them, walking together in God's perfect grace.

She reached for him, this time unconcerned about what the others would think. Why had she been so nervous before? These were her friends. They loved her and only wanted to see her happy. She took Joe's hand and wove her fingers through his and they stayed like that, hand in hand, until the final amen was said.

"Goldie. Joe." Peggy rushed toward them as soon as the group was dismissed. "I'm so glad you two came. Joe, I hope you enjoyed yourself."

"I did. Very much. Thank you for inviting me." He squeezed Goldie's hand and then released it to give Peggy a friendly hug. Goldie let him go, admittedly with a little reluctance.

Peggy giggled like a schoolgirl as Joe hugged her. "You're certainly welcome to come back anytime. I hope you'll join us again soon."

"Of course." He wrapped his arm around Goldie's shoulders and nestled her right by his side. "That is, if Goldie will have me back."

Goldie opened her mouth to say something charming, but before she could utter a syllable, Peggy beat her to the punch.

"Oh, you don't need to wait for Goldie to invite you. You have an open invitation." Peggy winked at Goldie, and that's when Goldie knew it was time to go. Peggy's matchmaking skills were kicking into overdrive.

"Goodnight everyone," Goldie called out to her friends, clustered once again around Joe's coffee.

"Night all. It was wonderful meeting all of you." Joe held up his Bible in a farewell gesture.

As they walked out the door, Goldie couldn't help but feel utterly delighted. It had been the perfect evening.

And then Peggy said the one thing that could possibly bring her back down to earth. "I'll see you two

Saturday at the dog show."

Without even thinking, Goldie waited for Joe's body to stiffen next to hers. But, to her astonishment, it didn't. She searched his face as he walked her back to her house next door, but his features remained smooth and relaxed. Where was the furrowed brow that had been there the last time someone had mentioned the dog show? Maybe it was just too dark under the soft glow of the moon to see anything.

"I had a really nice time tonight." Joe ran his hand in slow circles over her back while they walked. "Even though it wasn't a date."

Goldie laughed and rested her head on Joe's shoulder. She tried to forget about the dog show and concentrate on the here and now. After all, she didn't want to spoil such a lovely evening. "Aren't you going to ask me why I don't belong to a more, er, conventional Bible study group?"

"I think I can figure that one out." His voice carried a hint of melancholy. "And I think it's great that you're still part of their group."

Goldie looked up at him, expecting to find some sign of sarcasm or teasing on his face but found none. Eve could stand to take a page out of Joe's book. "You do?"

"Of course. They love you. You're one of them."

"You were a big hit." Then, without realizing exactly what she was saying, she added, "Everyone in that house tonight was madly in love with you."

Joe stopped in his tracks. At first, Goldie kept walking, right up the steps onto her porch. When she missed the warmth of his arm around her shoulders, she turned back to see him standing a few feet behind her with the oddest look on his face.

"Did you say everyone?" Then one corner of his mouth lifted into a half grin.

Goldie gasped, and her heart took flight on hummingbird wings.

In an instant, Joe was with her on the porch, cradling her face in the palms of his hands. "Your cheeks are warm, Bashful."

Then his lips came down on hers, soft and sweet.

Chapter Sixteen

Joe had never been less excited to be going to a dog show in all his life. Sitting in his car, with Goldie beside him and Java and Bliss tucked safely in the backseat, he had the sudden urge to yank the steering wheel in the direction of South Carolina and drive until they were clear to the other side of the Mississippi River. He couldn't shake the feeling that he was driving her to some sort of occasion for torture—say, an appointment for a root canal—instead of a dog show. He'd always had a great time with Java competing in Rally, but today he was hard-pressed to muster any enthusiasm.

Beside him, Goldie was quiet. Too quiet, as far as he was concerned. He wished they could fast-forward through this afternoon straight to his plans for the evening. Plans he knew he would scrap if Goldie had a difficult time at the show.

Everything is going to be fine. That's what she'd told him on the beach, and he'd promised to have faith. He wondered about his ability to keep that promise in the eerie silence of the car.

"Joe."

He glanced over at her and tried to loosen his

death grip on the steering wheel. "Yes?"

Goldie exhaled a shaky sigh. "I'm a little nervous."

Joe resisted the urge to maneuver the car into a screeching u-turn. Instead, he reached for Goldie's hand and brought it to his lips. Once he'd covered her knuckles with a tender kiss, he finally spoke. It took superhuman effort to keep his voice calm and steady. "We don't have to go, you know. Just say the word, and I'll take you someplace else."

"Don't be ridiculous." Goldie removed her hand from his and punched him lightly on the shoulder. "Bliss and I have been practicing all week, and the kids at the library are cheering for us to bring home a ribbon. I can't let a little stage fright get to me."

Stage fright. Of course. Goldie wasn't in the midst of another grief-riddled crisis. She simply had butterflies. Joe wondered what she would have thought if he'd given in to his desire to drive her in the opposite direction like a madman. *Everything is going to be fine, you idiot. Unless you screw it up yourself.* "I was, er, only joking."

"No you weren't." Goldie gave him a teasing jab to the ribs. "But, I am a tad bit curious. Where exactly would you have taken me if I'd changed my mind?"

The tightness in Joe's chest loosened somewhat, and he fell naturally back into their usual playful, flirtatious repartee. "I'll never tell."

"Oh, come on."

"Let's just say we could have started our date early." He wiggled his eyebrows at her until she giggled.

"I have to admit that does sound nice. But, we're not going home empty handed. We're going to win that ribbon for the kids. Right, Bliss?" Goldie looked over her shoulder at the two dogs riding in the backseat.

Not to be overlooked, Java made his presence known by craning his neck forward and giving Joe's ear a long, wet swipe of his tongue. "*Blech.* Settle down, you monster."

"Aw, don't pick on him." Goldie's words were punctuated with laughter, like music to Joe's soggy ear.

"Oh yeah? Let's see how you like it." Joe pointed at Goldie's face, now spread into a wide grin. "Java, give Goldie a kiss."

In a perfect display of obedience, the big Husky licked the side of her face with an audible slurp. Goldie squealed and squirmed to get away from Java, but the front seat left her little room for escape. By the time Joe pulled the car into the parking lot of the dog show, she was cowering in a giggling heap next to the window with Java looming over her.

"OK, Java. That's enough." Joe motioned toward the backseat, and Java shrank back to his usual spot, his tongue lolling sideways out of his mouth.

Goldie sat up straight and dabbed at the tears of laughter gathering at the corners of her eyes. "OK, OK. I get your point. I surrender. You weren't picking on him. He's a rather enthusiastic kisser."

After he'd pulled the car to a stop, Joe winked at her. "I hope you know he's the only other male I'm going to allow to kiss you."

"Really? The only other one?" Her blue eyes glowed bright aquamarine and pulled Joe away to another time and place...on the beach with Goldie in his arms.

Teri Wilson

He wanted to drown in those eyes for the rest of his life. With a gentle touch, he ran his fingers over the curve of her jaw and tilted her chin toward him. "That's right. No one else but me."

He gave her a tender kiss on her full lips, slow and easy. Despite the careful control of his movements, Goldie's heart at once began the familiar thump-thump that never failed to fill his soul with a thrilling combination of shock and joy. He let his gaze travel to the sweetheart neckline of her soft violet sweater and then back to those soulful blue eyes. "Is that stage fright, or is it me?"

"That's all you, mister." Her lips curved into a demure smile. Then, as if the mention of stage fright had reminded her of where they were, her head darted back and forth from one window to the other. "My, there are certainly a lot of cars here."

Joe waved a dismissive hand at the parking lot. At least he hoped it was dismissive. Now that they had actually arrived, his apprehension about the show was returning at full force. "Don't worry. You and Bliss are going to do great." He gulped and then said the words he'd been dreading all morning. "Shall we go in?"

Goldie bit her lip and nodded. Joe couldn't help but notice the color draining from her face as she blinked with wide eyes at the multitude of cars, vans and RVs in the parking lot.

"Hey." He cupped her face and forced her to meet his gaze. "Everything is going to be fine."

He felt like a complete and utter fraud as he repeated her own words back to her. Who was he to make such a promise? Everything within him screamed at him to drive away with her as fast as he could, but his faith kept him rooted to the spot. It was a small glimmer of faith, but it was enough.

"You're right." Goldie nodded, the pink returning to her cheeks ever so slowly. "Everything is going to be fine."

Then, to his great relief, she made a brave attempt at humor. "You know, Java's not such a bad kisser."

"Oh no." Joe clutched at his chest in mock horror. "Don't tell me I have competition from my own dog."

She peeked up at him from beneath her lashes. "Maybe later you can give it another shot."

"Yes, later." He squeezed her hand and thought of his plans for later that night. Plans he hoped with quiet desperation he would be able to carry out after whatever happened this afternoon.

❧

As she followed Joe into the crowded community center, Goldie clutched Bliss's leash as though it were her lifeline. She noticed he didn't steer her through the crowd with his hand in the small of her back, as he usually did, but instead walked in front of her with his shoulders squared and his jaw set. He looked like a human shield, standing between her and everything else. And as much as she hated to admit it, even to herself, she was glad.

Coming here proved to be more difficult than she had anticipated. After all her brave talk and her stubborn insistence on competing in the show, her feet suddenly felt as though they were made of concrete. She was having difficulty even forcing herself to walk inside. She was no longer convinced she was suffering from a simple case of pre-show jitters when she found herself peeking around Joe's strapping shoulders for a glimpse at Harold.

Where was he?

She didn't see him among the cluster of animated students from class. Granted, she didn't let her gaze linger too long on that crowd since they were all staring at her as if she might sprout another head at any given moment. Goldie waved and tried to flash a gracious smile in return. She could hardly blame the others for their reaction. What else could she expect after practically having a nervous breakdown at the last training class?

"Everything all right back there?" Joe shot her a glance over his shoulder.

"Sure." Goldie gulped. "A-OK."

She had never seen so many dogs in one place. There must have been at least a hundred, of all sizes and shapes. And, yet, the spacious room of the community center was strangely quiet. Most of the dogs waited in crates for their turn in the obedience ring. Near the far end of the room, handlers led dogs on leashes, practicing patterns Goldie recognized from her Rally class. Left circles, right circles, about-turns. One of the dogs, a thin wisp of a Whippet, looked so graceful as it wound in a circle around its handler, Goldie felt as if she were watching a ballet. She glanced down at Bliss, wondering if the spaniel would be overwhelmed by it all, but the little dog looked up at her with bright eyes, tail wagging, and Goldie knew her dog was fine.

"I see our group right over there." Joe motioned for her to follow him and winked, sending her insides tumbling.

Soft-sided, mesh dog crates lined all the walls, along with small gatherings of folding lawn chairs. Joe waved at one of the groupings and Goldie saw Eve and Peggy, perched on the edges of their seats and grinning from ear to ear. Next to them sat a familiar looking face, framed with a blaze of shocking red hair.

"Cinnamon, how great to see you here. Thanks so much for coming, Eve, Peggy." Goldie wondered if anyone could detect the nervous tremor in her voice.

The three women didn't seem to notice, but Joe pulled her close to his side. He didn't say anything, and for that, Goldie was grateful. He simply planted a kiss on her hair and held her with a steady arm.

"We're rooting for you and Bliss, Goldie." Eve flashed a thumbs-up, and Peggy nodded with unbridled enthusiasm.

"Your fans here tell me you've been practicing really hard." It was clear Cinnamon was talking to Goldie, but she seemed to be sending unspoken signals to Joe.

Goldie watched the silent interaction between them and wondered what it was all about. "Yes, I've been working poor little Bliss pretty hard. But, she's ready." *It's me I'm suddenly worried about...*

"I think we should get Java and Bliss settled in their crates so we can go get our armbands. The advanced class walk-through is about to start." Goldie's stomach leapt to her throat at Joe's words, but she zipped Bliss into her soft-sided crate as if everything was perfectly normal.

"Are you ready?" Joe clasped her hand and stood watching her with keen interest. In fact, they were all watching her. Eve, Peggy, Cinnamon. Even the dogs.

Goldie gulped. And by God's grace alone, was able to speak. "Sure. Let's go."

With her hand firmly clasped in his, Joe led her to

the steward's table where they stood in line with the other exhibitors. No one looked each other in the eye. In fact, most of the people around her gnawed on fingernails or tapped their toes.

At least I'm not the only nervous one around here.

The thought offered Goldie a brief moment of comfort until it was her turn in line. The steward looked at her and asked, "Number?"

"Um, I beg your pardon?"

Joe leaned in and explained. "She's asking for your number. It should have been listed on the entry confirmation you got in the mail."

"Oh." Goldie remembered opening the confirmation letter, but where had she put it? And the number was 12, right? Or maybe 14… She should have listened to Joe and forgotten about the dog show. This was already turning into a disaster and she hadn't even gotten in the ring yet. "I don't remember my number. What do I do?"

"Don't worry." Joe calmly wrapped his arm around her shoulders. "We can look it up right here in the catalog."

He showed her how to find her number in the steward's catalog, right next to Bliss's name. Everything seemed so official.

Once they both had armbands with bold black numbers fastened in place by rubber bands, Joe pointed out a stack of papers on the table.

"These are the course maps." He handed her a sheet with a square pattern of loops and squiggly lines printed on it. "You can look at this and know exactly what you'll need to do once you and Bliss get in the ring."

"Oh." Goldie pointed to a zigzag on the page

while her heart sank. "What does this mean? I don't think we've done this before."

Joe rested a calming hand on her shoulder. "The symbols can be a bit confusing at first. No worries. That's the exercise where you and Bliss weave through the orange cones. You've done that many times."

"Yes, we have." Goldie nodded, her confidence returning bit by bit. "This doesn't look so hard. Some of the more difficult exercises aren't even on here."

"That's the beauty of training with Harold. He always makes the Rally patterns at class much more difficult than the ones at the actual shows. So, when you get here it seems easier."

At the mention of Harold's name, Goldie's gaze flitted around the room once more. He was still nowhere to be seen. Even though her nerves about what to expect in the competition ring were settling down, she wouldn't feel completely sure of herself until she faced him. "Speaking of Harold," she cleared her throat. "Where do you suppose he is?"

"I've been wondering that myself." Joe's voice carried a distinct edge, which Goldie pretended not to notice. "He's supposed to be here."

Just then, the ring steward stood and called in a booming voice, "Attention all Rally Advanced competitors. It's time for the walk-through."

"That's me," Joe said, with some obvious reluctance.

Goldie knew he couldn't be terribly nervous. He and Java did this sort of thing all the time. His hesitation likely had much more to do with leaving her alone. She squared her shoulders and put on her best brave face. "I'll go join our cheering section. You knock'em dead out there."

He gave her hand a final squeeze and disappeared into the ring with the other more advanced competitors. Goldie watched them all walk single file through the maze of signs and cones, familiarizing themselves with the pattern before it was time to begin the actual show.

Only ten more minutes until the advanced competition started and still no sign of Harold. Goldie glanced around the room once more and then went to sit with her friends.

"What's going on?" Peggy's knitting needles paused midair while she looked at Joe and the others methodically walking around the large rectangular area separated from the rest of the room by a short, white lattice wall. "They're all just walking around. Why don't they have their dogs with them?"

Goldie lowered herself into one of the chairs and settled Bliss into a peaceful ball on her lap. "They have ten minutes to walk around the course and practice the pattern by themselves. This part is called the 'walk-through.' Once it's over, the first competitor in this class will start."

"When do you and Bliss get your turn?" Eve ran her hand over the spaniel's head, but her gaze remained on the action in the center of the room.

"Oh, we're only beginners. Our group, the Novice class, will go last. The highest level is the Excellent class. They went first and now, next is the Advanced class."

"I'm sure you'll do just fine, dear." Peggy nodded with encouragement.

"Wait until you see Joe and Java." Goldie couldn't help the trace of pride in her voice. As if he were commenting on the subject, the Husky let out a little groan from inside his crate. "They are so good. Have you ever seen them in action, Cinnamon?"

"No, I haven't. But, I was helping Joe out with some things at the shop this morning, and he invited me to come cheer you on to victory." Cinnamon's lips curved into a mysterious smile when she looked Goldie in the eye. Once again, Goldie was left with the impression that Cinnamon harbored some sort of secret.

Goldie shrugged it off. Then Joe was there, unzipping Java out of the crate and getting ready to head to the ring. He gave Goldie a farewell wink and led Java away. Java's attention never strayed from Joe. He looked up at his master with his mismatched eyes, his doggy steps perfectly in synch with Joe's.

"Here they go." Goldie bit her lip when the ring steward called Joe's number. She couldn't believe it, but she was actually a bit nervous for Joe and Java. Or maybe it was excitement coursing through her veins. Her emotions were such a tangled up mess right now, she couldn't make much sense of them.

"Oh, he's taking off Java's leash." Eve craned her neck to see around a rather large St. Bernard that had recently plopped in front of her chair.

"Yes, the more advanced dogs do the course off-lead. It's really something to see." Goldie twirled Bliss's leash around her fingers, grateful it would tether the two of them together when it was their turn.

True to Goldie's word, Java and Joe moved around the ring in perfect unison. Every so often, she heard a wondrous gasp of awe from the crowd. At the end of their performance, the room burst into applause.

Joe smiled amiably and gave Java a hug around his thick ruff of a neck. After receiving his green qualifying ribbon and taking first place honors, he didn't seem to waste any time getting back to Goldie's side.

"That was amazing. First place in your class. Congratulations." She flung her arms around him with a little more zeal than she had planned.

His eyes widened in surprise, and he almost tumbled backward over Java. "Thanks. Are you and Bliss about ready?"

"Yes." Goldie nodded and helped him regain his balance. "Eve's got Bliss, and I'm headed over to the walk-through right now."

"OK." He smiled, but it was a bit strained. Particularly for someone who had just collected a rather large first place ribbon in front of a cheering crowd. "I'll be waiting for you when you're finished."

A lump lodged in Goldie's throat. He was so sincere and obviously still dreadfully concerned about her. She desperately hoped she wouldn't let him down. She still hadn't found Harold. Maybe he wasn't even there. Maybe everything really would be just fine.

Maybe.

Not trusting herself to speak with any sort of confidence, Goldie gave Joe a quick peck on the cheek and headed for the ring. While she followed the other beginning exhibitors from cone to cone, she tried to concentrate on the task at hand. But everything around her seemed to move in a blur of motion. She put one foot in front of the other with careful exactness, but everyone else in the ring zipped around her, until it felt as though she was standing still. Even the barking of the dogs sounded short, clipped. Frantic.

"Goldie. Goldie!" Somehow, through Goldie's brief swirl of panic, Eve's voice broke through.

Goldie looked up and saw her standing ringside, clutching Bliss and looking rather panicked herself.

No wonder. When Goldie looked around, she realized the walk-through was over and she was the only person left standing in the ring. Besides the judge, that is, who was gathering papers together on his clipboard and hadn't seemed to notice Goldie lingering so far behind the others.

Thank You, Lord.

Goldie scurried to the other side of the lattice ring gates where Eve pounced on her and thrust Bliss into her arms.

"It's time," Eve whispered. Actually, it was more a hiss than a whisper. "And you and Bliss are first."

"We're first?" Goldie gripped Bliss's leash until her knuckles turned white as stone.

"Yes. Joe said the smaller dogs usually go first in each class."

That's right. Goldie knew that. Smallest to biggest. "Where is Joe?"

"He's right over there." Eve gestured toward the opposite side of the ring, near the exit gates. "He wanted to be there, waiting for you. And the rest of us are headed over there, too. Are you all right?"

Before Goldie could answer, the ring steward called her number.

"That's me." She waved her hand toward the steward. Good. At least she was able to move. That was a step in the right direction.

She looked back to say something, anything, to Eve. But she was gone.

"Exhibitor, take your place in the ring, please." The judge's rather business-like tone did nothing to calm her nerves.

Goldie took a deep breath and followed the judge's instructions, leading Bliss through the white lattice entrance. She paused beside the first cone with the laminated Start sign, just as Harold had taught her to do at class.

"Are you ready?" The judge stood looking at her from behind his clipboard, his bifocals perched on the very tip of his nose. Clearly, he was waiting for an answer.

Am I ready?

Goldie looked down at Bliss, and the spaniel peered up at her.

My dog is ready. But what about me? Am I ready?

Unsure exactly why, she glanced toward the exit gate. Perhaps she was looking for an answer to her question in the faces of her friends waiting for her ringside. But what she saw there caused her breath to skid to a halt.

Joe, Peggy, Eve, Cinnamon.

And Harold.

He stood sandwiched between Joe and Peggy. One of his puffy black poodles lounged at his feet and Harold himself was looking at Peggy like a dog eyeing a bone. Goldie would have laughed aloud at that look if she hadn't been so preoccupied trying to assess her feelings.

She waited for the terror balled up at the bottom of her stomach to rise up and strangle her, as it had done at class last week. But, by God's grace, it never happened. As Goldie let her gaze travel over Harold, she no longer saw a ghostly vision of her grandfather. She saw a friend. And when she looked at him together with Joe, Peggy, Eve and Cinnamon, she saw something beautiful. She saw a family. Not the family she had known all her life—but a family just the same. One God had stitched together while she'd been too busy grieving to realize what was happening around her.

"Ahem." The judge cleared his throat, dragging Goldie's attention back to the center of the ring. "Are you ready?"

"Yes." This time she knew the answer before the question left the judge's mouth. "Yes. I'm ready."

Chapter Seventeen

Goldie ran her fingers over the silky strips of blue ribbon dangling from her large first place rosette. Correction—Bliss's first place rosette. She could hardly believe how perfect the petite Cavalier King Charles Spaniel had performed. Even at the one sign when Goldie had hesitated before giving Bliss her command, the little orange and white dog had waited patiently for her instructions. At most of the *Halt* signs, Bliss had plopped into an automatic sit without Goldie having to say a word. When they exited the ring to the burst of cheers from Joe and the others, she'd known they had done well. Still, she never imagined their first place ranking would hold steady for the rest of the afternoon. One by one, the other novice dogs went through the course. Several of them, two low-slung Basset Hounds in particular, pressed their noses to the ground and refused to so much as bat an eye at their handlers. But plenty of the beginner dogs performed very well.

"Not as good as you did, huh, girl?" Goldie scooped Bliss into her arms and nuzzled her soft orange ears against her cheek. Bliss yawned with dramatic flair and her copper eyelids fluttered shut.

"Poor thing. You're exhausted after your big day."

Goldie settled Bliss on the new dog bed Peggy had given her as a congratulatory gift after the dog show. She had crocheted it herself, with a soft collection of pale pink yarns. Goldie smiled at Bliss as she burrowed in the cotton candy puff of a bed. The phone rang and the spaniel reacted with nothing more than a snore.

Goldie laughed and hurried to the phone, the delicate tulle of her dress swishing around her legs as she went. "Hello?"

"Hey, Bashful. Have you stopped looking at your first place ribbon yet?"

"Maybe." Goldie turned her back to the rosette, her cheeks prickling with heat. "Then again, maybe not."

Joe's laugh traveled through the phone line and caused her heart to beat a little faster. "I don't blame you. You and Bliss were amazing today."

Goldie glanced at Bliss, still burrowed into her new hand-crafted bed. "Well, we were pretty good. But you and Java brought the house down. I wish I hadn't been so nervous, that way I could have enjoyed your performance without my teeth chattering."

"Don't you worry." His voice softened. "There will be plenty of other times."

"Yes, I hope so."

"There will be. Consider that a promise." Something in Joe's tone told her he was serious, and a warm glow spread from the center of Goldie's chest to the tips of her fingers.

"I can't wait to bring her rosette to the library on Monday. The kids will be thrilled." Goldie had chosen a special book to read called *Blue Ribbon Mutt*, although she'd never imagined Bliss would win an actual blue ribbon to go along with the lesson.

"I think Eve took an entire roll of film, too. You should have plenty of pictures to share."

"All this reminiscing is nice, but do you know what would be even better?" Goldie twirled the phone cord around her fingers and thought she'd never been so ready for a date in all her life.

"I think I do." She could practically hear Joe grinning on the other end. "Why don't we finish this conversation in person?"

"That's exactly what I had in mind." She glanced at the clock and realized Joe should have been on the way to her house already. "Are you running late?"

"I've had a bit of trouble at the coffee shop." He cleared his throat. "Um, would you mind terribly meeting me here? Maybe I can get everything straightened out by the time you get here, and we'll still be able to get to our dinner reservations on time."

Goldie wondered what could have gone wrong. She hoped it wasn't something too serious. "That's fine. But, are you sure everything's OK? Do we need to postpone?"

"Absolutely not. This coffee shop could burn down around me, and I would still take you to dinner tonight."

She detected a note of humor in his voice, so she felt safe that the building wasn't actually in flames. "In that case, I'll be right over."

"Great. I'll see you shortly."

Once she hung up and gave Bliss a final pat, she checked her reflection in the mirror one last time. Joe was being charmingly secretive about their big date and wouldn't even tell her where they were having dinner. But she knew he'd made reservations, so that narrowed down the possibilities quite a bit in a town as small as Turtle Beach. In the end, she'd chosen her favorite cocktail dress from the back recesses of her closet. She'd purchased it a while ago on a shopping trip with Eve and never even had the chance to wear it before Grandpa had gotten sick. So, the tags had still dangled from the hanger when she removed it from the plastic garment bag. Thank goodness it still fit. The dress had spaghetti straps and a tight crimson velvet bodice leading to a full ballerina skirt of miles and miles of fine ruby silk tulle. The full effect was quite striking and perfect for a romantic first date. Eve had been so blown away by the sight of Goldie in that dress that she had forced her to buy it, even though she had no place to wear such a treasure at the time.

My, how things have changed.

Goldie smiled to herself and thought how silly it seemed that this was their first official date. Joe was such a part of her life now, it hardly seemed possible. She thought about this as she walked the short distance to his coffee shop in the cool autumn night.

How many people could say with utter certainty they were in love as they were on their way to a first date? Goldie shook her head. Not many, that's for sure. But Goldie was in love with Joe. She'd never been so sure of anything in her life. She knew it as sure as she knew the sun would rise in the morning and spill its radiance over the pale moonlight that glowed all around her while she walked to Joe's Coffee Shop.

She looked up at the stars twinkling overhead as if they were winking at her, and remembered a Bible verse that described God's love in a very similar way.

Though the mountains be shaken and the hills be removed, yet my unfailing love for you will not be shaken.

The holy words resonated in Goldie's soul and filled her with understanding. She had lived them in recent weeks. When she thought everything was over, God's love for her had never failed. And in the midst of her pain, He had given her the most unexpected, marvelous gift of all—Joe. She sighed with contentment and rounded the corner, expecting to get a glimpse of him through the windows of the coffee shop. But she couldn't see him. In fact, she couldn't see anything. The shop was pitch black. Not a sliver of light escaped from the closed blinds.

She paused for a moment and looked at the sign on the front door flipped over to the *closed* side. Of course, the shop was closed—she expected that—but why was it so dark? Her stomach sank as she realized the problem must have something to do with the electricity. The situation must be more serious than Joe had let on.

Goldie pushed open the door and poked her head inside. At once, the rich aroma of freshly brewed coffee invaded her senses. "Joe? Are you here?"

"Come on in, Goldie. Be careful." His voice came from deep inside the shop.

Goldie slipped through the door, stepping very carefully in her stiletto heels in the dark. "Is there something wrong with the elect..." Her voice trailed off as she heard a clicking sound.

All at once, the inside of the coffee shop sparkled with thousands of tiny twinkle lights. Goldie was so stunned, for a moment, she stood disoriented in the middle of the room trying to get her bearings. She barely noticed Joe until he stood right in front of her and cupped her face in his hands.

"You take my breath away, Goldie." Joe's whisper

was husky as his gaze swept over her. His fingers grazed the slender straps of her dress, sending a riot of shivers up and down her spine. "I've dreamed of this moment for a long time, and you're even more beautiful than in my imagination."

Goldie tried to tame the sudden racing of her heart, but when Joe took her lips with his own, it was no use. She lost herself in his kiss and forgot all about the blood pulsing with fury through her veins and the pounding of her heartbeat echoing in her ears. When he pulled back to take in her elegant scarlet dress, she noticed for the first time how debonair he looked himself. He wore a creamy ivory dinner jacket over a pair of tuxedo slacks and a smooth bowtie. She'd never seen him in formal dress, and it did strange things to her insides.

"You look pretty amazing yourself." She gestured to the room full of tiny glimmering lights. "And what is all this?"

"Just a little surprise." Even in the dim light, she could see the mischief flickering in his loving, cocoa eyes.

She was beginning to catch on. "There's no emergency is there? Everything's fine here, isn't it?"

"Oh, it's more than fine. Wouldn't you agree?" He wrapped his arms around her and buried his face in the crook of her neck.

When his lips nibbled against her collar bone, she nearly lost the ability to form a coherent sentence. "No arguments here." She buried her fingers in the smooth ivory fabric of his dinner jacket so her knees wouldn't buckle right underneath her.

Joe's shoulders shook with silent laughter. As usual, he was quite pleased with her reaction. "I have a little something for you."

Goldie blinked and tried to concentrate. But it was so hard when he made her dizzy like this. "Do you really? For me?"

"Yes, for you." He took her hand and tugged. "Follow me."

She followed him to the counter, where she saw a lone cup of coffee in the dim light. Even though they were right there in the coffee shop, it was a paper travel cup with a protective sleeve wrapped around it. The sight of it flooded Goldie with sweet memories. The cup looked identical to all the ones he'd left on her porch in the beginning.

"Coffee?" She let her gaze linger on the familiar paper cup with his name on the side. *Joe's Coffee Shop, Turtle Beach, North Carolina.* "Is it a *Goldie's Latte Macchiato*?"

"No." He grinned. "As a matter of fact, it's not. This is something entirely new."

She reached for the cup. When her hand trembled, Joe said, "Allow me."

He picked up the cup of coffee and brought it to her lips. Her gaze locked with his as he tilted the cup ever so slightly and the warm liquid reached the tip of her tongue. The taste was rich, sweet and wonderful. A hint of coffee mixed with something creamy, delectable and perfect.

"Mmm." Goldie licked her lips. "Is that white chocolate I taste?"

"Yes, it sure is. Do you like it?" Joe's gaze penetrated her to her soul, and she realized her answer to this question was much more important than merely her opinion of a simple cup of coffee.

"I love it." Just as she loved him. "What is it?"

Joe reached beside him and flicked a switch next to the counter. More light filled the room, this time from above Goldie's head. She looked at him, her eyes full of questions, and he pointed toward the ceiling.

Goldie's heart slammed into overdrive and she dragged her gaze from Joe's earnest face to the chalkboard menu hanging above her head. Glittering lights surrounded the board and the three solitary words printed on the menu in Joe's neat handwriting.

Marry Me Mocha.

Goldie gasped and clutched at her throat. She blinked at the words again and again, scarcely believing they were there. Peggy's insistence that Joe wanted to marry her had prepared her in no way for this moment. She couldn't have imagined feeling so overwhelmed with love and bliss. When at last she dared to look away from the board, she found Joe kneeling before her with a diamond ring resting in the palm of his hand. The sparkling lights bounced off the square diamond, sending a kaleidoscope of color dancing across the white canvas of Joe's tuxedo jacket.

"Goldie, I've loved you since the moment I met you." The determined set of his jaw told her every word was true. "And now God has blessed me more than I could have ever dreamed possible by bringing us together. Won't you be my wife?"

A sudden peacefulness flooded her heart and she was able to answer him with perfect clarity. "I'd love nothing more than to be your wife, Joe Montgomery."

When he slipped the ring on her finger and stood, Goldie threw herself into his waiting arms.

Epilogue

Three Months Later

Joe ran his hand through his hair, dampened by the ocean breeze, and paced in the sand.

"If you keep doing that, you're going to go bald." Harold pointed at his own thinning hair and grinned. "Trust me on this."

Joe didn't have the heart to mention that perhaps Harold's advanced age had more to do with the amount of hair on his head than anything else. Instead, he shoved his hands in the pockets of his tuxedo jacket. "Sorry. Nervous habit."

Harold's grin grew larger. "Along with the pacing, hmm? You're about up to your knees in sand now. How much deeper are you going to get?"

"Hey, stop teasing the groom. That's my job." Cinnamon crossed over the dune, lifting the hem of her pale blue bridesmaid gown so it barely skimmed the sand. Although, technically she wasn't a bridesmaid.

"Well, well." Harold let out a whistle. "You are one fine-looking best man."

For a brief moment, Cinnamon looked almost demure, and Joe could scarcely believe his eyes. He actually wondered if perhaps it hadn't been appropriate to ask her to be his best man, even though his barista hardly seemed the conventional type. Even without the nose ring.

"Watch it." She crossed her arms and narrowed her eyes at Harold. "I'm way too young for you."

Harold's jaw dropped open, and, after a pause, he laughed so hard he was forced to sit down on the worn wooden bench of the beach access. Even though it hardly made sense, Joe immediately felt better when he recognized Cinnamon as her usual handful.

Once Harold's laughter had died down long enough for him to form a rational sentence, he jerked a thumb towards Joe and pleaded with Cinnamon. "See if you can calm him down, will you? He's a nervous wreck."

"What's wrong, boss?" She slapped Joe on the back. "You're not getting a case of cold feet are you?"

"Not on your life." There wasn't a flicker of doubt in Joe's mind about marrying Goldie. To him, their short three-month engagement had seemed to last an eternity. Once this excruciating wait was over, Goldie would no longer be his fiancée, and he would at last be able to call her his bride.

"I didn't think so." Cinnamon pushed an unruly curl of red hair from her face. The sea breeze swirled around them, causing the sea oats on the dune to dance and sway, but fortunately the sand stayed put.

Those who didn't know Joe and Goldie very well had tried to talk them out of marrying on the beach. They cited blowing sand and fierce wind as only two of the many reasons to hold the ceremony in a more conventional place, but Joe and his bride couldn't be swayed. This pale ribbon of sand was the place where they worshipped together every Sunday. They couldn't imagine starting their life together as husband and wife anywhere else.

Of course, it was also where they'd shared their first kiss.

The memory brought with it a stir of longing. *The first of many more to come.*

At this thought, the restlessness gnawing at Joe's insides grew in its intensity until he couldn't stand still a moment longer. He plunged his hand back in his hair and resumed pacing, kicking up sand in his wake.

"Hey, watch it." Cinnamon frowned and brushed at the skirt of her dress. "You're making a mess."

Joe forced himself to stop moving and stand still. "Sorry. I'm a little restless."

Harold laughed. "You're a wreck. Plain and simple." He looked at Cinnamon. "I told you. Do something."

"What am I supposed to do? Believe it or not, this is my first stint as a best man." She crossed her arms and wagged a finger at Joe. "You need to chill. Now."

A look of utter confusion crossed Harold's features. Joe doubted anyone had ever told him to *chill* before. "She means I should calm down. You know, cool it?"

"Ahh." Harold nodded and Cinnamon rolled her eyes.

Joe shifted his weight and put his hands on his hips, to keep himself from raking them through his hair again. "The thing is…I'm not even nervous."

Cinnamon's eyeroll took on new life, until Joe thought her eyes might just roll right out of her head. "Whatever."

Harold snorted. "I beg to differ."

"I'm really not. I can't wait to marry Goldie." Joe

gulped. "I think that's the problem."

Harold and Cinnamon exchanged looks.

"You've got it bad, huh?" Harold shook his head and heaved out a long breath.

"Oh, you have no idea, Harold." Cinnamon's voice dripped with drama. "I see him day in and day out. It's pathetic." Then her gaze traveled to the white folding chairs lined in neat rows on the shore. She smiled wistfully at the arch of flowers where Joe and Goldie would stand and vow to love one another until death do them part. "Pathetic, but sweet."

"Actually Cinnamon, I owe you a world of thanks." Joe tried to keep his tone light and casual. He knew Cinnamon hated serious talk like this, but this needed to be said. "You're right. You do see me day in and day out. And you were rooting for me and Goldie all along. You helped bring us together."

Her face grew a shade or two closer to the flaming red of her hair. "I was just doing my job. Making coffee."

"It was more than that, and you know it."

"Well, someone had to step in and do something. Otherwise you might still be camped out on Goldie's porch." Cinnamon turned toward Harold and winked. "It was the *Goldie's Latte Macchiato* that eventually won her over and got him inside."

Or the *Blissful Whippaccino*. Or possibly the *Marry Me Mocha*. If Joe closed his eyes, he could picture the exact look on Goldie's face as she brought each of the drinks to her cherry-red lips. Every sip was a moment that would live in his memory until the day he died. And so long as Goldie was his wife, he'd die a happy man. "Isn't it time yet?" Joe groaned. "I don't think I can wait any longer."

"Almost," Harold planted a hand on Joe's shoulder. The firmness of his grip left no doubt in Joe's mind he aimed to stop the groom from pacing in case he got the urge again. "Almost."

"I know what we should do." Cinnamon picked up the pale blue fabric billowing around her legs and scooted closer. Whatever she had in mind had her eyes glowing with obvious excitement. "Let's pray."

Without waiting for a response, she grabbed Joe's hand. He noticed she seemed to forget all about the sand, the wind and her pretty blue dress. Before he knew it, he found himself standing in a circle, hands linked with Cinnamon and Harold.

"Dear Lord…"

As Cinnamon began to speak, Joe closed his eyes and bowed his head. At first, he had to strain to hear her over the roar of the ocean. Her quiet words weren't those of someone accustomed to praying aloud. But that precise bashfulness is what made the prayer all the more meaningful to Joe.

"Thank you for this beautiful morning, for the sun, the sea and the sand. But most of all, God, thank you for Joe and Goldie. Thank you for the love and happiness they've found with one another."

Over the past months, Joe had had the privilege of witnessing Cinnamon's gradual turn toward faith. She carried her Bible around in her backpack and her spiritual questions had become more probing than ever. He'd watched her bow her head on occasion at church and sometimes even at the coffee shop, but never like this.

"We ask you to bless their marriage and to watch over their life together. Joe and Goldie love you, Lord, just as they love each other. I pray that they will have many happy years together blessed with love, laughter and the joy of living in Your grace."

Each word was a balm to his restless soul, filling him with peace. He couldn't help but wonder when Cinnamon had become such a gifted prayer warrior. Sometimes he still saw her as that same girl with the rhinestone stud in her nose, searching for a reason to believe. Those times were growing few and far between.

"We pray this in the name of Your Son, Jesus Christ. Amen."

Harold added a gruff *Amen* as well. But when Joe tried to speak, he simply couldn't. He just shook his head at Cinnamon and squeezed her hand, hoping she knew how much her words, and her faith, had touched him.

"Just doing my job. I *am* the best man, after all." She shrugged, but Joe could see the tears welling up in the corners of her eyes. He did what he knew she would want—he pretended not to notice.

"Well, what are you two waiting for?" Harold waved a hand toward the guests, now all seated in the pristine white chairs, and Pastor Paul already standing beneath the floral arch. Joe's fellow members of the church worship team stood off to the side, strumming their guitars to the tune of *Ave Maria*, which was the cue for the groom to take his place beside the minister.

Joe stopped himself from running to the scene in a cloud of flying sand. "It's time."

"That's right, it's time." Cinnamon winked at Joe, once again reminding him of the twinkle of the forgotten nose ring. "C'mon boss. Let's go get you married!"

⥳⥲

"Hold still." Goldie bent down and fastened the ring of pink rosebuds circling Bliss's neck. The Cavalier swung her head, sending her thick orange ears flying, and nipped at the tiny flowers. "You just have to make it down the aisle with Java. Then, as soon as the ceremony is over, you can roll around in the sand if you like."

Beside Goldie, Eve let out a long, irritated sigh. "Here. Let me get the dogs ready." She nudged Goldie's hand out of the way and went to work straightening the floral wreath around Bliss's dainty neck. Bliss warily eyed Eve, but sat still and let Goldie's friend make the final adjustments.

"Really? You want to help with the dogs?" Goldie couldn't keep the surprise from her voice. She looked down at Java, waiting for his turn with the flowers. Even the Husky seemed confused about Eve's willing participation.

"Of course. I'm your maid of honor. It's my duty. Besides, I want to help. You just relax. I don't want you to worry about a thing." Finished with Bliss, Eve turned her attention toward Java. "But if this one drools on my bridesmaid dress, he's history."

As if Java would dare. The dog was a perfect gentleman, just like his master. Goldie smoothed down the front of her strapless Vera Wang and sighed. "I can't believe it's finally time. Joe and I are really getting married today."

"*Finally?* What do you mean, *finally?* You've only been engaged for three months." Eve straightened, planted her hands on her hips and scrutinized the appearance of the two dogs. "It hasn't exactly been a prolonged engagement."

"When you realize you want to spend the rest of your life with somebody, you want the rest of your life to start as soon as possible." Peggy swished into the room, the blue organza fabric of her dress swaying around her legs.

Eve bit her lip, like she always did when she was concentrating on something. "That sounds familiar. Is it a line from a movie?"

"Yes, dear." Peggy tsk-tsked at Eve. "*When Harry Met Sally*. We just watched it last night at Goldie's bachelorette party, remember?"

"That's right. Goldie's wild party. How could I forget?" Eve may have tried to sound sarcastic, but her wink told Goldie she was only teasing.

Besides, Goldie wasn't sure she had seen Eve have such a good time in months. The three of them had spent the night at Peggy's house, watching romantic movies and eating popcorn, even though Eve worried the whole night she wouldn't be able to fit in her bridesmaid dress if they didn't stop eating and drinking. Cinnamon had joined them midway through the evening and brought along an impressive array of coffee beverages. Each one was richer and frothier than the last. They had joked that Joe and Goldie didn't even need a wedding cake for the ceremony. Cinnamon's coffee drinks were just as delicious.

And now, here they were, hiding in Joe's Coffee Shop, while everyone waited on the beach for the bridal party's big entrance. A sign hung in the front window declaring the shop closed for the day in celebration of Joe and Goldie's wedding.

"Where's Cinnamon?" Peggy craned her neck and glanced around the coffee shop.

"She already went down to the beach to join the groom." Goldie practically giggled out the words. She couldn't get enough of calling Joe her *groom*. And to think, in a matter of minutes he would be her husband.

"Oh. Well, she did look lovely. Although not as stunning as you do, Goldie." Peggy shook her head, and tears began to shimmer in her eyes. "You are a vision. Joe won't know what hit him when he sees you walking down the aisle."

"You think so?" Goldie looked down at her beautiful gown and smiled. It, of course, was her *something new*. Peggy's antique diamond-drop earrings dangled from Goldie's ears and served as her *something borrowed*. Eve had provided the *something blue* – a very sexy, velvet, powder blue garter that she insisted was for Joe's eyes only. According to Goldie's friend, it was La Perla and much too nice to fling into a crowd of anxious bachelors. For that tradition, Eve had given her a substitute garter. Goldie couldn't help but notice Eve seemed to think quite a bit about the unattached men who would be in attendance at the wedding. Along with the fancy garter, Eve had given Goldie a matching set of La Perla blue satin bridal undergarments, the very sight of which made Goldie blush, which was a sure sign she and Joe would have a memorable wedding night. Eve, the official honeymoon pet-sitter, had threatened to "lose" Bliss if Goldie even thought about taking her Sponge Bob pajamas on the honeymoon.

"It's time for us to head down there." Eve glanced at her watch and then looked up at the bride in surprise. "Goldie! Where's your *something old?* We need to get going."

"Here, I'll help." Peggy lifted the lid of a worn

cardboard box sitting on the countertop.

The box was yellowed with age, but the delicate ivory veil nestled inside was in pristine condition. The three women held their collective breath as Peggy placed it on Goldie's head. Goldie peered through the fragile lace, thin as a whisper, at her friends. It was as though she were looking at them in a dream, which was fitting, in a way. Marrying Joe was a like a dream come true. "How do I look?"

"Oh, Goldie. You take my breath away." Eve's voice shook with emotion, and she blinked back tears. "I can't believe that is the same veil your grandmother wore when she married the big guy."

"He would be so proud of you right now, Goldie." Peggy reached over and squeezed Goldie's hand with both of her own. "Proud and happy. Joe is a good man. Your grandpa wouldn't have stood by and watched just anyone marry his Goldilocks. But he loved Joe."

Goldie's throat clogged with emotion, but it wasn't sadness exactly. More of a bittersweet wish. "I know. It would have been so nice if he could have been here and walked me down the aisle."

"Goldie, you don't have to walk down the aisle alone. Harold offered to do it. Or we could walk with you." Eve gestured toward Bliss and Java, holding their sits like veteran obedience dogs, so as not to crush the sweet floral wreaths around their necks. "After all, this isn't the most conventional wedding party. Your flower girls are dogs and the best man is a woman." Eve's gaze darted toward Peggy, and Goldie knew she was thinking about the elderly members of the wedding party. But, wisely, Eve kept her mouth shut about that subject.

"It's okay. I won't be alone." Goldie fingered the

edge of the lacey veil and smiled. She wouldn't be alone walking down the beach. She had Joe waiting for her at the end of the aisle, her friends, the memories of her loved ones who were now in Heaven and, best of all, she had God by her side. She wasn't alone. She never had been. She'd learned that lesson and would always remember it. "I'm ready."

The three women linked arms as they traveled over the dune and headed toward the ceremony with Bliss and Java following close on their heels. The dogs were the first to go down the aisle. As soon as Joe gave a *come* signal, the Husky and the Cavalier trotted down the aisle like seasoned flower girls, or flower dogs as Goldie liked to call them. Their performance caused quite a stir of excitement among the guests. Eve stood shielding Goldie from view, but even from behind, Goldie could tell her friend was impressed as well. Perhaps pet-sitting for the dogs during the honeymoon would give Eve a greater appreciation for animals. Somehow, Goldie doubted it.

The dogs were followed by Peggy, then Eve, each as lovely as ever in their billowing dresses the color of the sea. And all at once, Goldie was the lone figure at the end of the aisle. The guests all stood to get a good glimpse of the bride and Goldie was sure several of them spoke to her and smiled. But all she could see was the man she loved, watching her with a look filled with hope and adoration. She could scarcely believe the one he waited for, longed for, was her. She'd never felt so blessed in her life.

With each slow step down the aisle, she closed the gap between them. When at last she reached him, Goldie handed her bouquet of pink roses and calla lilies to Eve. Joe wrapped his strong hands around

Goldie's and she realized she was trembling. The shaking subsided when Joe brought her hands to his lips and grazed her knuckles with a tender kiss of assurance.

Pastor Paul began to recite the words of the ceremony, words Goldie and Joe had gone over time and again. Goldie was suddenly very glad they'd pored over the verses and vows, because now the time was finally here, everything was happening so fast. Even if the pastor spoke in slow motion, she would have been unable to focus on exactly what he was saying because she was lost in Joe's gaze. In the entire history of weddings had a groom ever looked at a bride quite that way before? Goldie didn't think so. She could see every ounce of love he felt for her pouring through the warm brown glow of his eyes. And when he spoke his vows, his voice never wavered, but held steady and true. "I Joe, take you Goldie, to be my wedded wife. To have and to hold, from this day forward, for better, for worse, for richer, for poorer, in sickness or in health, to love and to cherish 'til death do us part. And hereto I pledge you my faithfulness."

Goldie repeated the words back to him, willing herself not to cry. "I Goldie, take you Joe, to be my wedded husband. To have and to hold, from this day forward, for better, for worse, for richer, for poorer, in sickness or in health, to love and to cherish 'til death do us part. And hereto I pledge you my faithfulness."

Goldie had been to her fair share of weddings in the past and, like many people, the vows had always been her favorite part. They'd always sounded so dreamy and romantic. But now, since living through the death of a loved one, she knew these weren't mere words. And she still meant them with all her heart. She would stand by Joe in sickness, even in death.

"By the power vested in me by the State of North Carolina, I now pronounce you husband and wife." Pastor Paul's voice rang with joy, and Goldie finally tore her gaze from Joe to look at the clergyman. His eyes twinkled with mischief and he said, "Joe, you may now kiss your bride."

Goldie held her breath with sweet anticipation as her husband lifted the fine lace veil away from her face. She wondered if her grandmother's heart had beat anywhere near as fiercely as hers was now when Grandpa removed this same veil from his own bride's face so many years ago. She hoped so.

If only every wife could feel this way about her husband. Even for just a moment. Thank you, Lord, for blessing me so.

As the lace came up over her head, Goldie said a silent prayer that she wouldn't be the last bride to wear this veil. Maybe someday Eve would wear it. Or perhaps Joe and Goldie might have a daughter or granddaughter of their own. Goldie felt herself glow from the inside out at the very thought.

Joe took a sharp intake of breath as he lifted the sheer fabric and unveiled Goldie's features. His gasp made her heart pump even faster. "You are so, so beautiful." He cradled her face in his hands, and as he tilted her chin to kiss her, he whispered, "My wife."

The kiss was tender at first, but as the emotions within Goldie swelled to the surface, their lips moved with greater intensity. Goldie thought she had experienced the best of Joe's kisses before now, but she was wrong. Dead wrong. She clutched at the fabric of his tuxedo jacket and hung on for dear life, lest she melt into a puddle at his feet in front of all their closest friends and family. Joe sighed when he finally pulled away.

They turned to face their cheering guests and, as they made their way back down the aisle, Goldie leaned in and gave Joe's earlobe a little nibble. "Do you think we'll have time later today for you to kiss me like that again?"

Joe pulled her closer against him and breathed against the sensitive skin of her neck, sending a riot of shivers up her spine. "Don't you worry, Bashful. Now, we have all the time in the world. And I fully intend to spend a good portion of it kissing you. Capeesh?"

Goldie smiled, wrapped her arm around her husband's waist and leaned into his embrace. "Capeesh."

About the Author

Teri's son once wrote in a third-grade paper, "My Mom loves dogs and Jesus." He may have gotten the order reversed, but the sentiment was right on target. Her romance stories are often filled with happy endings, splashes of humor and a loveable critter or two. After all, Cinderella never would have lived happily ever after without a little help from her animal friends!

Cup of Joe, written in memory of Teri's grandfather, won second place in the 2009 San Antonio Romance Authors Merritt Contest. Teri is also the winner of the 2008 Pet Sitters International Humor Writing Award, the 2008 Spaniel Journal Writing Contest, the 2006 Westminster Kennel Club Angel on a Leash Writing Award and the 3rd place winner of the 21st Annual American Kennel Club Short Fiction Contest. Teri lives in San Antonio, Texas, in a house full of delightful dogs.

Thank you for purchasing this White Rose Publishing title. For other wonderful stories of romance, please visit our on-line bookstore at
www.whiterosepublishing.com.

For questions or more information contact us at info@whiterosepublishing.com.

White Rose Publishing
www.WhiteRosePublishing.com

LaVergne, TN USA
20 October 2010
201584LV00001B/2/P